WHAT READERS ARE SAYING -

Praise for *Ericksen*

"This book is a beautiful unraveling of self-assurance to new self-discovery, and this couple was absolutely perfect."

Nikita – BookSirens Reviewer

"Ericksen is an action-packed adventure that will take its readers on a thrilling, shocking, but above all, incredibly entertaining journey!"

Di – Booksprout Reviewer

"One of the most compulsive marriages of fantasy and romance, Ericksen is an absorbing story that will warm you from the inside out."

Nicky Flowers – Indies Today

Praise for *Asherwick* –

"I adored this story. Ms. Westill has created the most fantastic world with these amazing characters... I love the complex mystery, the romance, the world itself, and all the fabulous characters."

Baroness Book Trove

"Westill's books never disappoint. They're suspenseful, romantic, sexy, and mysterious, and the writing pulls you into this unique and captivating world from the first pages."

One Book More

"... much better than the box that genre put it in. I thoroughly enjoyed the intrigue of the mystery interspersed with the sexual tension between the characters."

BookSirens Reader Review

Praise for *Kynhaven* –

"...emotional and heart-breaking while still having elements of mystery that keep you hooked and wanting more. Overall, Kynhaven is an amazing book to read."

Miche Ardense for Readers' Favorite

"...a brilliant addition to the series and highly recommended..."

ERICKSEN

GEN-HEIRS: THE GUARDIANS OF SZIVERIA

SARAH WESTILL

ERICKSEN

Gen-Heirs: The Guardians of Sziveria – Book 5

Copyright 2022 by Sarah Westill

ISBN 978-1-955293-11-2

Cover Design by For the Muse Designs

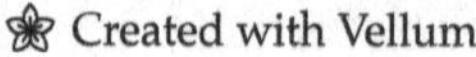 Created with Vellum

OTHER TITLES BY SARAH WESTILL

GEN-HEIRS: The Guardians of Sziveria

(in reading order)

Levkaseon – A Prequel

Wintersfall

Raiventon

Kynhaven

Asherwick

Ericksen - A Wintervail Special

Survaine (April 27, 2023)

Bella and the Beast Master

(Gen-Heirs world novella series)

Frozen Flowers Fallen (Dec. 2022)

For world maps be sure to visit www.sarahwestill.com

To get the latest updates, follow Sarah on Instagram

@authorsarahwestill

Dedication and Acknowledgement

For my amazing mom, who has loved her daughters, with our crazy quirks and all.

CONTENT WARNING:
This book contains mature content, including but not limited to –
Consensual sex (non-graphic)
Action violence
Crime scene depiction
Death of a spouse and child (secondary character)

Reader discretion is advised.

1

THE *TICK, TICK, TICK* OF A CLOCK BROKE THE BLEAK SILENCE permeating the house. Once laughter, life, and love had filled the brick home. Now, the lone steady clunk of cogs ticking away time sank the space deeper into melancholy. Vayden Dossett sighed and went in search of his mentor, wishing he had something, *anything* of value to reveal.

Vayden looked around the single-level home, each empty room a reminder of all Henry Castien had lost. A scattering of toys still covered the living room rug. A half-read book rested pages down, open and waiting for a reader who would never again discover what the novel held. The only clue to the emotional distress of the owner were the torn down and discarded Wintervail decorations littering the floors and hallway. Dishes sat stacked in the sink. Four plates and cups. Henry hadn't used the room since tragedy had struck. Continuing through the dining room and a short hall to the library, he found Henry sitting in the wash of gray light filtering from the wide greenhouse doors. Not even a fire burned in the hearth to ward off the deep-set chill of impending winter.

On another sigh, Vayden went to the stone hearth and started a fire, hoping the soft glow of light and heat would alert Henry to his presence. One did not surprise an ex-assassin. Especially one suffering in the midst of a personal nightmare no man ever wanted to face.

The chair creaked. Henry's flinty, dark brown eyes widened when he noted Vayden crouched before the fireplace. His hands moved in the rapid motions of his language. "How long have you been here?"

Not wanting to disrupt the quiet, even if Henry couldn't hear, Vayden used only his hands to answer. "Long enough to notice you haven't eaten. When was your last meal?"

"I'm not hungry," he signed with jerky, angry motions.

Vayden crossed the distance between them, dragging a chair along with him. He positioned it next to Henry and sat. "Lucianna is still out there, somewhere. You know she is." Vayden waved a hand up and down before signing, "What will she come home to? A starved husk of her father?"

Henry shook his head, his face aging before Vayden into harsh lines. "You don't know anything. She could be lying in a field somewhere, worm food, like her mother and brother."

Vayden clenched his jaw at the ugly imagery, at the furious delivery, and at the pain, the words brought to his own heart. He took a moment to compose himself, looking out over the stunning greenhouse grounds Fiona Castien had been so proud of. "Do you know something I don't?"

An odd snorting puff of air escaped from Henry's nose and mouth. He waved a dismissive hand. His signs were equal parts frustration and annoyance. "The First Intelligence Office thinks they can make sense of it all."

"You don't?"

Henry shook his head. "There is no sense to be made when a nine-year-old is murdered."

Okay, Vayden would give Henry that truth. "What about learning why? Did whoever visited say they would try to find out why, or even who? Did they give you any information?"

"The man's name was Ryan Voklanc," Henry signed. "He had no information to give me, only questions to ask."

"What sort of questions? And is this Voklane a ranked guardian?"

"No, just a guardian, no rank. He asked about the day, a complete account." Henry's attention shifted back to the greenhouse. Long moments passed before he faced Vayden again and signed, "Why would he need that when Haven City Enforcement Services met me at the crime scene? Wouldn't they have everything he needed?"

Vayden shrugged. "You are asking the wrong person, Henry. HCES wanted nothing to do with a gencommon like me."

A grunt of aggravation accompanied a flippant wave. "Idiots, all of them, I told you that when I was training you. I trust your opinion over any of those *guardians* any day. Now, tell me, what do you think it means?"

Knowing he needed to tread carefully here, that his

mentor, a man more like an uncle than a friend, suffered. However, Henry was smart. Vayden couldn't ignore or gloss over the question. "I think he either wanted to hear the information from you himself, or HCES didn't share."

"FIO has dominion, they can request access to any case the HCES has."

"Yes, but that doesn't mean they gave it."

Henry seemed to mull the information over, his focus once again sliding to the immaculate greenery past the windows. When his attention returned, determination hardened his tired face and edged the aggressive motions of his hands. "I want you on this case."

Vayden slowly shook his head. "We've talked about this already. The situation is too high profile, I won't get any information and I'll be stonewalled at every turn when I do go looking. Government services don't like their territory intruded upon."

"You've taken harder jobs and succeeded. I know you have."

Vayden scrubbed his hands down his face. He had. But never so personal. Never with so much to lose and someone so important to him to disappoint. In a rare move, Henry reached out and grabbed Vayden's fore-arm. Squeezed. Vayden stared at the stark grief in Henry's eyes. The desperation.

"Cia won't be found without you," Henry signed, each elegant sweep of his hand emphasized with the fear blazing in his eyes for his only living child. His daughter, not even seventeen yet.

"I learned some information that may or may not make a difference," Vayden signed. "I came to share it with you, so you could pass it on to whoever is handling the case."

"You," Henry snapped the gesture, "are handling it."

"I don't think it's a good idea," Vayden tried to disagree again.

Henry jumped from his chair and paced before the conservatory doors. His signing aggressive and over-exaggerated in his anger. "They don't care about her! She is a no one to them."

"She is a missing child," Vayden insisted. "Of course, she matters."

"I have received no other visit except by that Voklane man. No updates. No assurances. How is that mattering? If you don't do this, Vayden, she is lost to us."

Vayden flexed his jaw in thought. Drawing out an exhale, he dropped his head in defeat. "Very well, I will do all I can. But you know I can't promise anything. HCES doesn't have to share anything with me."

"But they can't stop you from talking to people, from doing your own investigation."

"No, they can't," Vayden acknowledged. But past experience told him the behemoth government agencies filled with men and women who looked down upon his gen-common status, regardless of his mother being a shield guardian, could make things considerably difficult.

"What did you learn?" Henry asked and sat back down.

"Have you heard of a family named Cyrano? They own a small shipping company out of Italyssa."

Henry shook his head. "I have not, why?"

"There is evidence they are kidnapping people from the streets of Sziveria and shipping them off to be sold," Vayden explained.

"Why kill Fiona and Joshua, only to take Cia to be sold, then?"

"I don't know," Vayden admitted. "I just thought the information was interesting, since she has gone missing. I wanted to tell you about it. The two may be unrelated."

"Or not." Henry sighed. "She is young, female, and beautiful. Perhaps too beautiful to kill to punish me for my past."

Vayden agreed. If the order to murder the Castien family had been from a past grudge, the assailant could have decided to make extra income by stealing the girl instead of killing her. Henry suffered all the same. He lifted his hands to say as much when a knock echoed from the front.

Henry's gaze narrowed on Vayden. "What is it?"

"Someone is at the door."

Henry glanced over his shoulder at the doorway and then back to Vayden. "I am not deaf to anyone who is there. If they come in, speak," Henry said.

Rising, Vayden nodded. He knew Henry liked to keep the upper hand. Only those the retired assassin decided ever knew he couldn't hear. Had never been able to. On wit, his Gen-Heir talent, and a drive few exhibited, Henry Castien had built a career as a dangerous man working for the Sziverian crown. "Very well."

Before answering the door, Vayden picked up the stranded garlands of silvery birds, flowers, and greenery cast aside in the hall. He tossed the glittery mass into the living room and closed the door on the expressed chaos of loss. One final look assured the home appeared more like a bachelor's residence than that of a broken man.

He opened the door, not sure which surprised him more, the cold shock of air or the visitor with her hand poised to deliver another knock. Unable to control the inner-troublemaker she seemed to bring out in him, Vayden crossed his arms and leaned against the door-frame. Lazily, he allowed his gaze to wander from the top of the pretty, chestnut curls brushing her shoulders, down the length of her petite frame, to her booted feet. He tried not to enjoy the visual journey. And failed. Everything about Melody Ericksen worked for him. She squared her shoulders and straightened her spine, pulling up all her five-foot-six-inches, issuing the clear challenge of who had authority over whom.

Ah yes, how dare he forget his lowly gen-common status.

Vayden smiled.

"Guardian Ericksen, how may I assist you this morning?"

The light smattering of freckles covering her cheeks and nose stood out as color crept up her face. Her spring-green eyes nearly glowed with annoyance. She pointed a finger at the bright gold lettering printed on the front of her black HCES uniform jacket. "Tribunii Ericksen, Dossett. Respect my ranking, I worked hard to earn it."

"Ah." Vayden straightened and grabbed the edge of the door. "All right then, easy enough. Hope you have a great rest of your day, *Tribunii*."

With another smile, Vayden let the door slam on Melody's attractive face.

Dumbstruck, Melody stared at the closed teal-painted door and blinked. What had just happened? Her cheeks burned with mortification and anger. The pounding of her heart made her chest ache. Taking a calming breath, she pressed her hand to her chest and willed a sentiment of calm to flow through her.

Okay, so she hadn't expected the overly handsome reward seeker to answer the door to her current case. A man she'd turned down months ago when matched to him by a matchmaker she figured understood the necessity of proper genetic compatibility. As a Gen-Heir, Melody *needed* to marry another strong Gen-Heir talent. The rejection on her part had been nothing personal. Only the gen-common seeker had never seen it that way. No, the infernal man had taken it entirely *too* personally.

Unsure how the enterprising seeker had found out about poor Henry Castien's situation, Melody raised her hand and pounded on the door, determined to make sure the man didn't squander any money on hiring Vayden. Cold wind blew at her back, skittering leaves and scraping naked branches together. Winter teased the edges of fall. Soon the short days would never thaw. Melody shivered in her pants and thin uniform jacket, not having expected to spend more time outside than what it would take her to walk from her Ariot, a vehicle powered by a magnetic engine harnessing the power of positive and negative attraction, to a building. She pounded on the door again, hoping this time the owner would answer.

To her disappointment, Vayden swept the door open. With his breathtaking golden-blue eyes, dark brown hair a little too long to be considered professional, and a masculine physique Melody couldn't seem to make her own traitorous body ignore. He quirked an eyebrow. "Yes?"

"I would like to speak with Mr. Castien, please," Melody ground out.

The much too sensual curve of his mouth tilted up. Mischief danced in his gaze. He took a step back and swept his arm wide in an invite to enter. "By all means, I'll take you to him. I'm sure he'll be interested to know the latest development on his case."

Anxiety churned her stomach. Melody swallowed and stepped past him. She tried to ignore the earthy, citrusy, dark scent of him. Somehow, she resisted the urge to breathe deep, to inhale his essence, thereby thoroughly embarrassing herself. In the end, she resorted to holding her breath. After closing the door, he led her down a short corridor, where they turned right into a kitchen and dining area, through another short hall, and into a cozy library. A fire warmed the space.

Henry stood when he spotted her and held out his hand in greeting. Melody accepted, squeezing his rough, textured fingers. "Mr. Castien, thank you for seeing me."

"Do you have news for me?" he asked, his dark eyes full of hope.

Melody removed her hand from his and cleared her throat. "Not exactly, no, I'm sorry."

Henry looked at her and then over her shoulder to

Vayden, who must have made some sort of expression, for Henry's changed to one of resignation and disappointment. "Ah, I see. Please sit."

Melody took one of the two chairs situated in front of the greenhouse doors. She couldn't help but admire the beautifully cultivated garden with a brick path for viewing and benches for leisure.

"So," Henry began with a slap to his thighs, "if no news, what is the reason for your visit?"

"I had some additional questions for you, if that's okay?" She reached into her inner jacket pocket and removed a pencil and small notebook. "My master prefect has given your case to me, and I had some things I wanted to clarify."

"Is anyone looking for my daughter?"

Melody glanced over at Vayden, noting his scowl and crossed arms. A new set of nerves danced in her belly. She had to play this right. Henry watched her intently, which only served to increase her anxiety. "Um, yes, we… we're doing what we can, but the information is um, as you know, limited. I haven't been able to find any leads, as of yet, which is why I was hoping you could give me a more detailed statement of patrons in the park that day."

"I told the MT who took my statement of every person I saw. I pointed them out, most were still in the crowd of onlookers," Henry said, a heavy frown settling across his face.

Melody looked down at her notepad. "Well, I—"

"The least you can do is look at him when you tell him bad news," Vayden said, his deep voice low and dangerous.

A shiver raced up her spine. "Who said I'm going to give him bad news?"

"Bad news?" Henry's back straightened, and he looked at Vayden in concern. "What is this bad news?"

Vayden made down motions. "Relax, she has said nothing yet." He turned his beautiful eyes in her direction. Like sapphire wrapped in gold, Melody mused. She must have pondered a little too long, for he snapped, "Tribunii?"

Blinking, she looked from him, to Henry and back to the empty notebook page. "Yes?"

"You have something to tell Henry?"

"No, I have questions to ask, that's all," she assured. "You are the one who made assumptions. There is no news to report."

Henry chuffed an odd snort and stood. "I have no answers to give that you don't already have. I have asked Vayden to find my daughter. From now on, you can deal with him, he's my agent in this whole affair."

Melody hastily closed her notebook and stood, shoving everything into her pockets. "Mr. Castien, I highly recommend you leave this case to the professionals. HCES is more qualified than a reward seeker to find your child."

For long moments, Henry stared at her, then his gaze shifted to Vayden, who'd leaned against the mantle, hands in his pockets. Annoyance flashed through Melody. She forced the unhelpful emotion down and cleared her throat.

"Look, I know it seems like we haven't been able to do much so far, but HCES is committed to helping Haven City residents in any way we can," Melody said.

Henry barked a laugh. "You should have been a saleswoman, Tribunii Ericksen."

Heat suffused Melody's cheeks. "Have I convinced you?"

"No."

"Then I would have made a poor saleswoman," Melody stated.

"Are you a better investigator?"

Vayden's deep voice drew her attention back to him. Really, she decided, a man shouldn't be allowed to look *that* good. The faint shadow of stubble covering his jaw accentuated the hard edges of his face. Long, thick, black lashes made the unique coloring of his eyes seem more intense than they probably would be otherwise. Maybe. The rich caramel of his skin had to be an inherited trait from one of his parents, unlike her milky white so common in the sun-poor nation of Sziveria. She blinked to reset her thoughts. She *had* to stop getting lost in his looks.

In her world, the people she crossed paths with most daily, had a single shade of color to their irises. Pure blue, green, amber, or any other shade, with variants of the same color, but never a mixture of one with another. Eye-color was the general way to determine if someone was Gen-Heir or gen-common. The first time she'd met Vayden, she'd been speechless. He'd taken her breath away. Then she'd been angry, because he shouldn't have, and she couldn't do anything about her attraction anyway.

"They didn't promote me because I'm pretty," she said dryly.

"And yet you've made no progress," he pointed out.

She wanted to glare and snap he needn't be Mr.

Obvious, but that would take down her professionalism a notch or two, and she wouldn't give him the satisfaction. Melody decided the truth, or at least a version of it, would serve best. "The case is new to me. I took it on this morning. Any lack of development to this point is due to the rise in crime across the city. We're under-strength, as you well know."

Vayden smiled, an expression she was learning had nothing to do with happiness. "That happens when hiring is a restricted process."

Uneasy, she shifted her weight. The prejudice against the gen-common population of Sziveria was known and accepted. For the greater good of all, the elevation of Gen-Heirs within society served on many levels, ensuring the best, most capable of protecting were chosen. They were called guardians for a reason. Some, like Melody, hadn't achieved a ranking within the guardian system, but the title was still theirs to claim. A fact Vayden usually never failed to mention in some snide manner, reminding her of her failure so far to procure the greatest honor of her nation. Someday she'd be able to affix a rank before her name that had nothing to do with her Enforcement position. She'd achieve the status her parents had bred and groomed her for.

The problem was, she realized as she stared at Vayden, she'd never actually met a gen-common individual affected by the genetic inheritance guardian law. Being faced with the bias, knowing she'd never truly understand, made her uncomfortable to admit. She sighed and looked away from him. "The genetic inheritance law is—"

"Put in place to best serve the nation as a whole

with no intent to harm, or hinder, the professional growth of any Sziverian citizen… blah, blah, blah," Vayden flapped his fingers together in mock speaking. "I know the law."

"Vayden will handle the investigation for me personally," Henry cut in. "If you work together, all the better, but he *is* handling it."

Work? With Vayden? Melody glanced between the two of them and wondered when her reality had taken a sharp turn. "But he's… a reward seeker."

"Yes," Henry said. "I am aware. I suggested the profession to him when he was told he'd never be able to be a guardian. The next best thing, a reward seeker. Helping those the government can't, or simply won't, assist. I trained him myself."

"I can't be seen working with a reward seeker," Melody choked out before she could stop herself. Diplomacy had never been her strength.

"Vayden, would you mind seeing the Tribunii out, please? I have told HCES all I need to," Henry stated, looking past her as if she'd already left.

Great. She'd really stuck her foot in it this time. If she didn't find a way to salvage the situation, she'd never forgive herself. Henry may think Vayden qualified for the task, but Melody was a *Gen-Heir* for the love of sun, she was better equipped, and more capable. Finding the missing girl couldn't fall into the hands of someone who *might* be able to see the recovery through.

"All right," she conceded, holding her hands up in defeat. "I will work with him."

Henry narrowed his eyes. "On all things?"

Melody worried her bottom lip between her teeth. "I'm not sure—"

The earthy, citrusy scent of Vayden reached her before he did. He took hold of her elbow and steered her toward the library door. "Come on, guardianess, the owner of the house has spoken."

Shocked by the heat of his touch through the layer of her jacket, and the strength of his fingers wrapped around her bicep, Melody gaped at him. She stumbled, failing to send the message to her feet to move. Before she could fall, she found herself hauled up against solid man.

"Sorry," he said, taking a step back. "I shouldn't have moved so fast."

Would her entire visit to the Castien house be one, long string of mortification? At this point, she'd be lucky if her cheeks didn't remain stained red for the rest of the day. Huffing her aggravation, she yanked her arm free. "I can walk on my own, thanks."

Vayden made an *after you* sweep of his arm. Melody cast one last glance at Henry. Lost in thought, he'd settled back in his chair before the greenhouse, ignoring both of them. "How long have you known Mr. Castien?"

"Almost my entire life. He's friends with my father."

"He is very fond of you."

"Because he trusts me to handle something so important?" He stopped at the front door, his hand on the knob.

Melody tucked a curl behind her ear. "Well, yeah, I suppose. I mean you charge people for something enforcement handles for free."

He held up an index finger. "Actually, I charge people for what enforcement deems too unimportant to take on. There is a difference."

Melody pursed her lips. "No one ever said the Castien case wasn't important."

Vayden crossed his arms over his chest and leaned back against the door. "And yet we're going on three weeks and no movement. A sixteen-year-old girl is missing. You do realize at this point she may not even be in Sziveria anymore, right? The incompetence of HCES is staggering."

Melody looked around the small entry hall, noting the lack of festive decorations for the Wintervail season. Then again, her own house was decidedly bleak, without the excuse of personal loss. She wished she could refute his claim. She also knew if she didn't fix the mess she'd made of things, there would never be answers for Castien. "Actually, you're correct, I am embarrassed to admit. I wasn't so much assigned this case, as I've taken it upon myself."

Melody took a deep, bracing breath and forged ahead. "All the evidence and testimony has gone missing."

____

2

Vayden assumed he had misheard. Because there was *no way* she'd just disclosed Henry's entire case was gone. "I'm sorry, say again?"

She had the good graces to look sheepish. "I know it's not ideal, but I did have a chance to review the original file, so not everything is lost. I've made as many notes about the case as I could remember."

A pounding started directly between his eyeballs. Vayden pressed a knuckle to his forehead and grimaced. "Let me see if I have this correct – you have the *audacity* to question my professionalism, experience, and talent when your own department has lost a complete case, which includes a missing child?"

Only a pitiful squeak and the scrunching of her face and shoulders were his answers.

"Right." Vayden sighed and straightened from the door. Anger would solve nothing. Between the two of them, he clearly had to be the voice of reason. "Here's how this is going to go. At Henry's request, which I feel the need to remind you is the victim in this awful situation, I am taking over the case. You've pretty much told me HCES doesn't even have documentation of it anymore, which means there's not a trail to follow. I could use the help, I will admit. We can work together, or I can work alone. The choice is yours."

Weariness shone from her leafy green eyes and slouched frame. "I admitted to the mess-up at Division because I wanted to be honest. However, my reputation will be ruined if I'm seen working with a reward seeker."

"And a gen-common," Vayden added for her, knowing she'd left the words unsaid.

She flushed and looked away from him. "I didn't—"

Vayden held his hand up, cutting off her attempt at a denial. The misconceptions about his genetics had long ago stopped bothering him. When he'd first met Melody, he'd admit to holding out hope she'd be different. The idealistic expectation lasted all of two seconds. One look at him and she'd wished him a good life and walked away. Unfortunately, his attraction hadn't vacated when she had. Masochist that he seemed to be, he looked at her, and the primitive side of his brain went *mine*.

Pushing the unpleasant thoughts aside, he met her guarded stare. "I know, you didn't mean to be offensive, you don't mean to imply, I've heard it all, guardian. I am capable of doing my job, *my* reputation speaks for itself. I don't need your approval to do what I know I'm good at. I am taking on Henry's case, with or without your assistance."

He opened the front door. A gust of wind swept inside, fluttering the curls around her face. The urge to know if the glossy mass was as soft as he imagined had him clenching a fist. She made no move to exit, simply stared at him, a pinch between her brows.

"All that matters is finding the girl," she said softly.

"Yes," Vayden agreed. "Three weeks is too long to think any trail we find will still be hot enough to follow. I can't allow any more time to be wasted."

"We," she breathed out, glancing around the now illuminated entry. "I guess I don't really have much choice."

"Nope," he said without an ounce of sympathy.

Her lush mouth flattened into a hard line. She nodded. "Very well. You can close the door, I agree. I need Henry's statement, though, as much as he can remember."

"I already have it," Vayden disclosed, stepping outside. "I took it the day of the murders and abduction, at his insistence."

Melody frowned anew. "He didn't trust HCES?"

"Apparently, he had good reason not to." He waited until she walked out before closing the door. "I have it all at my place."

"Great," she drew out with a clear lack of enthusiasm.

Vayden waited a beat at the sidewalk for her to offer direction since she'd insisted on taking the case and was, in all honesty, the officially trained investigator between the two of them. While Vayden had Henry's exceptional instruction under his belt and had passed the required testing to obtain his seeker license, professional courtesy dictated he let her take the lead if possible. When she made no attempt, Vayden raised his face to the shifting gray clouds above and took a deep breath.

Fine. He would continue to be an adult about this. If he figured correctly, he had a few years on her anyway, maybe she was deferring to his wisdom. The sarcastic thought almost made him snort. So much for being a grown-up.

"I'm going to the crime scene. Do you want to come with?" he asked.

"After three weeks? What could you possibly hope to find?"

"Were you there the day it happened?"

"No. My MT was, but..." She looked away, worrying her bottom lip.

A niggle zipped up his spine, a sensation he'd learned long ago never to ignore. "What is it?"

"No one was assigned the case when it happened," she said, her voice low, as if someone could be listening on the empty street. "My MT asked me to take a file about the case to MT Hunter the day it happened, but he didn't include all the case specifics, only...." She took a shaky breath. "Only what it seemed he could shove into the file as fast as possible. After that, everything went missing."

"Key Guardian Asherwick?" Vayden asked. Melody nodded in confirmation. "Why him?"

"I don't know, MT Hunter has been helping MT Rainier with several odd cases in South Row. I thought at first the cases must be related, but now, I'm not so sure."

"I need to see the crime scene, if nothing else. Do you have any notes at all from the investigator's perspective? Was there a crime scene diagram done, do you know?" he asked, heading for his Ariot at the curb.

She shook her head. "I have no idea, and if there was, it's missing too. *Everything* is missing, except for what I handed to MT Hunter."

Last Vayden knew, the key guardian and his lovely bride were soaking up the sun in Italyssa. "Okay, I'll work from memory based on what Henry told me. Do you know how to get there?"

"I can follow you." She motioned to the little beat-up HCES issued Ariot parked behind his.

Vayden kept his thoughts about her piece of crap ride to himself. He'd have to drive slowly.

A FROSTY WIND HAD BLOWN UP ON THEIR DRIVE TO CARIS City Park. The immaculate park, with bark trails, rolling hills for play and picnicking, benches and swings, looked too tranquil for such a horrific moment in time to have occurred weeks ago. Melody tried to huddle deeper into her jacket, the sudden chill from more than just the weather aching to her bones.

"How long have you been a Tribunii?" Vayden asked, stopping beside her on the entry trail into the park.

The frigid air burned her fingers. She shoved them deep into her pockets. "I was promoted six months ago."

"Ah," he said as if that answered a different question.

Curious, she glanced at him. "Why?"

"Just wondering. Shall we?" He bundled tighter into his thick jacket, which he must have had in his vehicle.

The edges of a cream, knit scarf fluttered out behind him.

The warm scent of leather and man drifted to her on a passing gust. Melody shivered and glared at his toasty back. Her feet kicked up wooden chunks glittery with ice. "You sure are prepared."

He glanced over his shoulder and shrugged. "I better be after ten years working the streets. In this country, you never know when the cold will hit."

Melody's teeth chattered. "I am learning that. As a First Guardsman, I worked a few cases with my MT, but most were indoors."

"No surveillance?"

"Not yet, no," she admitted. She tucked her chin into her chest. "How long do you think this will take? The roads aren't going to be safe for too much longer this far out of the city."

"Yes, that has made me curious. Why is this a HCES investigation to begin with?" He left the trail. Grass crunched under his booted feet.

Melody paused for a moment and regarded the rising hill. Ice seemed to collect with each new sweep of wind. Knowing her luck, she'd make it halfway, slip, and end up sliding right back down. Vayden didn't appear to have the same misconceptions. Sighing, Melody scrambled after him.

"Caris City fell under HCES jurisdiction when they ran the rails to the city," she panted out on huge puffs of vapor.

"Are they expecting Haveners to flock to the city?"

"I don't know. Would make sense, though, wouldn't it?"

He stopped at the crest of the hill, hands braced on

his hips as he surveyed the area around them. "Might put a kink in development if people are being shot and kidnapped in the parks."

Melody pressed her arms into her sides and fisted her hands in her pockets. On top of the slope, the harrowing wind tugged at her coat and sent her hair flying in all directions. Tiny flecks of ice stung her cheeks. "What exactly are you hoping to find up here?"

Sighing, he unwound the thick scarf from around his neck. Before she could utter a protest, he'd draped the length over her head and around her throat, still warm from his body. She couldn't help the groan of pleasure. Her ears, cheeks, and neck all delighted in the sudden barrier against the elements.

"There are pockets at the end for your hands," he said, tucking the edges down around her neck like he would a child. "Perhaps next time you won't get caught in the cold."

She slipped her hands into the silky softness. The unexpected kindness made her fidget in embarrassment. She hadn't exactly been the nicest to him, and here he was, making sure she didn't catch frostbite. "Thank you."

He nodded curtly, surveying the grounds again. Leaning close enough for her to catch his heat again, he pointed. "The attack happened right over that knoll."

Melody looked at the gentle rise and then beyond. A bulky, gnarled oak devoid of all but a few stubborn brown leaves stood out among the skinnier pine population. "That tree would have provided suitable cover, not only from the family, but anyone walking by at the time."

"I had the same thought." Shoving his hands into

his jacket pockets, he headed down the frosty hillside toward the tree.

When he didn't slip or otherwise tumble down the treacherous looking landscape, Melody took a deep breath and braved after him. The grass crunched and broke beneath her boots. At the ancient oak, they both walked in a slow circle. Overcast, the muted light made seeing any detail tough. Especially, Melody mused, an old detail, out in the elements for weeks now.

Vayden crouched behind the tree. He reached into his jacket and removed a small rectangular box. Melody tilted her head in curiosity. After removing tweezers and a small glass tube, he plucked something from a crevice near the roots. He dropped the object into the tube, sealed it, and then held it up for inspection.

"What is it?" Melody stepped closer, trying to see inside.

"I'm not sure, some sort of plant."

"We're in a park."

Vayden shook his head and handed her the container. He put the box back into his jacket. "No, it was left here, placed inside the crevice right here."

"How could you tell?" She inspected the vivid purple flower. "I've never seen this before, what is it?"

"It's not native. I'm not a botanist, but I bet that particular beauty is only grown in a greenhouse."

"Like the Wintervail Iris," Melody said more to herself than to him, lost in the beauty of the flower. "Have you ever seen it?"

"I don't think so. My mother grows an extensive garden, maybe she'll know." Vayden held out his palm.

Hesitating, Melody wrapped her hand around the evidence. "Shouldn't I take it with me, back to HCES?"

Vayden lifted a brow. "Do you really think that's wise, considering? Besides, my kit, my evidence."

She really didn't have an argument on either account. With a huff of frustration, she dropped the tube into his waiting hand. Shoving her fists back into the warmth of the scarf, she glanced back around. "So, he laid here, or do you think he was up in the tree?"

Rising, Vayden gazed up. He took several steps back and took another long sweeping look. "What do you think?"

Surprised, Melody stared, too stunned to formulate a rational opinion. No one ever asked her opinion on investigations, and she certainly never expected him to extend the courtesy.

Vayden laughed and shook his head, dislodging flecks of ice. "Six months, huh?"

"Um…"

"I think he laid on the ground to take the shots." Vayden took more steps back and spun in a slow circle. He crouched down again and removed the box. "Put this away too soon."

Using the tweezers, he picked up a spent rifle casing. Holding up the brassy shell, he tilted it back and forth. "Guess this answers our question," he said. "No one bothered to examine the scene."

His gaze met hers. "Still think the evidence is safe with you?"

Melody hated the insecurity that welled in her gut. Haven City Enforcement Services was a bastion of guardian duty. If a family couldn't trust the local enforcement division to handle a crime, who could they trust? The travesty rolled like a hot, heavy stone in her stomach.

"I guess not," she whispered. "What will you do with it?"

He stood, pocketing all the evidence. "Keep it safe until I can find someone trustworthy to take it. When we find Cia, we'll need all the proof we can for the accusation hearing."

"You're assuming her kidnapper and the killer are the same people."

"They're connected, at the very least."

"Perhaps," she said, falling in step beside him on the trail out of the park.

At her vehicle, she went to unwrap the scarf. Vayden waved her efforts off. "Keep it, that sorry excuse for an Ariot isn't near warm enough."

Melody sighed, thankful. The temperature would only continue to plummet as the sun fell from the sky. She tried to open her door, but the thin wood had frozen shut. Vayden took one hard tug and broke the seal. "Thanks."

He shook his head. "I'll follow you."

"I wanted to see your evidence, though," she argued.

An unreadable mask slid over his face. He glanced down the road, soupy with an icy slush. "Do you think that's such a good idea, what with you not wanting to be seen with me and all, to come up to my apartment?"

Grateful the cold disguised the heat of her cheeks, Melody tugged on the edge of the scarf and cleared her throat. "I'm sorry, if I made you feel—"

He held up a hand and shook his head. "Never mind. I'll still follow you." He rattled off his address, letting her know he lived on the same street as Harold's Book Emporium, which was a Haven City staple.

Melody climbed into her frigid vehicle, blowing on her hands before touching the blistering cold steering column. HCES had better Ariot's, but they were reserved, or assigned, to higher ranking enforcers. Since she'd obtained a high enough ranking to utilize a mode of transportation she could never hope to afford, not yet anyway, she wasn't going to complain. The rickety, should-have-been-recycled-for-parts ride was preferable to walking or taking a hired carriage.

Navigating the near-frozen roads was a slow journey. By the time she pulled into an available parking space at Vayden's building, the sun had long set, and her little ride barely managed to creak in, weighed down with a layer of ice. Shivering, Melody slammed her shoulder into the door. Vayden arrived, yanking while she applied her weight. The door rushed open. She would have tumbled onto the icy ground if he hadn't been so quick, snatching her mid-fall.

The solid strength of his arms wrapped around her and hauled her from the vehicle. Her feet slipped on the glassy bricks, forcing her to dig her fingers into his biceps for balance. His hold tightened around her waist. The action crushed her to his frame, every inch hard and so very male. Melody gasped, her attention shifting from trying to stand upright to being held.

A cloud of vapor puffed from between his full lips. Melody had the crazy urge to feel the warmth of his breath, to catch the mist on her mouth. He leaned closer, and for an expectant moment, Melody thought he would kiss her. Then he snapped his head back as if wanting no part of realizing what he was about to do. He took a step away, putting space, and cold air, between them.

After closing her Ariot's door, which required a firm kick to keep it shut, he maintained a hold on her upper arm and headed to his building. The cold kept her too occupied to be disappointed. Then again, what did she expect? She'd pushed him away at every opportunity. Shaking the cobwebs of the embrace from her mind, she reminded herself she had a duty to honor her family name. Vayden Dossett was not an attraction she could afford to have.

The double glass doors to the five-story building opened into a lush indoor garden. The first three stories of the front of the building were glass. Set deep, the first three floors looked out over the conservatory. Melody shook off the chill, breathing in the moist, warm air. The entry trail branched in three directions, straight, right, and left.

"I know this building," she said.

Vayden released his hold and motioned to the left path. "I'm sure you do."

Following behind him, unwinding the now too warm scarf, she shook her head. "No, I mean this is where Madeleine Fenwick lives."

"Yes, she's on the fifth floor." Vayden held open the door leading to the stairs.

"What floor are you on?" Melody asked, having learned when she visited the infamous matchmaker that the apartments became larger the higher the floor number. The top floor had only four residences.

"Fourth."

Melody lifted her brows at the announcement. "I see."

Vayden brushed past her on the stairs, leading the

way. "Did you expect me to be on the first floor, in a studio?"

"You are a bachelor, aren't you?" Melody felt the need to point it out. He had, after all, used the same matchmaker she had.

"Yes, but that doesn't mean I don't like space."

Expensive space. "Do you own or rent?"

"I own."

Melody choked on a cough. A year of her Tribunii salary wouldn't cover even a quarter of the cost of one of the apartments to purchase. "The private sector is good to you."

He cast one of his sly smiles over his shoulder. "I know it may come as a shock to you, but I am good at what I do, despite being gen-common."

On his floor, he held the door for her once more. An old-fashioned gesture a lot of the men she worked with never bothered to observe. Perhaps because most women considered themselves equal, or in some regards, even above their fellow men. In some instances, such as Vayden's shield guardian mother, they were. Yet Melody found herself enjoying his consideration.

The thick maroon carpet lining the corridor ate their footsteps, maintaining a still silence Melody was uneasy about interrupting. Vayden stopped and unlocked the second door on the left side of the wide hall. As usual, he let Melody enter first. Nervousness fluttered in her stomach as she crossed the threshold into his personal domain. After locking them in, he lit lamps and went to work on the pellet stove in the living room.

She'd expected sparse, masculine furniture and, if she were honest, a bit of a mess. Her father's personal spaces were always cluttered with discarded clothing, papers, and trash until the cleaning staff arrived once a week to do their magic. A long corridor stretched at an angle into an open floorplan for the living area. Four closed doors, a small narrow table for his personal items when he walked in the door, and framed art projects done by children, lined his hall.

The neatly organized shelves, polished hardwood floors, clean rugs, place set dining table, and empty sink all took her by surprise. Paper Wintervail birds coated in all shades of glitter, from brilliant pink to emerald green and diamond silver, hung from the ceiling in draping strands. Crystal Wintervail irises suspended from ribbons over the windows caught the weak light from the street below. Melody imagined during the day they cast rainbows in all directions around the interior.

At the end of a comfortable, blanket-covered couch, a black lacquered chest left her breathless. Hand-painted vines of bright green and gold framed a mother of pearl inlaid floralscape of flowers, birds, and butter-flies. Melody knelt in front of the Wintervail chest and traced the delicate scene in wonder. Carefully, she opened the lid and spied the beautifully wrapped pack-ages inside waiting to be opened Wintervail night. A tradition her parents had never fostered. Melody let loose a shaky breath and shoved old disappointments aside, slowly closing the lid.

When she sat back on her hunches, she found Vayden watching her closely. A little embarrassed to be caught snooping in his gift chest, she asked, "Does your family come here to celebrate?"

"No, we celebrate at my parent's estate. But my nieces won't let me get away with not having a Wintervail chest, so I store all my presents in there until Wintervail night."

Melody's heart fluttered in warmth. "That is sweet of you."

"It's self-preserving of me," he stated dryly, removing his jacket and hanging it on a set of pegs along the living room wall off the hallway. "You don't know my nieces."

Rising, Melody took another glance around his home. Under the bright colors of Wintervail, which would remain hanging for months to come, meant to get a family through the bleak, endless white and gray of the snow, were rich masculine colors. Dark brown trim along the pine floors brought out the warm hue of the wood and the cream of his walls. A subdued shade of burnt orange trimmed the ceiling and corners, accenting the medium brown of his furniture.

Inviting landscapes of rolling green wild-flower-covered hills, sun-drenched forests, and wildlife-infused ruins, brought a sense of vitality and life. In front of each floor-to-ceiling window overlooking the city beyond, large potted plants soaked up sun during the daylight hours and provided a sense of fresh renewal to the open space.

Unlike the house she'd grown up in, still sadly lived in, the apartment welcomed, invited, and even comforted. A sense of *right* settled over Melody, which she had no business feeling, or thinking on. Shoving the unwanted sensation from her mind, she held out the scarf she'd been carrying like a security blanket. "Thank you again, for letting me borrow this. And for allowing me into your home, it's very nice."

He blew out a heavy breath and glanced around.

"Thanks. Took me a couple years to get it the way I liked it, but all the effort paid off, I think."

"Not many people live outside their family home when they're unmarried."

Vayden laughed and hung up the scarf next to his jacket. "I haven't lived at my parents' home since my first contract at nineteen."

Melody gaped at him. "You've been married?"

"Three times." He held up his fingers.

Unwarranted jealousy zipped through her. Who were these women, and why wasn't even one of them in his life anymore? "Wow, is that why you went to Madeleine? To try to find a more suitable match?"

A dark brow arched toward his hair hairline. "The contracts weren't meant for a lasting relationship, Melody. They were for safe affairs. Of course, if something came of them, none of the women I'd married would have objected. But they never amounted to more than a year or two of comfort. And I didn't see Madeleine, she cornered me at the message boxes."

Melody stared at him. Surely, she misunderstood. "You married for… sex?"

"Safe sex," he clarified, heading down the hall. Her cheeks burned at his easy mention of something so intimate. "I've never been interested in playing the *maybe* game and wondering for two whole weeks if I'll become an infected zombie because I let my hormones rule me. Nor do I like to be with a stranger. The women I married felt the same. We ended each contract period on amicable terms."

Confusion, and if she were honest, a little frustration, made her trail after him. "You didn't love any of them?"

He shrugged as he lit a lamp just inside the door to what appeared to be his office. "Sure, they were all remarkable women that I wouldn't have asked to share my life for a time if I didn't care about and respect them. But, in the end, each of us decided, for whatever reason, when the contract expired, not to renew."

"I see."

Crossing his arms over his chest, which caused the fabric to pull tight across the thick muscles of his biceps, he regarded her in a manner that made her feet shift in discomfort. "How old are you?"

"Twenty-four."

"And you've never been contracted?"

Melody shook her head.

"Promised?"

"Once," she admitted, though she wished now she hadn't. She shoved her hands into her back pockets and rocked on her heels. The conversation had taken a dangerous turn she didn't want to expand on. "Why did Madeleine corner you if you aren't in the market for a love match?"

"I have known Madeleine for a long time. She was the one who let me know when this apartment came available for purchase. She's been trying to set me up since, as she put it, my first hussy-of-a-wife."

Melody's lips twitched. "She doesn't approve of your contracts of convenience?"

"Madeleine is a romantic to the marrow of her bones. She believes in one husband, one wife, forever after, the end," he stated with an eyeroll.

A wishful sigh yearned to escape from Melody's chest. Didn't all women dream of such? "Still, sounds like everyone was adult about the relationships, why was she upset? Really?"

His gorgeous eyes looked her over, from the top of her head to her toes, the sapphire melting into the gold. "I'll answer that, if you tell me more about your former promised."

3

———

Vayden knew he tread on dangerous ground.
Getting to know the beautiful young woman looking
vulnerable in his home couldn't lead to anything good.
At thirty-one and gen-common, he'd made peace with
the temporary relationships he'd found himself in. Not
for lack of trying to achieve something more perma-
nent. Kids were awesome, and having little humans of
his own running around would delight him in ways he
could only imagine. And Guardianess Melody Ericksen
was *not* for him. As she'd made clear months ago, and
continued to remind him of their opposite social status.
She needed another Gen-Heir to round out her life.
Vayden did not.

No, usually, he went for mutual attraction, strong
desire, and a personality he knew he could live with for
a year or more. The pull to Melody was there for him,
along with longing. Ah, but could he live with her?
Looking her over, from her pretty, rich brown curls, to
her sensibly booted toes, and the possibilities in-

between, he found himself imagining all the ways they could definitely *live*.

Her already pink cheeks flushed further. The teasing tip of her tongue darted across her lips, making them glossy. Needing something to do other than stare at her and feel his pants growing uncomfortably tight, he turned and searched for Henry's file. Since he'd been the one to share about his past, he'd wait her out. The reaction she'd had to his Wintervail chest, the wonder, excitement, curbed quickly by sadness and shuttered completely when she'd noticed him watching, told him things weren't all nice and tidy for Melody.

Patience paid off moments later. The whisper of fabric told him she'd walked deeper into the room. A covert glance found her studying the framed license allowing him to be a reward seeker in Sziveria, along with several awards from both the Sziverian National Investigative Division, and the Immigration and Import Regulation Agency for cases he'd assisted in.

"I was promised when I was sixteen," she said, her finger tracing the dark frame of his license.

The file open in his hands, Vayden turned to face her. "Not a legal age to marry."

"No," she agreed. Still refusing to look in his direction, she shifted to the floor-to-ceiling bookcase where all his investigative research books were shelved. "I can't believe I'm saying any of this to you. I've never told anyone."

Early in his career, he'd learned people confided in him, of their own accord, with little insistence from him. He simply had to be attentive. Focused solely on them and their problem. While he couldn't claim a Gen-Heir talent, the natural-born charisma from his father seemed to be Vayden's all the same. He allowed the file to flip closed and his weight to settle back onto the desks edge.

Continuing to face away from him, her ears cherry red, she trailed the binding of several books. "The man was old, seventy-nine. My parents found him through their family tree mapping. He didn't have any heirs, and the line ended with him. He was a primary guardian, who somehow, even at his advanced age, maintained his seat."

Vayden frowned, sadly knowing where her tale went. "If he married you, you could take over his ranked position."

"Providing the E&R committee agreed to award it to me on his death, yes."

"And your parents were willing to marry you to a man old enough to be your great-grandfather?"

A harsh breath left her. "My mother said it would be a short-lived marriage. My father said I'd probably remain a virgin, the man was too old to do anything useful to me."

"And?" Vayden pressed when silence reigned.

She shrugged and heaved another sigh. "And the man insisted on the contract signing being the day I was legal enough to wed. He asked for fifteen minutes alone with me, where he explained in graphic detail what he expected of his child-bride. Also, proving my father wrong. He would indeed be capable of a wedding night."

Vayden's gut clenched. "He didn't... do anything to you... did he?"

"No," Melody assured quickly. "No, he never

touched me. He did, however, touch himself quite often during our *alone time*."

Anger simmered in his veins over the innocence she'd been robbed of early in her teenage years. Of the excitement she should have had over her first promising, the idea of marriage, and love. Instead, she'd been forced to view her future through a lens of perversion, brought on her by those who should have been protecting her.

The petite line of her shoulders was as stiff as her spine. Vayden looked over the length of her legs, hidden by her pants. The cut of the fabric couldn't hide the soft swell of her butt, the attractive flare of her hips, or her narrow waist. His gaze shifted to her front, to breasts that wouldn't even fill his palm, and to her pretty face most would describe as charming. Could that awful moment be the only sexual experience she'd ever had? Despite the idea of another man touching all that creamy, delicately freckled skin, causing a rise of possessive jealousy, Vayden hoped not.

"What happened?"

"He died a week before we were to be contracted," she said. "And my parents weren't able to find anyone else willing to marry to help keep Gen-Heir genes in the family *and* ensure a ranked guardianship in the process. At least, they haven't been able to yet. Most marriages in ranked families appear to happen within the community, or beyond our borders."

"Yes, Ruthenia and Italyssa are popular choices."

Melody frowned. "I've seen."

"Asherwick's situation was unique, and personal. He truly loves her," Vayden said softly, recalling weeks ago when he'd run into Melody at the key guardian's house.

A forced smile spread across her face. "I have no doubt."

"Is what happened your sixteenth year the reason *you* sought out Madeleine Fenwick's services?"

She pulled a random book free and began flipping the pages. "Yes. I made an agreement with my mother."

When she didn't elaborate, and her spine remained taut, and her motions jerky searching the book, Vayden figured he'd let the topic drop. For now. He held up the file. "This is what you came for, yes?"

Her attention lifted from the book, her spring-green eyes wide. "Castien's interview?"

"The very one." He held the documents out to her. "You can use my desk or the dining table, wherever you're more comfortable."

She finally seemed to notice what she'd pulled from the shelf, if the surprise on her face as she closed the cover and took in the title. "Your collection of research is impressive."

"You're welcome to any of it, any time."

After shelving the book, she accepted the folder from him. An awkward smile tugged at her lips. The memory of her within kissing distance, her breath a lacy flutter of temptation, made him hyper-focused on her delectable pink mouth. Would she allow him to kiss her now, if he tried? The question blindsided him, just as the earlier desire to see if she tasted as sweet as her strawberry and jasmine scent. Melody Ericksen was off-limits.

Off limits, he repeated to himself, because he didn't

seem to be able to remember the Gen-Heir obsessed female wanted nothing to do with him.

"You keep surprising me," she said, opening the file. "I haven't exactly given you any reason to be nice to me or help me, and yet… you are."

Vayden sighed and crossed his arms over his chest. "Well, thanks for being honest. I like to think of myself as a pretty decent human being, when I choose to be."

"I think you choose to be pretty often," she surmised. "You took on this case, despite all the obstacles, because your friend asked you to."

Vayden shook his head at her misunderstanding. A fist tightened in his gut and around his heart as the grief he still admitted to not processing threatened. "Cia is like a little sister to me. Her mother was basically my aunt. Joshua was a little brother…."

His voice failed, and he cleared his throat and tried again. "A little brother I helped Henry bury." He looked away from her and took a centering breath. "This has impacted my family, deeply. The difficulty is only an obstacle if I choose it to be, and I don't, because it doesn't matter in the end. I *need* to find Lucianna."

Sympathy lighted her eyes. She reached across the short space separating them and laid a hand on his arm. "I'm sorry, I had no idea. We will find her, I promise."

THE MOMENT THE DECLARATION SLIPPED FROM HER LIPS, Melody stared at Vayden, shocked by her impulsiveness. There was no taking it back. She had to own the pledge.

He seemed aware of her discomfort and smiled. "I

appreciate it, but I'm used to working alone. If I have to find her on my own, it won't bother me any."

Melody hugged the folder to her chest. "No, we'll work together, as we agreed. Two heads are better than one in any investigation. This particular situation has extremes one person shouldn't handle alone."

Especially when the investigation was so personal. Melody would have suggested that he, like Henry, should rely on the HCES. Her faith in the service had been shaken, though. She agreed with Vayden, finding Lucianna Castien was the top priority. After being in his office and seeing the level of dedication he put into his work, Melody acknowledged her mistake. Vayden Dossett had turned out to be nothing like the predatory seekers she'd encountered in her career. He even had accolades from agencies she'd give just about anything to work for.

Nothing cluttered the small office space, not even stacks of papers. A polished wood desk sat against the wall, and a filing cabinet was behind the door. A large bookcase filled with research books on investigating, crime scene details, missing persons, and much more was positioned for easy access across from the desk. Her mind spun at all the information he had at his fingertips. She didn't think her division could claim the same.

Underneath her feet, an area rug in chocolate brown with sage green and crimson accents kept the room cozy and warm. If he happened to see a client in his office, an upholstered chair with an end table was positioned at an angle on the far wall. A green plant, which he must swap out with ones in the living room because not one window was in the office, kept the room from feeling gloomy. More landscapes Melody could get lost in if she allowed herself to graced the walls.

The inviting study, along with everything else she'd seen about his home, made Melody want to explore the other rooms. All that kept her from asking was knowing one of those rooms belonged to him. Where he slept. Melody turned and headed back to the safety of the living room, refusing to allow her brain to conjure the picture of Vayden in pajama pants and nothing else. Or worse… in the shower. Melody's heart stuttered as a wicked vision danced in her mind. Hot steam, cascading water, soap flowing a glistening trail down his naked chest to his…

Stop!

She gulped in air and blinked away the vivid fantasy.

"Are you okay?" his deep voice asked behind her.

Oh great, he'd noticed her little foray into dreamland. Clearing her throat, she pulled a chair out at his dining room table. "Of course." Her voice squeaked, and she tried again. "Yes, I'm fine."

"Can I get you anything? Tea? Coffee?" He opened a cupboard and took out a mug.

"If you're making some, sure. Thank you."

"Is Wintervail tea okay?"

Melody stared at him. The expensive, yet essential, Wintervail drink had been another tradition her parents refused to partake in. Actually, anything considered a direct connection to the global day of celebration never made it past her parents' threshold. Their reason for shunning the holiday had never been explained, and whenever Melody asked as a child, she'd been told they didn't answer to her.

By her teenage years, she'd given up. When her sister Lyrica was born, Melody vowed the little girl would have a special Wintervail, even if the two of them had to celebrate in secret. For several years, she'd managed to sneak a gift, and a few paper birds, into the house to make the season special when her sister was home on break from boarding school.

"Melody?" Vayden asked when she failed to respond.

"Yes, I'm sorry, that sounds perfect." *Better than perfect.* A sliver of anxiety wedged into her stomach, mixing with anticipation. How was she supposed to pretend she knew, even expected, what he'd place in front of her?

While he made their tea, Melody tried to focus on the neatly organized notes and interview of the Castien case. But the efficient, comfortable way he moved about in his kitchen, fascinated her. At home, her parents hired a cook for their meals and prepare snacks for the day. The cost was worth it to them to get a taste of ranked life. At least, they figured that must be how *the other half* lived. Having been in many ranked guardian homes, Melody had learned most of Szlverian's guardian population lived like any other family, cooking, and cleaning their own homes. Her mother had claimed Melody lied when she divulged that information, accusing her of trying to get out of her familial duty.

She'd finally settled into reading the information in front of her, making notes and writing out questions, when the sweet, spiced fragrance of the tea pulled her focus. Melody breathed in deep and raised her head. Vayden carefully set a steaming cup of creamy brown liquid in front of her. Melody's mouth watered, and every ounce of her self-control went into not snatching up the drink.

"Find any interesting observations?" he asked, sitting in the seat next to her. Close enough that the citrusy scent of him competed with the delicate orange wafting from the cups.

"Um…" Melody eyed the tea. Her fingers twitched. Would it taste as sugary as it smelled? Would she like it or find the flavor too sweet? "I'm not sure yet, still reading."

Vayden watched her closely. Those jewel-toned eyes missed nothing. "How is it you're twenty-four and have never had Wintervail tea?"

Melody's cheeks flamed. She fiddled with the pen. "That obvious, am I?"

"You look terrified." He brought the rim of his cup to his mouth and sipped. Melody couldn't stop the fascination of watching his lips take in the liquid, and his throat work. "You'll like it, I promise."

"I could never justify the expense, you know?" she managed, drawing the pretty painted porcelain closer. "Can't miss what you've never tried."

He didn't ask for more information, and Melody almost thanked him for the restraint. Motioning at her cup, he urged her on. "Well, go on then, it's not going to drink itself."

Feeling ridiculous, Melody took a small taste. The robust flavors of orange, cinnamon, black tea, and vanilla skated across her tongue. Pulling back, she blinked down at the cup. "Wow."

Vayden smiled. "Yep."

Melody took another sip, unable to stop a giggle of delight. "Thank you."

He lifted his mug with another smile. His gaze shifted to the window, where the inside reflected on the glass against a dark night. "It's getting late. Is anyone going to worry about you at home?"

Melody sighed and returned to the task at hand. No way would Vayden allow his notes to leave his apartment, not that she blamed him, she wouldn't either. "Probably not. My parents stopped keeping up with me a long time ago."

And as long as she kept attempting to secure a ranking in some form or fashion, they'd continue to leave her alone. Melody kept *that* depressing information to herself.

A pattern drummed on the table from his fingertips. "Well, I'm going to go take care of what we found today and do some other work. If you need me, I'll be in my office."

Tea in hand, he disappeared down the hall. An odd sense of loneliness filled her at his missing presence. She scoffed at the nonsensical reaction. She barely knew the man, and yet here she pined like some love-sick teenager. Forcing her attention back to the case, *the important thing*, she made several more notes.

Finally, the end of the interview allowed her to stop and stretch her aching back. Vayden had been meticulous in recording every word, every memory, even sketching a rough version of the crime scene Castien had relayed. The families were close, which could account for his precise attention to detail. But somehow, Melody knew he gave every case the same thorough treatment. She heaved a sigh. Darn it, she did not want to be impressed by him. Yet, here she sat, once again completely stunned by his competence.

After making sure she'd reorganized everything the way he had it, she went to find him in his office. The soft glow of two lamps highlighted his dark hair and made his already rich skin decadently colored. Faint scratches from his pen filled the room.

"Give me just a second, and we'll head to your place."

Melody slid the folder onto his desk, trying not to notice the warm, masculine scent of him or that he was close enough to touch. "I can drive myself."

"How? Your vehicle is probably a block of ice by now."

She lifted a brow. "And yours isn't?"

His broad shoulders rose and fell on a heavy sigh. "If that's the case, I'll take you up to Madeleine's."

"Why?"

He swiveled in the chair until he faced her. The elegant length of his body sprawled comfortably, looking every inch male with his arm draped over the rest and his legs stretched out. His black boots looked impossibly large so close to her smaller feet. Locks of hair framed his handsome face, and she shoved her hands in her pockets to keep from reaching out to smooth the strands back. The shadow of a beard darkened his strong jaw, defining the rugged lines of his face.

"You have to ask me why?" he questioned, his voice husky.

Faster than she could react, Vayden leapt from the chair and pinned her to the wall between his desk and the edge of the bookcase. Awareness tingled along her nerves. An unexpected excitement coiled in her stomach. His gaze, more gold than blue, swept over her face to land on her mouth. Two large hands circled her wrists, as though she'd be able to escape. For the second time this evening, she found masculine strength pressed over almost every inch of her. Her heart thrummed a fast echo in her ears.

Somehow, he managed to move closer, his knee shifting between her thighs, making her gasp, which seemed to be what he had planned all along. He swept in, his mouth fastening to hers. His tongue invaded, demanded, and explored in hot, wet strokes. The kiss wasn't the inexperienced, sloppy attempts she'd had from her virgin lover so many years ago. No, Vayden kissed like the man he was. Strong. Assertive. Skilled.

Time fell away. Melody's world reduced to Vayden's lips devouring any notions of intimacy she'd once had. Her past familiarity with the male gender became a pathetic memory. Need burned into a hot ache at her center. Pulsing waves of desire made her tremble. At some point, she had no recollection of when, her hands had been restrained to the wall above her head. Vayden's chest crushed to hers. The hard proof she wasn't alone in her wanting pressed into the soft flesh of her belly.

Melody knew sex with Vayden would be nothing like the frantic moments she'd stolen when she'd decided her virginity would not be lost to an old man, but on her terms with who *she* decided. At a house party her parents had thrown celebrating a successful lineage certification for a client, she'd managed without much difficulty to seduce a boy her age in the darkness of their vacant greenhouse. The uncomfortable, over much too fast encounter, had left her knowing sex wasn't something she'd ever miss.

Until now.

Every inch of Melody yearned to know what he would do to her. How he could make her *feel*. Rashness had her forgetting decorum. A haze of desire had her forgetting every promise she'd made to herself, to her parents. When his mouth tore from hers, she whimpered and followed, trying to pull him back in.

"Now you know why you'll be staying far away from me," he growled, his lips trailing down her jaw to the sensitive flesh of her throat.

"No," she groaned in denial. She was exactly where she needed to be.

"Oh, yes." He lifted his head, the sapphire completely gone now, leaving only blazing gold. "Unless you marry me. I don't take anyone but my wife to my bed."

Yes almost slipped for her. Biting her tongue, she stared at him, shocked over the seductive power he'd wielded. He leaned in again and stole her breath for the second time with another open-mouthed kiss. Her toes curled in her boots, and her nails bit into her palms, still held captive above her head. Over and over again, his tongue teased and stroked, making promises her body wanted to discover. The euphoric sensation of floating forced a groan of pleasure from deep inside.

He broke free and rained gentle, fluttering kisses along her cheek, jaw, and down her throat to her collarbone, where he licked. "You taste as sweet as you smell. Like strawberries and flowers," he whispered against her skin, sending a delicious shiver through her.

"Vayden," she whimpered, not sure what she expected, only knowing she needed *something*.

"Ah," he drew out, breathing deep as he sought out her mouth again. "Too bad I'm not good enough for you, hmm, guardianess?"

4

———

VAYDEN WANTED TO REGRET HIS TAUNT. BUT COULDN'T make himself feel anything other than vindicated as another shudder ran the length of her frame pressed so deliciously against him, allowing him to feel every womanly curve she possessed. He was pretty sure the buttons on his pants and front seam were in danger of ripping from the pressure of his massive hard-on. Melody Ericksen's passionate responses came as a pleasant surprise. Her innocence, not so much.

He'd always preferred his women to know what happened between a couple. To know what they liked and didn't like. To be able to express expectations and restraints. Only one time had he allowed himself to court an innocent. The frustrating results had left him kissing her hand and wishing her luck with her future husband. No promises made. No virgin territory ventured onto.

And yet, here he stood, seducing a woman he should be hauling upstairs, far away from him, to the safety of a chaperone. Caressing an index finger down her cheek, he circled a hand around her throat. Her pulse beat strong and rapid against his palm. "How innocent are you, Guardianess Ericksen?"

Her cheeks, already flushed, darkened further. "I don't see how that's any of your business."

He stroked his thumb over her plump bottom lip, smearing the damp evidence of their kiss. Slowly, he pressed inside her mouth, curious to see what she'd do. He almost fell to his knees when her hot tongue stroked along the pad of his thumb. Her gaze stared at him in defiance, and she bit with enough force to send a sizzle straight to his painful erection.

Smiling, Vayden pulled his finger free. "I shared with you. Is it a secret?"

"I wasn't contracted." She glanced away, and he figured if he didn't have her restrained to the wall, she would have fidgeted.

"Ah." He used his knuckle under her chin to force her gaze back to him. "And he was?"

She blinked, startled. "What? No! Oh wow, no. We were… sixteen. Well, he might have been seventeen. Definitely not contracted."

This time Vayden stared at her in shock. "Sixteen?"

She licked those kiss-swollen lips, and he had to swallow a groan. "Yes?"

"Has there been anyone else?"

A heavy sigh feathered across his neck. "I haven't wanted there to be anyone else. Not really."

He quirked a brow. "Not really?"

She shrugged and looked away from him again.

The answer came to him in a flash of insight, and he grinned. "Asherwick."

"Briefly," she admitted with a huff.

Vayden slid his fingers into the silky riot of her curls, smoothing them away from her face. "Lucky for me."

Her fingers wrapped around his wrists and held him captive this time. Vayden took her mouth in another leisurely kiss, needing with a force he couldn't deny to taste her again. He didn't know how long he spent exploring the mysteries of her mouth. Her little whimpers of longing urged him on. By the time he allowed reality to sink back in, she was wrapped around him in a manner that if they were naked, he'd be inside her. When had that happened?

"I know better," he said more to himself than to her, even as he flexed his hips and made them both gasp with pleasure.

"I don't," she whispered, her body trembling against his.

Resignation brought reality crashing back. "But you won't marry me."

"I barely know you," she said, unwrapping from around him.

"You know me well enough to stand here kissing me for an hour."

Melody rolled her eyes and gave his chest a gentle shove. "An hour is not a year, Vayden."

He looked her over. At the pretty, passion-filled glaze in her eyes, lips swollen from his attention, and a flushed chest showcasing her arousal, and couldn't stop an arrogant smile from crossing his face. "I could convince you a year would be worth it."

Determination flashed in her gaze. "There will be no convincing."

"No, there won't be," he admitted, helping her

straighten from the wall. "Because I'm not going to persuade you that I have value, despite my genetics. I shouldn't have to."

But damn if he didn't want to anyway.

Thankfully his head managed to stay engaged, the one that had more thought process than *right now*, and he could hold onto his self-respect for another day. Untucking his shirt to cover her effect on him because it wasn't going away anytime soon, he grabbed his keys and led her out of the apartment. They took the stairs down in silence. The greenhouse only had a few late evening walkers.

The moment he opened the door leading onto the sidewalk, he knew travel would be unlikely. Ice shimmered on the vacant street and coated the bricks at the edge of the sidewalk. Melody shrugged from the warmth of the greenhouse, her expression resigned. There'd be no going home for her tonight. They took the stairs to the fifth floor, and Melody's steps lagged behind.

"Are you sure about this?" she asked halfway to Madeleine's door.

"Yes. Madeleine won't mind. She has the space, and she'll understand. Trust me." He paused at the matchmaker's door. "Are you sure your parents will be okay with you not coming home?"

"They probably haven't even noticed."

Vayden opted not to reflect on what kind of parents didn't care when their child never came home for the night. Parents who seemed to have so much control over their daughter, she wouldn't, couldn't, think about a relationship outside of a ranked guardianship. When he raised his hand to knock, she grabbed the back of his shirt.

"Wait," she said, breathing deeply. "Would you really contract with me?"

Vayden rapped his knuckles on the door before she said something she'd regret. But he answered anyway, "In a heartbeat, guardianess."

MELODY SAT CURLED ON PLUSH CUSHIONS IN A WINDOW seat. The room she'd been shown to graciously by Madeleine Fenwick was nicer than any room she'd seen in her life. Thick, navy-blue brocade curtains draped from the ceiling to enclose the bed in warmth if the pellet stove in the bedroom ran out. A chest-style dresser made of highly polished cherry wood with a mirror rising to the ceiling dominated the front wall. Paintings of songbirds and flowering fields brightened the already cheery, yellow-painted walls. On every surface and draped in all the corners, Wintervail birds and irises hung in a cheery reminder of the celebration denied to her year after year. The cloying scent of vanilla, orange, and cinnamon filled the room.

All in all, the sophisticated elegance made Melody uneasy. She wanted to return to the comfortable home Vayden had built around himself. Tracing an abstract shape in the vapor covering the frosty window panes, she swallowed a sigh. Confusion warred inside her.

She shouldn't want anything to do with Vayden. Yet, his brutally honest words struck a nerve. As did his fiery kisses. Her body still hummed, alive and desperate for his touch.

She didn't like the image he drew of her. One of prejudice, and she now had to admit, misinformation. Vayden was intelligent. Smarter than many of the guardians, ranked and unranked, she worked with. Honestly, she struggled to figure out where he was deficient. At least by her parent's standards. She expected him to be slower, to take more time to figure out where important information fit, or even *what* may be imperative to a case.

Yet, at every turn in the case, he'd proven her equal on multiple levels. Where exactly did *her* Gen-Heir ability come into play? A niggle of doubt crept inside her mind. What if her testing had been wrong?

Melody laid her head on her drawn knees and stared at the night. Ice and snow blanketed the empty street five-stories below. Amber lights twinkled across the city like sporadic stars. In the quiet, loneliness settled in deep.

I could convince you a year would be worth it.

The words echoed in her mind. Enticed and seduced with the same depth as his kisses. Eight years ago, her future lay in the hands of a seventy-something predator.

For a ranked guardianship.

No love. Selfish passion. For almost a year, she'd dreaded the dark because visions of an old man rutting away, using her young body, had stolen her nights. Thankfully, her parent's subsequent attempts to marry her off had failed, leaving little choice but to allow her to search for a mate on her own.

Sadly, they had two qualifiers. The potential match had to be either a Gen-Heir capable of obtaining a ranking, or already within a seat. Vayden failed on both counts. And didn't that crack her heart a little? Melody stilled at the shocking revelation.

Deep inside, she conceded a year wouldn't be near long enough. While Vayden didn't promise love, he tempted her with a mutual passion. A chance to know what a normal life could entail. Hugging her knees, she worried for her self-control, or lack of where he seemed to be concerned. If, after only eighteen hours, the man left her fantasizing about an impossible future, what would happen a week from now? Melody squeezed her eyes shut.

No.

She slammed the door closed on any further illusions. A young woman was somewhere being held captive, alone, hurting over the loss of her mother and little brother, scared. Finding Lucianna Castien was all Melody needed to focus on.

A sharp rap on the door pulled her from the troubling thoughts. Unfolding herself from the bench, she called for the person to enter. Madeleine swept in, arms laden with fabric. Her silver-threaded dark hair fell to her hips in a thick curtain. The long, pink nightgown she wore brushed the carpeted floor with each step.

"I have some clothes here for you and a towel." Madeleine set the small stack on the corner of the dresser. Her hand patted the load. "Delanee is a bit taller than you, but I think the dress and nightgown will be fine."

Melody glanced at the black boots tucked under the edge of the bed and smiled. Good thing she had tomorrow off. At least where her HCES duties were concerned. "Thank you, I appreciate it. I would have been fine in what I'm wearing."

Madeleine waved a hand. "Child, you can't wear the same clothes all day, sleep in them, and expect to wear them yet again. What kind of a hostess would I be if I let you walk out of my house looking like a street person?"

Deciding not to point out that leaving the house in a dress and boots wouldn't prove much better of a fashion statement, she did like her Mistress of Etiquette had taught and made the appropriate noises of gratuity. "Do you get stranded, unexpected guests often?"

A twinkle danced in her beautiful eyes, not quite golden but not quite green either. An odd mix between the colors, pure in its intensity, marking her a Gen-Heir. "Everyone in this building knows if someone needs a chaperoned evening, I am always available."

Melody threaded her fingers together. "Yes, Vayden mentioned you are a firm believer in contracts."

"I am a firm believer in living somewhere I don't have to worry about an HRS episode," Madeleine stated. "Of which the occupants of this building can proudly say hasn't occurred in almost five years now."

Melody's eyes widened. "That is impressive."

"Even if people don't stay exclusive in a contract, being aware of the danger, and reminded to be responsible is important to me." Madeleine went to the bed and turned the blankets down. An echo of a motherly chore she once did nightly. Across the spacious mattress, she met Melody's curious stare. "As is reminding young ladies genetics are a lottery, not a guarantee, so therefore who we tie ourselves to in marriage matters."

"Gen-Heir traits—"

"Are never promised unless one parent is Ruthenian

and the other a confirmed Gen-Heir. Here in Sziveria, only two bloodlines have a pedigree, the Dandridge and Edmond families. Who, until this generation, married only into genetic families with records as meticulous as theirs. Not even our own monarchy-elect is without a gen-common, Guardianess Ericksen." Madeleine smoothed away imaginary wrinkles from the sheets. "And if I am not mistaken, child, you are a second-generation Gen-Heir, which means you wouldn't even qualify for certification to marry a Ruthenian. Your children perhaps will qualify if the man you marry is also a second or third generation, and your union doesn't produce a gen-common."

Which was why, after two children, most couples looking to keep their genetics *pure* opted not to risk the chance of having more if both turned out to be a genetic heir. Her parents had calculated the statistics, and Melody, if married to the correct man, had a less than twenty-five percent chance of producing a *g-c* child. By the same degree, her numbers dwindled to the same percentage for producing a Gen-Heir if she married the wrong man.

"My youngest daughter married a Ruthenian, Delanee's father, did you know that?" Madeleine asked.

Melody shook her head.

"Oh yes, and Bella is a second-generation Gen-Heir on my side, and a first generation on her fathers," Madeleine said, propping a hip on the bed. She folded her hands on her knee and offered a small, yet cutting smile. "They have given me eleven grand-babies"

Melody couldn't contain the choked gasp. "Eleven?"

Madeleine's smile grew. "Yes. Markus tried to warn her about what marrying a Ruthenian meant. She had to have him anyway. So, he has given her eleven beautiful children. All but one of them are beast masters, but each of them may carry a normal, common gene instead of a talent. By marrying her, he had to give up his entire country due to that possible common thread. Do you think he regrets his decision?"

Words failed Melody. She honestly didn't know how a pure-blooded Gen-Heir felt about having common genetics in his line.

"He doesn't," Madeleine answered. "His fourth born is the Arch Guardian Wolvenguard. My grandson agreed to take on the most dangerous job in our nation because he's capable, not because of his genetics. Which, I will point out, are as strong as anything Ruthenia has produced, despite his mother's gen-common trait in the mix."

"Why are you telling me all this?" Melody asked, inching closer to the bed.

Madeleine raised a brow and cast a pointed look. "That beard burn on her chin, darling, tells me Vayden brought you up here because he couldn't trust you to stay put in his niece's sweet pink bedroom."

Heat bloomed across Melody's cheeks. Her skin tingled at the mention of Vayden's stubbled chin, having done a number to her softer skin while he kissed her senselessly. "Okay, yes, we may have kissed a little."

"When you came to me for guidance about a future spouse, I chose correctly, Melody Ericksen. Vayden may have a dreaded *g-c* next to his name on your parent's little family tree chart for the Dossett line, but I'm not convinced that means anything except eye color." Madeleine stood with a grace that belied her age. "He can afford to live in this building because he's good at what he does. Even the very agencies that won't hire him for a guardian position recognize his talent. They've utilized him enough, that's for sure. Don't let your parents bias stand in the way of your happiness."

Madeleine's expression turned even more sober. "Be your own woman, Melody. Make your *own* choices."

5

———

THE SCENT OF SALTY BACON MIXED WITH SWEET PASTRY pulled Melody from sleep. The fragrances were strong enough to taste. Groaning, she reached for a pillow and wrapped her body around the comforting fluff. After her day yesterday, she wasn't quite ready to face reality.

"Not a morning person, eh guardianess?" a deep voice rumbled with laughter.

Lethargy fogged her mind and slowed her thought process. Smacking the nasty taste of sleep from her mouth, she buried deeper into the cozy warmth of the covers. A niggle that she'd missed something important had her blinking her eyes open.

And stared straight into an amused golden-blue gaze.

He was close enough for her to see the various flecks of richer azure and amber saturating the intense hues. Melody squeaked in alarm and scooted away from him. Too far, too fast. On another squeal, she found herself on the floor, the blankets covering her head. *Oh, sweet summer sun, Vayden was here!* Perhaps if she squeezed her eyes shut and pretended she hadn't seen him, that her morning would start in an entirely different manner, and he'd disappear.

"Are you going to cower over there all morning? I brought you food," he said, clearly unaware he wasn't supposed to still be around.

Melody's hands fisted in the tan fabric cocooning her. Every inch of her skin burned with mortification. "Um...Wha..." Her voice cracked and failed. She cleared her throat and tried again. "What are you doing in here?"

The mattress bumped and jostled her shoulders. The wood frame groaned. Melody held tighter to the blankets, alarmed to realize he'd climbed onto the bed.

"You must be hiding because you're naked under there," he said with a hint of smugness.

"Even more reason for you to *leave*."

The sheets shifted and billowed. Vayden's face appeared at the edge of the bed. Lying on his stomach, under the covers, he folded his arms under his chin and peered down at her. The sun glowed through the thin fabric, making the already intimate setting one of complete isolation. They were in their own little bubble. Melody curled into herself, feeling small and uncertain. The nightgown she'd borrowed pooled on the floor around her.

"Not naked," he said, grinning.

His bed-diving escapade had left his hair a wispy mess around his face. He'd shaved this morning. The harder lines of his face seemed muted without the gruff hair covering his jaw. Melody found she missed them.

The provocative scent of him filled the enclosed space. She pressed her lips closed, far too aware that she hadn't brushed her teeth yet, and he was temptingly close.

"I brought you food," he said again, his voice going as soft as his gaze. "Good morning."

Melody's heart stuttered. "Good morning," she whispered.

"You look good when you first wake up," he said.

His eyes swept over her, starting at her toes peeking out from underneath her nightgown to the tangled chaos of curls Melody wanted to smooth into some semblance of order. Somehow, she refrained, not wanting him to know he affected her the way he did.

Seemingly satisfied, his gaze returned to hers. "A man could get used to seeing you like this."

"Why are you in here?" Maybe if she inquired enough times, he'd answer.

"Madeleine asked me to bring you breakfast."

"To my room?"

He grinned again. "She said we'll be sharing one soon enough; no point in playing the modesty card now."

Melody whimpered and dropped her head to her knees. This was a disaster. "I should have walked home in the ice last night."

Vayden laughed as he rose. The sound sent heat through her body. He was so alive, vital. She wanted to wrap herself around him and experience all that male energy. With the sweep of his arm, he sent the covers curling away from them. The bright light from the windows made her squint. Still chuckling, he braced with his knees on the mattress, thighs spread and held his hand down to her.

"Come on, guardianess." He made an up motion.

She wanted to bat his hand away and tell him to leave. She could get up and eat on her own. No help necessary. Yet, she reached for him. Her fingers slipped onto his large, rough palm. On a one-armed tug, he pulled her up like she weighed nothing. Only he didn't stop once she was up. With a swift pull, he set her off balance, and she tumbled toward the bed into his arms.

Two things slammed into her at once. Vayden's body and the awareness that they were on the bed. Together. Panic and desire seized her. The emotions warred for dominance. She wasn't ready to fall into bed with him, even though she couldn't think of anywhere else she'd rather be than in his arms, experiencing the delicious arcs of yearning he sent through her. Then again, she rationalized, since she hadn't agreed to a contract, he wouldn't touch her.

And why did that bring a pang of loss to her heart?

His hands moved to her shoulders, where he steadied her. Smiling, he pressed a kiss to her forehead. Then he was gone, sliding off the bed. The wicked gleam she'd come to recognize still filled his eyes. "That's an excellent view. I will see it again, *soon*."

He left before she could utter a word, the door clicking softly closed behind him. Melody clenched her fists into her nightgown and noted how she knelt on the mattress, her nipples pebbled and pronounced through the thin fabric, looking like a woman bent on seduction. Which she knew nothing about. Convincing a teenage boy to a tryst didn't count, she was pretty sure he wouldn't have said yes any faster, regardless. Sighing, she waddled on her knees to the nightstand, where her breakfast waited.

Two frosted scones, crisp fried bacon, a bowl of fruit, and a cup of Wintervail tea, awaited and looked divine. The amount of food made her wonder if Madeleine had intended the meal to be shared. Nibbling on bacon, Melody bounced off the bed and went to the clothes neatly folded on the dresser. Perhaps Vayden struggled with temptation, too, more than he let on. The idea should have brought a sense of relief that she wasn't alone in her desires. Her shoulders slumped, and she frowned at her reflection in the mirror. Nothing would ever happen between them, no matter what the confident matchmaker claimed.

Melody dressed and then gathered together the tray. Her work boots were bulky and heavy compared to the near weightless rose-colored silk floating around her ankles. The simple gown was a touch too big, almost sweeping the floor. Without a shower, and the special cream she used in her hair, there was no hope for her curls. They surrounded her head in a frizzy, unsightly mess.

The soft hum of conversation and laughter made Melody slow at the end of the hall leading to the main living area. Like Vayden's apartment, Madeleine's floor plan was spacious and open, the outfacing walls mostly glass, allowing in abundant natural light. Gathered around a circular table, Madeleine, Vayden, and a stunning woman with spiral wine-colored curls and milk-in-tea skin sat conversing comfortably. The woman turned to look at her, and Melody almost gasped at the unusual golden shade of her eyes. They were almost... feline. A smile lit up her entire face, drawing attention to her full mouth and straight, white teeth.

"Melody, isn't it?" The woman rose, all tall, lithe lines and an elegant grace Melody could never hope to achieve.

"Yes," Melody replied, feeling ridiculous in the borrowed clothes and her boots, with crazy hair. She sighed at how she must look.

"I'm Delanee Ralston." Smiling, Delanee reached for the tray. "I hope you slept well."

Melody tried not to be overwhelmed, knowing she spoke to the sister of an arch guardian. If her mother were here, she would be fawning all over Delanee as if she were royalty. "Really great, thank you."

"I'm so pleased to hear that, child," Melanie chimed in. "I know the rooms can get a bit cold this time of year."

Vayden stood, stretched in a way that sent the muscles of his shoulders, chest, and biceps rolling. A quiver danced deep in Melody's stomach. All her willpower went into not pressing her hand to her disloyal body part.

"Do you have everything?" he asked, pushing his chair back into place at the table.

"Why? I can see myself down and to my Ariot," she replied.

Vayden shoved his hands into his jacket pockets and smiled. "I'll walk you down, make sure it starts in this cold."

Melody wanted to argue, but the sad fact was she couldn't deny her vehicle may not start. "Okay, thank you. I'll go grab my clothes." She turned to Delanee. "How do I return your dress to you?"

Delanee waved the concern away. "The next time you're visiting with Vayden, bring it up."

Melody glanced at Vayden, who raised a brow as if daring her to say she wouldn't be at his apartment again anytime soon. Another fact she couldn't refute. Imagining this was how a cat felt cornered by dogs, Melody simply nodded in understanding and disappeared back to the room she'd slept in. Clothes gathered in her arms, she said her polite goodbyes, filled with all the proper gratitude. Not difficult, since she *was* very grateful for the warm bed and delicious food. She forced herself once again to not be overwhelmed by their position in a society she only dreamt of moving within.

Hugging her clothes to her chest, she fell instep beside him in the public corridor. "You seem very comfortable with them."

Vayden shrugged and held open the stair doorway. "Delanee's brother Deklan is the newest Wolvenguard. He sometimes has to work with my mother in Transport, especially where the rail lines are concerned. I've worked with three other guardians in the Ralston family, or ran into."

"Madeleine said there are eleven children." Melody still had a hard time wrapping her head around the huge family and the woman who birthed them.

Vayden grinned. "That's kind of what happens when a Ruthenian male marries outside his country. I know of another blended family that blossomed, just not as fully."

"I knew Ruthenians were different, I didn't realize by so much."

"Yes, their biology is different from the rest of the

world. Not so much that they can't make babies, obviously, but if their lore is to be believed, they were a genetically created race, before the cataclysm. Their sole purpose was to be able to make more perfect babies with exceptional abilities."

"Gen-Heirs," Melody murmured.

Vayden still heard. "Supposedly, yes. The first Gen-Heirs are recorded in Sziveria shortly after the Primal Years ended when inhabited world exploration finally began. So, many, if not all, Gen-Heirs can trace their lineage back to Ruthenia if their family has kept correct records."

Which, Melody had learned, most had. And with a little research help, her parents provided those wishing to return to their Ruthenian roots to seek a mate that required certification verifying strong genetic inheritance traits. Something the Ericksen's couldn't deliver. Not yet. That was Melody's familial task. To produce a Gen-Heir child with a ranked guardian. Or even better, obtain a ranking herself, therefore ensuring whomever she married took on her name.

On days like today, when she encountered families who seemed so comfortable in their place within society, the duty weighed her down like a heavy stone and threatened to overwhelm. Why couldn't her parents be satisfied with the life and name they'd built for themselves? They were the premier couple for ancestry research and authentication. Ruthenia trusted their results because they were grueling in their methods and honest with their conclusions. The prestige was never enough. Gregory and Willow Ericksen set the expectations high and expected them to be met. Regardless of how their daughter felt about the matter. A lot of money and time had gone into Melody's education to ensure her eventual place within a ranked society.

Then an arrogant gen-common swept everything away and, for the first time, made Melody question all she'd been taught to achieve.

The echo of their shoes on the stairs pulled her from the depressing thoughts. In the greenhouse, residents walked the bark trail. Birds trilled softly overhead while squirrels smart enough to seek shelter in the wild enclosure scurried up trees and between underbrush. The massive conservatory soothed, made Melody inhale the moist, earthen air in deep. All the lush green life helped ground her. She wanted to stop and bury her hands into the rich loam, feel the heartbeat of the plants growing healthy indoors. Her fingers twitched, and she picked up the pace before temptation could get the best of her.

A cold gust swept curls around her face and bit into her fingers the second they stepped outside. Ice crunched beneath her boots. Without the extra layers usually worn in the winter, the silk dress did little to keep the wind out. A shiver raced along Melody's body.

Once again, Vayden had to help with her vehicle. The door had iced over. Only his strength cracked the seal open. Melody leaned her weight on the doorframe to swing inside. Halfway in, a harsh crack rent the air. Her boot slipped on the slick brick as the thin wooden frame fell away. Cursing, Vayden grabbed for her, his thick arm banding around her chest.

Before she could take another breath, she found her back pressed against his solid torso. His hand gripped her ribs, pressing his thumb into the side of her breast. Melody used his forearm for leverage. Her fingers dug into the muscle beneath the thick layer of leather. The soles of her boots fought for purchase on the frozen ground. She tried, *so hard*, to ignore the heat of his body, the scent of him, to keep the flashes of memories of his mouth on hers skittering across her mind.

"Are you all right?" he asked, his mouth so close his breath fanned her ear.

A sizzle of desire shot straight through her. She gritted her teeth. "I'm fine."

He helped her upright and then reached for the door, hanging precariously on one hinge. One swift yank, and the door popped free. Melody sighed.

"Well, at least I can still drive," she said, sliding onto the stretch canvas seat. Bitter wind swirled around the interior.

He leaned his arm on top of the Ariot and looked inside. "I can drive you. I don't mind."

"No, I'll be fine," she assured. She started the ignition process. The vehicle trembled awake. Melody smiled at him.

Her confidence came too soon. An awful, humiliating tear preceded her butt slamming to the floor. Melody stared at the center of the steering wheel.

"Still think you can drive it," Vayden asked, his voice devoid of emotion.

Melody flexed her hands on the wooden wheel and took a calming breath. "I can't imagine what you must think of me."

"That's probably for the best."

The husky edge to his words had her snapping her attention to him. Heat filled his gaze. She swallowed and quickly looked away. "I'll..."

"Accept my offer?"

All she could manage was a nod.

. . .

AFTER MELODY SLIPPED INSIDE, VAYDEN CLOSED THE DOOR to his Ariot. He glanced at her broken ride and shook his head. How Haven City could allow their enforcers to drive around in such pathetic excuses for a safe mode of transport, Vayden would never know. He'd asked his mother about it once since she oversaw the transportation division of Haven City, which included all the government-assigned vehicles. She'd had no decent answer other than the patrons of the city could only afford so much.

Halfway through the drive, he gave up and tried to pull Melody into comfortable conversation. Stiff as a board, she stared out the window, her hands clasped in her lap. Vayden sighed and made a slow turn when she motioned.

"It would be easier if you spoke," he said, easing around a horse-drawn carriage on the sleepy street. When she continued to remain silent, he tried again. "It's not your fault HCES provided you with an unsafe Ariot. Not like the vehicle is yours, personally."

She glanced around his ride, to the small space behind the front seats for personal items, or even a baby holder, making the vehicle family friendly, to the polished wood of the interior and soft padded leather seats. The gears shifted smoothly under his direction. The magnetically powered engine hummed an elegant sound under the hood. Her fingers brushed the edge of her seat.

"I've never been in an Ariot this nice before," she said quietly. "Must have cost a fortune."

"Nothing I couldn't afford," he replied. "I need a

reliable vehicle to not only navigate the city, but some of the wilder roads beyond, often at higher speeds." Vayden smoothed a hand along the polished dash. "This was worth every raimark."

"You must be very good at what you do."

He glanced at her. "I don't think the upper agencies would have given me awards if I sucked at my job," he said, chuckling.

"That's not what I meant." She took a deep breath and tucked her hands underneath her dress. "You must be able to request a great fee for your services because you're worth the amount."

Vayden shrugged. "I charge what people can honestly afford. If I'm able and I have the time, I don't turn anyone away. A mother living in the rows with a missing son is as important as a primary guardian with a wayward husband."

"That's very noble of you."

Vayden cut her another glimpse. "Noble? Not so much. A good neighbor, yeah, I'll take that."

"This is it," she whispered, motioning to a two-story, pale blue house with white trim and a short stone porch.

A bricked in bronze plaque set in a pillar before the walkway read *Ericksen Ancestry Research and Verification.* Melody gathered together the small pile of clothing she'd set at her feet. She made no move to leave, simply stared out the window, silent. Vayden drummed his fingers on the steering wheel. Anxiety and nervousness practically rolled off her in visible waves.

"I thought you said they wouldn't be upset you didn't return home last night," he said, breaking the quiet. He reached for the door handle.

"They won't."

He flexed his jaw and stared at the picturesque house and the tidy landscaping surrounding it. "Then what's wrong?"

"They…" her voice cracked. She cleared her throat and tried again. "I don't think they'll understand you."

Vayden frowned. His fingers tightened on the handle. "What is there to understand?"

Her lips disappeared as she pressed her mouth into a grim line. He imagined she bit them inside by the faint quiver of her chin. "Their prejudice runs deep, and…." She shook her head and breathed out a long sigh. "I can see myself to the door."

The shock of hurt left Vayden staring at her. He wasn't sure *why* he felt the unfamiliar emotion, he'd certainly been rejected in such a manner enough times to no longer feel much where his status was concerned. However, for some reason, perhaps because he'd allowed her to get a little too under his skin, he'd expected more of Melody. In what way, he wasn't sure. Did he really expect her to march him to her parent's steps and flaunt his common status in their face? Or perhaps he'd simply hoped she wouldn't care at all.

Vayden released the handle and clenched his jaw in disappointment. Foolish ideology had no place in his life. He'd proven himself, time and again, with his peers. If he were honest with himself. If she chose to continue to allow her parents bias to shadow her world, there was nothing he could do. Nor did he want to. Melody Ericksen had to come to her own conclusions, form her own thoughts. Which he hoped she would at some point. Even if for no other reason than to help her see the world from a different perspective. One not formed by the opinions of others, but by hers.

As he took hold of the wheel, he had to remind himself not everyone had been raised by open, accepting parents like the Dossetts. And Amari Dossett's family held the plaque for Worst-Parents-in-History where Vayden was concerned. His mother had learned the hard way how far an elder generation was willing to go to seek power for an ancestral line. Vayden figured Melody and his mother had a lot in common. He quirked a brow. Maybe they needed to meet.

"Very well," he said with a calm he didn't feel. "I'll give you until lunch today. The roads should have thawed out enough between here and Caris to travel safely. If I don't see or hear from you, I'll begin the investigation on my own. I can't wait any longer."

"I'll be there." She paused halfway out of the vehicle. "Thank you, for everything. And… I'm sorry."

Vayden tsked and shook his head. "Yeah, see, that's the thing, guardianess. If you were truly sorry, you wouldn't need to apologize to me because nothing worth apologizing over would have happened."

A vibrant flush spread across her cheeks. She didn't deny the accusation, simply nodded and slipped from his Ariot, leaving behind the delicate feminine scent of strawberries and jasmine. Vayden watched her amble along the neatly laid stone walk to the door, her gate almost unsure in her work boots and the dress floating around her ankles. The glossy mane of her dark curls danced in a riot around her head, fluttered and teased by the wind. His hands tightened around the wheel at the memory of all that silk against his palm.

She'd been so close this morning, pressed into his

body on a bed no less. *A bed*. Where if he'd been less of a man, he would have dragged her down and shown her how good they would be together. He shook his head and pulled from the curb when she opened the front door. If he didn't change the direction of his thoughts real fast, he'd be chasing her up those steps, her parents be damned. Literally. He could care less about them. Convincing Melody that spending a year under his roof wouldn't be an awful, career-killing, parent-disowning mistake seemed a stellar plan in his book.

The problem, he mused, pulling into traffic turning heavier as the ice thinned and commuters began their day, was keeping his hands to himself in the process. If she somehow decided his asking her into a contract wasn't a joke on his part – because he'd been absolutely serious – he didn't want her doing it for the intimacy alone. No, he wanted a life with her. One that would hopefully reach well beyond the year and include little ones. If she could learn to see past her taught preconception, he could learn to see past how she'd once felt, too.

While he didn't know a lot about the beautiful young guardian, he knew enough to realize he wanted, needed, to know more. A lot more. About every part of her. From her luscious body to her equally lovely mind.

But now wasn't the time to be thinking about such things. He needed to engage his mind on finding a missing teenager. Cia deserved his full focus. Not split between the concern for finding her and the desire for a woman who wanted nothing to do with him. On the way back to his apartment, he formulated the route he'd take from the park to get the most out of bystander interviews. Who was likely to have seen something, and who would have possibly heard second hand near the park and could direct him toward a possible witness.

Someone had seen something. Vayden only had to discover what. Soon.

6

—————

MELODY TUCKED THE BOXES OF PREPARED SANDWICHES under one arm and gripped two paper bags dotted with fresh oil between her teeth to open the door to Vayden's building. She figured since her spoken apology had fallen short, perhaps the way back into his good graces would be through his stomach. Melody knew every decent food vendor between her house and South Row Division and decided to pick up lunch on her way to feed them both. His place wasn't exactly on the route, being closer to Extilis Square, and therefore under East Street Division's jurisdiction, she figured him trying a new food from the city would be a bonus.

She headed through the soothing greenhouse, her feet kicking up bark and chipped wood in her haste to get upstairs with a still-warm meal. On the way up the stairs, she tried not to think about how her parents had barely noted her presence when she'd walked in. Hadn't even noticed her mismatched attire, or asked where she'd been. As she'd figured, they hadn't realized she'd never returned home last night. The ravaged face and desperate, pain-filled eyes of Henry Castien came to Melody's mind. How long would she have to be missing before her parents became as worried as he'd been? Would they ever?

At Vayden's door, Melody squared her shoulders and positioned the food in front of her, using the toe of her boot to knock. When the door swung open, the fresh scent of citrus and dark, earthy notes surrounded her. Damp hair curled around Vayden's neck and face. He wore a comfortable, burnt orange cotton shirt and black slacks. His feet were bare. Melody blinked, taken by surprise, expecting him to be ready to head straight to Caris.

His long fingers combed through his hair as he stepped back and motioned her in. "Good, right on time, I was just about to put my shoes on and get my jacket."

Her feet had somehow become glued to the carpet. "Your hair is wet."

"Happens when I take a shower."

Oh, summer sun, *those* words brought all sorts of images she didn't need to be having to mind. She shoved the food at him. "I brought food."

He rushed to accept the boxes and bags before everything tumbled to the floor. "I had plenty."

"We can eat it on the road. If you eat in your Ariot that is, I didn't mean to assume." She blinked again, trying, so, *so* hard not to imagine him naked and covered in slick soap, the muscles he kept hidden under clothes gleaming in the low light of his bathroom. She was failing. Miserably. "That you ate in your vehicle. We can eat here. I don't mind. I mean... of course, I don't mind."

And great. Now, she babbled like an idiot. Her brain had been reduced to useless mush.

"Melody," he said, his tone grounding and firm. "Just come inside. We'll eat while I finish getting ready, okay?"

She shrugged and shoved her hands in her back pockets. "Sure, yeah, that sounds fine."

He smiled and waited. "Are you going to come in?"

A hole needed to open underneath her and allow her to disappear. Heat scorched her cheeks. She lowered her chin to her chest and stalked into his apartment. The soft click of the door closing made her nerves jump. She was alone with him again. After last night, and now her little side fantasy of him in the shower, she wasn't so sure if being alone was wise.

He brushed past her into the living area. Melody clamped her jaw tight to keep from inhaling his scent deeper as he went by. She trailed behind, her attention going to his space in the bright light of day. As she'd expected, the crystal flowers hanging in the windows sparkled and shimmered in the noon-day sun. Little rainbows danced off the walls and floor, adding to the colorful glitter of the decorated paper birds draped from his ceiling. A warm fire burned in the pellet stove. The potted trees drew Melody like a beacon. She found herself going to the one nearest to the table, where he set the food down.

Carefully, she brushed her finger along a dark green leaf. The leaf trembled and seemed to curl toward her. She gasped and snatched her hand away. When she looked up, she found Vayden watching her closely. Unsure what had happened, Melody plopped down in the seat next to her and reached for the closest set of food.

"Are you sure you don't want to eat this on the way?" she asked, opening her box with a perfectly pressed sandwich nestled inside.

He sat, boots in hand. "No, I have some notes to make for the interviews I want to conduct. I can do that while I eat."

Melody opened her bag of spicy, seasoned fried pork fat. "Anything I can help with?"

After he tied his boots, he stood. "Yeah, I think there is. Let me go get the file."

An impossible to ignore rush of happiness swelled in her chest at his willingness to let her assist. Yes, he'd agreed to, but he didn't *have* to let her do much of anything than tag along. Melody was eyeing the position of Master Tribunii at the East Street Division for fraud occurrences, which were mostly research-based. Being able to assist in the research side of casework wasn't something she had much experience doing.

He returned with a notebook and the file he'd had last night. The notebook slid in front of her, along with a pen. She accepted both. Vayden arranged his meal and the file opposite each other and then began dividing his attention between the two. He murmured his approval of the food while positioning papers. Melody tried not to let his praise affect her, but she found pleasing him brought her a sense of... contentment. How odd.

They ate while working. Vayden rattled off names, addresses, and questions he wanted answered while she made a structured list that would allow them to maximize their time and hopefully meet up with witnesses fast enough to keep the knowledge of their presence and their questions from spreading. Just in case someone had something to hide.

When they finished, Vayden cleaned up, and Melody organized everything back into his folder, including his inquiries. Behind her, a gentle rustle made her glance over her shoulder. The branches and leaves of the tree seemed to arch and stretch closer. Melody gasped and leapt back, bumping the chair. The feet scratched along the hardwood.

"Are you okay?" Vayden asked, closing the cupboard where the trashcan was housed.

Melody stared at the little clementine and tried to slow the pound of her heart. The plant sat inert, still. If she told Vayden what had happened, he'd probably insist on taking her to the nearest medical scientist for a mental health review. And she wouldn't blame him. Clearly, she'd seen things twice now where it was concerned. She took a cautious step away from the tree. "Yes, sorry, tripped over the chair."

Suspicion bracketed his mouth and pinched between his brows, but thankfully he let her odd behavior go. "Ready?"

File in hand, she practically ran from the living room. "Yes, let's go. Before the frost hits again."

And before a leafy bit of produce tried to make another imaginary grab for her.

Countless conversations, introductions, and dead ends later, Vayden stood poised on the edge of a real break. He could feel it to the very center of his bones. Nerves made the witness's pale, age-spotted hands shake while he arranged flowers in black clay pots brimming with water. A colorful painted sign tacked onto the side of the carriage informed customers they shopped at Cosmos's Botanicals.

The vendor leaned forward and whispered, "I saw two men pull a young lady into a carriage."

Vayden leaned an arm against the top of the cart. "Why didn't you tell the investigators the day it happened?"

The flower peddler wouldn't meet Vayden's eyes, instead he fiddled with bright yellow daffodils. "I have my reasons."

A quick look around the quaint cart didn't reveal anything out of place. Vayden glanced at Melody, who waited on the curb, hands shoved in her back pockets. She spoke with a local pastry shop owner in what appeared to be a casual conversation. Her pretty chestnut curls were pinned back, and he found he missed the riotous way the breeze would tease them when unbound. Forcing his attention back to the witness, he leaned further forward, plucking a beautiful pink carnation from a pot. Water dripped off the stem.

"Why speak now?" Vayden asked, twirling the flower.

"I can't sleep," Cosmos revealed on another whisper. "I keep seeing *her*. She keeps tormenting my dreams, accusing me." He shuddered and shook his head. Shaggy lengths of dark gray hair fell into his eyes. "I just want to sleep."

Vayden plucked a white carnation to join his pink one. Okay. So, his witness wasn't all together *there*. Wouldn't be the first time, or likely the last, he had to deal with an adult who somehow managed to function despite being on the unstable side. "You can talk to me about what you saw if it'll make you feel better."

He squeezed his eyes shut and rocked toward the daffodils. "She will go away if I tell you, so I will tell you."

Vayden waited, patient and careful not to make any motions to spook the already rattled man.

"Okay," Cosmos breathed out as if bracing himself. "All right. It was a carriage. A hired carriage. But the driver seemed to know, you know? To expect them. I'm not sure. I didn't see anyone clearly, but he pulled up, they shoved the screaming girl into the ride, and it sped away."

Vayden forced away the gut-wrenching vision of Cia, terrified and heartbroken, being pushed into a vehicle by strangers. "No one cared about her screaming?"

Cosmos sniffed and arranged a row of pink roses. "Everyone was screaming."

Only the occasional carriage, bicyclist, or pedestrian meandered by this time of day, with the air quickly cooling and the dark clouds heavy with the promise of snow. Vayden looked it all over, trying to imagine the warmer autumn afternoon when everything fell apart for the Castien family. The arches for the park entrance seemed ominous in wrought iron, flanked by naked trees. He narrowed his vision on the stone roadway, his imagination playing out the terror of people fleeing the echo of three consecutive gunshots. The chaos of fear. The ease with which two men dragged a young woman through the confusion unnoticed, except by a slightly unhinged flower vendor.

"Who did the hired carriage belong to?" Vayden asked.

The man shrugged and handed Vayden two more carnations to go with the ones he held. Then he seemed to change his mind, taking the whole bunch from Vayden's hand. Cosmos arranged the blossoms on a simple piece of green tissue paper, randomly adding color without much attention to what he reached for. "I don't know, we only have five in all of Caris, must have been one of those."

Vayden was inclined to agree. Doubtful, whoever did the kidnapping would have paid a company all the way from Haven City to make the drive when a local was willing to take their money. He thanked the vendor, who handed him an impressively simple yet elegant arrangement, and reached into his pocket to pull out enough raimarks to cover the flowers and a hefty tip for the information.

Melody noticed him walking away and wrapped up the conversation with the baker. She met him at the park entrance, where he casually threaded his fingers through hers and handed her the small bouquet. Her gasp of surprise made him smile.

"They're beautiful." Then she frowned, looking them over, turning them in the golden light of sunset.

"What's wrong?" he asked, pulling them deeper into the park. He'd parked his Ariot on the other side.

"I'm not sure...." She looked the flowers over again. "They're dying."

"Yes." He squeezed her hand. "Even attached to their roots, once they fully bloom, they begin to wilt and die."

"Perhaps."

"Do you not like them?"

She hugged the vibrant array to her chest and beamed him another smile. "They're really for me?"

Vayden stopped and stared down at her. "Have you never received flowers before?"

Leaning forward, she brushed the arrangement under her nose and even along her lips. Her eyes fluttered closed as she breathed in deep. "No. We don't keep plants of any kind in our house."

"No greenhouse?"

"No, my parents said it's too much maintain, and they'd rather hire a chef than a horticulturist, so ours is empty. They have silk plants to keep up appearances. My parents dust twice a year to keep them fresh looking."

A flash from earlier in the day when she'd stood before one of his clementine trees, the shock on her face and the tremble of the plant, went through his mind. The investigator in him stood up and took notice. Things clicked into place like puzzle pieces laid out on a table. Vayden's insides coiled, and he clenched his jaw to keep from speaking his suspicions to her and turning her world upside down. Somehow, he didn't think Melody would appreciate his sudden revelation. No, she'd probably throw the flowers in his face and run fast and far, in complete denial the entire way.

Deciding a change of subject was mandatory, Vayden began walking again. "What did you learn from the baker?"

"The family had purchased some bread from her before their picnic. She's still shaken over what happened. What about you?"

He motioned to the blooms still held close to her face. "The vendor witnessed Cia's kidnapping."

"What?" she asked, eyes wide. She shook the bouquet at him. "You didn't think to start with that? Maybe say it when you handed me these flowers?"

"And ruin the experience?" Vayden tsked and shook his head. "I can't get the next bit of information any faster than our walk to the Ariot."

Excitement shone in her leafy green eyes. "Where are we going?"

"The carriage Cosmos saw her shoved into was hired. I think only one company services Caris, so we'll start there." He guided them down a trail to the left, spotting his ride parked on the curb.

"You know where they're located?"

Vayden opened the vehicle door for her, holding the flowers until she reached for them once inside. "I'm sure they won't be hard to find."

"Just follow a carriage?" she asked as he slipped into the driver's seat.

Laughing, Vayden started the engine. The magnetic components whirred to life. The first fat snowflake of the evening drifted onto the windshield. He leaned forward and surveyed the angry sky. "However we find the place, we better make it quick."

Melody clutched the flowers to her chest and followed his view. "Do you think we have enough time?"

Vayden shifted the gears into drive. "We don't have a choice. I have this lead, I'm following it. We're a step closer to Cia than we were five minutes ago, I'm not letting this thread get away from us."

• • •

MELODY TRIED HARD NOT TO LET VAYDEN'S USE OF THE plural mean anything. But being part of a *we* and an *us* warmed something deep inside. The flowers he'd gifted, though lacking the vibrancy and pull of life she always seemed to encounter around plants, sparked another glow of happiness she wanted to ignore. At every opportunity, Vayden chipped at her defenses, at the reasons she'd stacked up like bricks around herself to keep him away.

Caris turned out to be a quaint town. Melody could see the appeal for those who could afford the rail commute to work daily to avoid living in the city. Finding the transport company was surprisingly easy. Vayden spotted a driver not far from the park, along with the name of the business. A short trip around the small town yielded a tiny building nestled between two, three-story apartment complexes.

Vayden parked and then sat with his hands on his thighs, staring at the building. "I think you should handle the request."

Melody glanced at him and then at the lonesome shop front. "Why?"

"I don't have HCES embroidered on my clothes. You'll get results faster, and with minimal threats."

She glanced down at her jacket. "Right. Okay. I can do that."

Gathering witness testimony and documentation was routine for her. She had to remind herself this case wasn't any different from any other. Except everything about it seemed to have gone missing. And her *partner* wasn't officially recognized. Not to mention, at some point, the matter had become personal. Melody cast all that aside. If she allowed all the exterior influences to affect her, she'd walk into the business and behave like a rookie and get precisely nowhere.

Four years of training and hard work weren't going to be wasted because she couldn't keep her emotions in check. Holding out her hand, she exchanged her flowers for the file. Armed with official evidence and a legitimate need for an acquisition, Melody exited into the cold, waning light. She straightened her jacket and shoulders and marched into the transportation office. Not once did she glance back at Vayden, despite wanting to. Desiring the strength he seemed to give her was bad enough, acknowledging it couldn't happen. She'd gone her entire career without him, she sure didn't need him now.

A little bell chimed as she entered the small, poorly lit shop. The sweet scent of good smoking tobacco hit her. The hazy evidence of a cigarette permeated the air. Melody wanted to prop the door open and allow some of the smell to dissipate, never having appreciated the scent of burnt tobacco in her hair. Behind the counter, a man sat hunched over a paper. He flicked ash into a glass bowl and brought the brown paper wrapped smoke to his lips. Gray streaked his dark hair, and if the lines around his mouth and eyes weren't premature, Melody figured him in his forties.

He glanced up when she approached the counter. Coffee-brown flecked with darker shades of green looked her over. "You here for the desk position?"

Melody cocked a brow and pointed at the golden embroidered letters on her jacket. "Tribunii Ericksen, HCES, I'm here to see the owner."

The man sat back in his chair, deep wrinkles settling in his forehead as he frowned. "I am the owner."

Melody set the file on the counter and gave her best cooperate-with-me-or-else smile. "I need to see your records from three weeks ago, please."

He set the smoldering stub in the glass bowl and reached under the counter. "Yeah, sure, what's this about?"

"There was a shooting in the park a couple weeks ago, just doing some routine investigating," Melody said with a vague shrug.

"I remember reading about that." He set a thick bound book before her. "But none of my drivers said anything, so I don't think any of them were in the area."

"Great, I'll just take a look." Melody opened the book and flipped through the pages to the date she needed. "I'm sure you understand needing to obey orders."

The owner sat back in his seat, the cigarette hanging from his mouth again. "Sure wish my drivers listened so well."

Melody gave him a gracious smile. Growing up in her parent's house, she'd learned from an early age how to read what people desired from her. This man wished for obedience. From the speculative look in his eye, she figured he was wondering *how* submissive he could make her. Melody kept from meeting his gaze again while she copied the short list of fares on the day of the Castien event. She reminded herself she wasn't alone, Vayden waited in his Ariot only a few steps away. If she took too long, he'd investigate.

The last entry recorded, Melody closed the book and slid it away. "Thank you for cooperating. If I need anything further, do you have a radio number where I can contact you?"

Clenching the smoke between his teeth, he leaned back and slipped a card free from a holder. Melody thanked him again, took the card, and left before he could speak another word. Her breath escaped in a rush once the fresh, crisp air of the approaching night washed over her.

Fat snowflakes danced and fluttered on the breeze. A dusting of white gathered on the sidewalk and street. Tonight promised to be drier than the night before, perhaps sparing the city of an icy build-up. Disappointment took Melody by surprise. She'd be able to return home after she and Vayden consulted all the evidence they'd gathered.

She forced a neutral expression on her face as she slid into the much warmer Ariot. Vayden shifted and pulled onto the road. The warm glow of the setting sun made his dark hair look almost red and defined the smooth planes of his handsome face. Melody clutched the file and forced her attention to the street and the powder accumulating on every surface.

"What were you able to find?" he asked, making a smooth right turn.

"I copied every entry from the day of the incident. Hopefully, the driver wasn't thinking about covering any tracks and logged his passenger destinations like usual."

"That would be ideal," Vayden agreed. He tapped his thumb on the steering wheel and glanced her way. "Tell me your favorite Wintervail memory."

The request took Melody by surprise. She turned and stared at him. "Why?"

He shrugged. "Why not? We have a thirty-minute

drive and nothing else to talk about. I want to know more about you."

Melody's heart did an odd turn in her chest. At least, that's what it felt like. A strange, twisting twirl, almost unpleasant and yet, exciting. She swallowed and tried to keep her breathing normal. No one had ever asked anything personal of her in her entire life. The question, however, left nerves dancing in her stomach. She rubbed her neck and swallowed. "Why do you care to know anything about me?"

He reached across the short space between them and grasped her hand. The action made her jump. His warm fingers slid between hers. "I want to know anything you'll tell me. So? What is your favorite memory?"

Melody's chest tightened, and she licked her suddenly dry lips. "I'm not sure. Probably when my little sister Lyrica opened the first gift I ever bought her."

His fingers traced a random pattern on her palm. "You have a little sister? How old is she?"

Focused on his distracting touch, Melody answered without thinking. "Twelve."

"Big age gap."

"Yes. My parents lost two pregnancies between us."

His fingers slid between hers again and squeezed. "I'm sorry. That must have been rough to go through as a family."

Old anxiety curled in her belly. "No more difficult than keeping their secret about the losses."

"I don't understand."

Melody stared down at their clasped hands resting on her thigh. The contrast between his larger, darker hand

and hers held her fascinated. "The Medical Scientists deemed both miscarriages as genetic incompatibility. Lyrica only confirmed their suspicions when she was born. Healthy but… different." She looked up at him, his frown a mirror of her own. "Do you know what would happen if their clients realized they couldn't even predict how their own union would match when it's their job to ensure good fits between Gen-Heirs? How they've failed to produce anyone else to take over the family name and ensure a future in our society except for one genetic success?"

"You aren't some successful science experiment, Melody. You're their child. Their daughter." He stopped the car at a traffic sign and turned in his seat. No other vehicles, man or horse driven, ambled by them. Exasperation shone in his gaze. "Please tell me you've been treated as their child and not the result of some effective breeding program."

Confusion made her separate their hands. "But I am. My parents don't love each other, they never have. They both agreed their marriage, their partnership, would result in the highest chance for either of them to see their genes mapped into greater and greater genetic heirs. Their names would become part of a genetic dynasty, like the Dandridges, the Hunters, or the emerging house of Ralston."

"Which has gen-commons in the mix, like me."

"Yes, but they have more Gen-Heirs, and they are in powerful positions," Melody argued. "They'll form alliances in marriage that will ensure future generations of Ralston's will go on to be history makers, like them."

"This is what they've told you?" he asked, staring at her in shock as if her skin had suddenly changed to blue and she'd sprouted two more arms. "You're supposed to be like them, marrying for genetic power so they can see *their* names immortalized on some piece of paper no one may ever care about?"

Melody started and pressed her body closer to the door. How could he not understand? "Everyone cares about genes."

Growling, he shifted the car hard. The normally quiet engine roared, and the slender car trembled. "Not everyone, guardianess."

7

AFTER ARRIVING BACK AT HIS APARTMENT, MELODY insisted on putting her flowers in water. Vayden found her a tall glass, and once the flowers were cared for, they'd settled into working the case. Uncomfortable silence filled the room. Melody studied a map of Haven City that included a small cut out of Caris while he organized the list she'd copied into drivers and their destinations. At least, Vayden figured she made a good show of being absorbed in the intersecting roadways, which kept her from having to speak to him. The company had three drivers working that day, they serviced twenty-eight patrons. Four of the fares went beyond Caris into the outskirts of Haven City. Vayden wanted to think one of those four were his kidnappers, but he couldn't be certain.

Not coming unhinged when he eventually met the Ericksen's was also an uncertainty in his future. Because he *would* meet them. If Melody's earlier words were true, she was in more trouble than he originally thought. His assessment of her situation being a lot like his mother's had once been rang all the truer. A victim of those desperate for power. He had so many questions and figured he'd get few answers. At least not yet. She had no reason to part with anything more than she'd given, and he didn't have the right to ask.

Vayden wrote the last name on his grid and stood. Paper in hand, he handed her two pigmented wax highlighters and set the list at the top of the map. He held up his blue and orange markers. "I'll take these two colors, you do the other two."

She accepted the green and purple. "What am I doing?"

"You're highlighting their routes. From pick up, to drop off."

Vayden shifted to the side of the table to give them both room to maneuver. When their lines intersected, they'd take turns waiting patiently for the other to work through the area. Almost an hour later, with his back killing him and his fingers cramping, they each drew their last line. Vayden overlooked their work.

"Okay, I only see six pickups around the park, and this one," he touched a finger to the fare two blocks away, "is close, but not near the flower cart."

"He could have lied about his pickup point."

"Then we'd have to assume he lied about his drop-off location, too." Vayden braced himself over the map and sighed. "And I really don't want to think about that."

Melody trudged over to the couch and flopped down. Her feet dangled over the arm, the rest of her hid from view. "Where do we go from here?"

Vayden's stomach rumbled. He rubbed a hand along his belly. "Tea and some food, I think."

Melody's head appeared over the back of the couch, her eyes wide. "Food?"

"Can't send you home on an empty stomach, can I? What kind of host would I be then?" he asked with a grin.

She sank down until only her pretty green eyes were visible. "I'll be okay."

Vayden lit wood in the cast-iron stove and then gathered all the ingredients together to make a quick meal. He flashed her another smile as he set a cutting board out. "I won't be. If you don't want to eat, you can watch me."

Her arms folded over the back of the couch as she rose on her knees. "Where did you learn to cook?"

The edge of his knife clacked on the cutting board with each quick move of his wrist. "My father. While he had the money to hire a full time cook by the time he married my mother, he enjoyed feeding her and then us." Vayden shrugged, dumping cut vegetables into a pot. "It's not a big deal and usually not difficult."

"Usually?"

"Some things, like Italyssian orange bread, can be a challenge." He thought about his favorite foods for a second, cutting strips of rabbit. "Oh, and Westican hot chicken. Have to have a bit of patience for that one, too."

"The cooks my parents hire only cook Sziverian meals," Melody said, frowning. "What are you making now?"

"Rabbit sauté with vegetables." When she licked her lips, Vayden took a deep breath and shifted his focus back to preparing. "Sound good?"

"Sounds amazing. Thank you." Her fingers

thrummed on the back of the couch. She chewed on her bottom lip, her gaze shifting between him and the table piled with their investigation efforts.

Vayden cast glances at her between pouring white wine over the sizzling ingredients and stirring. "What are you thinking about?"

She rested her chin on her folded hands. The vivid, clear depths of her gaze looked him over. "You're very good at what you do."

"This surprises you?" He stirred in fresh herbs. A cloud of steam sent the aroma sizzling into the air.

"Yes."

Her honesty made him chuckle. "Why?"

A rich flush bloomed across her cheeks. She looked away from him. "It just does."

Vayden let loose a burst of air, shaking his head. He didn't bother to hide his frustration. "Let me guess, your parents told you gen-commons sweep the streets and wash windows, but we're good for little else. Meant to be at the bottom rung of society, doing menial tasks because we aren't talented or smart enough to do much else."

"Not just my parents," she said, the rest of her face flaming to match her cheeks.

The information didn't shock Vayden. He grunted, adding broth-soaked grains to the pan. "You must have gone to one of those prep academia's. The ones promising to get young boys and girls into the upper echelons of society."

"I went to Honor Grace Academia for Young Women."

"I've met two other women who attended that particular school," Vayden said neutrally. "They both tried to hand me their empty wine glasses in my own house."

Melody winced.

He pointed his wooden spoon at her. "My thoughts exactly. What kind of school teaches the next generation to look down on their fellow Sziverian's?" He shook his head. "My children will be going to no such place."

"My parents only wanted...." She took a deep breath. "*Want*, what is best for me."

Vayden set the spoon aside and propped his weight on the counter. He met her wide-eyed stare. "And what is best for you?"

The moment the question left his lips, he knew he shouldn't have asked. He didn't want to know the answer. No good would come from whatever she had to say. From the way she shifted her focus to the windows, where outside heavy gray clouds muted the city beyond, he knew she wasn't ready to acknowledge much more than her surprise at his degree of aptitude. Which was fine. Vayden would take the victories where he could at the moment.

"I don't know anymore," she said so quietly, the crackling in the pan almost drowned out the words.

Vayden removed the pan from the heat, setting it on the cooler side of the stove. He covered their meal to make sure it'd stay warm before crossing the short distance. Hunching before the back of the couch, he folded his arms in front of hers. To his amusement, she didn't move, leaving them nose-to-nose and close enough for him to see the faceted peridot depths of her eyes. The smattering of freckles across her nose and cheeks and hairline fascinated him, as did the pout of her pretty pink mouth. *Lovely* wasn't strong enough a word for her.

He tucked an errant curl behind her ear, his thumb tracing the curve of her jaw. "What is your dream? Your goals?"

Her bright eyes disappeared beneath the sweep of her lashes. The flutter of her breath caressed his knuckles. "You already know the answer to that."

Vayden slid his fingers under her chin and forced her gaze back to him. "To be a ranked guardian? Has that always been what you wanted?"

"There is no *what I want*," she stated, sliding away from him.

Vayden stood, bracing his hands on the back of the couch. "You aren't a dog, and your parents aren't your master for you to obey, Melody. You're a person. You're allowed to have your own goals and dreams."

"I do." She stood and wrapped her arms around her waist. She looked small and much younger than her twenty-four years. Lost. "I want to bring honor to my family and help secure a seat for our name."

He had the urge to point out she sounded as though she were trying to convince herself, not convicted in a decision he figured had been spoon fed to her since the cradle. Sighing, he raked a hand through his hair. "The food's ready, let's eat before it gets cold."

He ladled the sautéed meal onto plates and then placed salt and pepper on the counter between them. Melody collected her plate in silence. At the table, she moved an edge of the map away before taking a seat. Vayden sat next to her and waited in anticipation for her to take the first bite. She didn't disappoint. A smile of wonder crossed her face. She dug deeper into the mixture of meat, vegetables, and grains. The discomfort of their conversation forgotten.

"This is so good, thank you."

"You're welcome." Vayden had to remind himself he needed to eat, too. The food was good, but he found more pleasure in watching her mouth accept what he'd cooked, the slide of her fork pulling free from her sensual lips.

She inched his notes closer, flipping through the pages between bites. "How many cases have you solved?"

"I have no idea," he answered honestly. His fork clanked on the empty plate. "I have a cabinet full of files. Some I've never been able to solve. Others I solved in a day. Each case is unique. Haven't you found that in your career?"

"I've only been working cases six months now. I helped assist when I was a First Guardsman, but you only get to work cases on your own once you make Tribunii." She looked over the map. "And no one I ever worked with, except maybe Key Guardian Asherwick, seems to care like you do."

"Do you care? About your cases?"

THE QUESTION CAUGHT MELODY OFF-GUARD. SHE immediately wanted to say *yes, of course*, she cared about the assignments she was given, the chance to make a difference and help someone or their family. But as she looked over all Vayden's hard work, the meticulous method's he used to map out a crime and hope to make connections, Melody couldn't help but admit she wouldn't have put in half as much effort. The revelation made guilt rise.

How many of her cases had she left with loose ends or a lack of enough evidence to allow for proof of guilt? Could she blame ignorance? Not being taught any better? Or did attention to detail and the desire to follow any thread given, come with being a Gen-Heir with a burning inherited desire to solve the unsolvable? She looked at Vayden and his sapphire-wrapped-in-gold eyes and knew he couldn't have such a trait. Yet, he sought the answer like a wolf seeking his prey all the same.

His pupils narrowed. Small muscles bunched beneath his eyes and across his cheeks. He seemed to wait for something. Her answer, she figured. Or her lie. Melody took a deep, shuddering breath and picked up her plate. "I used to think I did. Now, I'm thinking maybe I haven't cared enough."

Vayden twisted in his seat. "I think I can safely get you home. We can finish this up tomorrow. I need to visit with Henry and let him know what we've learned. Did you want to go?"

"Yes," Melody answered. "And I can get home. As I said yesterday, I'm an adult, an enforceman for HCES, I can take care of myself."

He rose and took the plates from her. "I think I also remember saying I prefer knowing you've arrived safely."

The fall of his booted feet echoed in the open room as he went to the kitchen. He made quick work of cleaning up from dinner, offering her no chance to help. Melody found herself drawn to the little clementine from earlier in the day. The nearest branch seemed to stretch, beckoning. Melody shoved her hands in her pockets even as she moved closer. Lamplight shimmered off of the leaves, making them appear to quiver in the colder air near the windows.

"It's okay to touch them," Vayden said softly.

Melody jumped. He stood right behind her. When had he left the kitchen? She wiggled her fingers deeper into her pockets. "Why would I want to? They're just plants."

He moved in so close the heat of his body washed along her back. His fingers curled around her wrist, forcing her hand from her pocket. "I want to show you something if you'll let me."

An unexpected sliver of fear raced through her. How ridiculous. What did she have to be frightened of? Rolling her eyes at her reaction, she straightened her back and held her palm up for him. "Sure, okay."

His fingers slid along the back of her hand. An entirely different shiver slid along her spine. Little crackles of lightning seemed to spark at every point where his touch brushed her skin, leading her hand to the plant. So absorbed in the unfamiliar sensation he created within her, Melody failed to notice when a leaf curled around her index finger.

"Look," Vayden whispered into her ear, forcing her attention to the tree.

Melody gasped. Another leaf stretched and coiled around her middle finger. Little tremors danced through the stems. Every muscle froze within her. She stared in wonder and a bit of anxiety. "What is this? What is happening?"

Vayden held his other hand out, caressing a branch

beside the one that seemed alive to Melody. Nothing happened. "It's you. All you."

When she tried to pull free, the leaves tightened. "I don't understand."

Vayden carefully unwrapped the clinging plant from her hand. "You will when you're ready. I just wanted you to see. Did you feel anything?"

Faint wisps of information coalesced at the edges of her mind. She tried to grasp them, but they faded before she could make sense of what was trying to form. "I'm not sure."

Slowly, Vayden released his hold on her hand. "You will, someday. Come on, let's get you home."

Melody cast a glance at the clementine, allowing Vayden to lead her to the front door. A sense of melancholy settled in her chest. She wanted to stay, to explore what the tree seemed to be trying to tell her. A tree, communicating? The idea seemed preposterous, and yet somehow, she *knew* that had almost happened.

If she remained at his apartment, her parents wouldn't miss her, and only silk plants awaited her at home. Nothing living. The thought made her frown. Then again, in her entire life, she never remembered her parents using their greenhouse space or keeping plants of any kind within the house. They were simply too busy to care for anything, often even their own children.

The urge to beg Vayden to let her stay, regardless of his self-imposed rule, rode her hard. She clenched her teeth and fisted her hands. No. Her job was as an investigator for HCES. She was a guardian, and she had a task to do to help find a missing girl, and try to figure out why her case had gone missing. Curious plants had no place to distract her.

Henry's sigh echoed in the quiet library. The crackle and pop of the fire Vayden had lit seemed to mimic the mournful complaint. "I wish I had better news for you," Vayden said, clasping his hands between his knees.

Henry's fingers tightened, crinkling the edges of the papers. "You have more now than before, and confirmation she was alive when they took her."

The shift in perspective hadn't crossed Vayden's mind, and he took it as a good sign Henry saw a more positive side. "She's still alive." Vayden held his hands together in an effort to keep from signing to make sure Henry understood his words without error. When his friend looked up, eyes glistening with moisture, Vayden repeated the words with more conviction. "She's still alive, Henry. I'm going to find her."

"We're going to find her," Melody repeated softly. Her hand touched Vayden's shoulder, giving a faint squeeze of encouragement.

Vayden touched the paper still clutched in Henry's hand. "Do you recognize any of these addresses?"

Henry sat back and waved the pages at Vayden. "No, not a single one. I am useless. I can't leave this house because I don't know why they wanted my family dead or what they wanted with Cia. I can't help because if anyone learns I am, I could put her further at risk. I don't know anyone because I've kept my head low, trying to..." Henry shook his head and dragged a hand down his weary face. "None of it mattered."

"You aren't useless." Vayden held up the list. "I don't know any of these addresses either, but I'm going to learn about them."

Henry stared at the dancing flames for silent moments. Vayden let the quiet settle in the room. Behind him, Melody shifted, oblivious to knowing the world Henry existed in was noiseless and one Vayden had become used to whenever he visited with his friend. Grief rode Henry hard today, and Vayden needed to let the distraught man handle things in his own time. In his own way.

When Henry finally spoke, Melody jumped, and Vayden had to keep his amusement hidden. The flush of her cheeks and sudden attention in a nearby book spoke of her embarrassment.

"I think you need to see this Ryan Voklane man from the FIO," Henry said to the fire. "I've been thinking more about why he'd be interested, and I believe he knows something. Take your evidence and convince him to help."

Vayden glanced at Melody. She chewed her bottom lip and met his stare. Uncertainty darkened her eyes. To her, the First Intelligence Office was a giant in the guardian world. Where the best of the best Gen-Heirs were recruited and assigned to work for one of the highest levels of security in the nation of Sziveria. As the son of a shield guardian, he knew a lot of the guardians, ranked and unranked, who walked the halls of the FIO. And when they needed someone they *knew* was intelligent and capable, but to anyone else, an average guy, they came to him. Visiting their offices didn't intimidate him.

"Okay, I'll go ask. The worst he can do is send me on my way, right?" Vayden said with a shrug.

A hard glint shone in Henry's dark eyes. "If he sends you away, tell him I'll be coming by to see him."

Vayden snorted and stood. "Yeah, threatening an Intel Guardian will go over really well, Henry."

The harsh expression didn't fade from the retired assassins face. "If he withholds the information I need because of FIO politics, you know I won't be making a threat."

"He may not have anything to disclose," Vayden said.

Henry's chin lifted in acknowledgment. "You'll know if that's true, I have no doubt."

Vayden handed Melody the documents. "Do you mind if I have a moment with him in private?"

Nodding her agreement, she accepted the papers. He waited until she was clear of the library before turning his back to the entry and signing, "Are you sure about my going to the FIO?"

"Yes. The guardian knows something, I can feel it," Henry signed in return, his motions insistent. "Don't let him fool you into believing otherwise."

Vayden ran a hand down his face and sighed. "Okay."

Henry grasped Vayden's hand and held tight. "Thank you."

Returning the gesture of friendship and trust, Vayden squeezed Henry's grip. "I already told you, no need to thank me."

In the foyer, Melody waited by the front door. She chewed on her bottom lip, a hand shoved deep in her back pocket, the other holding the papers. "Are we really going to the FIO?"

"Yes."

Vayden opened the door. Cold air rushed in, ruffling the loose curls around Melody's pale face. Her freckles stood out in starker contrast, her eyes a little too big in her nervousness. The urge to kiss her and replace the anxiety with something much nicer, for both of them, had Vayden slipping outside into ice-laden mist.

A thin layer of crystalized frost covered his Ariot. He used a scraper across the windshield and back window. He'd probably have to repeat the process at least once on the way to the FIO building. Melody bundled into the front seat. A visible shiver trembled along her entire body. Vayden dug around in the back space until he found a bin where he kept supplies. He pulled out a soft, thick knit blanket his sister gifted each family last Wintervail for them to keep in their vehicles. The vivid pinks, yellows, and greens brightened the space in the gray light.

Melody accepted the warmth with a gasp. Her fingers buried deep into the rich cotton. "This is beautiful."

"My older sister, Bree, knit each of us one last year." He started the vehicle and shifted into gear. "I will admit to being very thankful and wondering why I never kept a blanket in here before."

Smiling, she gathered the vibrant cover around herself. "How many siblings do you have?"

"There are four of us Dossett offspring, though Bree is a Charters now. I'm the second born. Third born is Elianna, she's on her second contract. If they re-sign, he'll probably take on our family name, since he's a first-generation genetic heir, and our surname has more influence than his. The baby in the family is Luka. She's sixteen, and so far, it's looking like she'll be our mother's genetic heir."

"Is Elianna a Gen-Heir?"

"Yes, from my father's side, for commerce and trade. She helps my father run his import company."

Melody seemed to ponder that information. "But your father is gen-common."

"Maybe. He's whip-smart and has a mind for business transactions, which he inherited from his father, all the same. He just had to work a little harder because of preconceived notions due to his eye color. And because everyone assumed he wasn't as good as my grandfather, he was able to get the upper hand on a lot of competition that neglected their company's contracts as a result."

Vayden thrummed his fingers on the steering wheel and slowed for a carriage ambling along in front of him. A bicyclist zipped by on his left. Melody's fingers poked through the small holes in the blankets design.

"So, your father, who isn't a Gen-Heir, but still has a level of talent, passed on a genetically inherited gene all the same from his side of the family?"

"Yep," Vayden answered, easing around the carriage. The horse shook his head as Vayden sped by and whipped around him before oncoming traffic came too close. "How much do you know about genetics?"

She shrugged. "As much as anyone else, I suppose. My parents never really explained it to me, and Honor Grace Academia was more worried about making sure I turned into a guardian than the past."

Vayden quirked a brow. "The past?"

"Yeah, what we've learned through books but can't prove because we don't have what humanity used to before the Cataclysm."

"Technically, all that information was proven through their scientific methods, which they outline in very concise manners. We *know* when two people create life together, half the genetics come from the mother, the other half the father. No one knows which genes will be given to a child, but each parent contributes. Some are dominant, others recessive, but still able to be passed on. Genetically inherited abilities are the same."

"So if a parent has a genetic gift, it'll always be passed on?" she asked, shifting in her seat to face him.

"If the gene marker is one that gets into the fifty percent, yes. Since it's believed Ruthenian DNA was fiddled with, all Ruthenians will pass on some form of genetic talent."

Her face scrunched up. "What do you mean?"

Vayden considered the easiest way to give a history *and* genetics lesson while in a moving vehicle. "In the early days of genetic inheritance, since it's theorized the genes were created as some sort of a pre-cataclysm experiment, it's likely each original Gen-Heir was given a dominant and recessive ability to pass on to their progeny. This would have ensured a genetic inheritance always occurred among the population. Another theory being argued for those in Ruthenia wanting to widen the available gene-pool is the eye-color test may be inaccurate in Gen-Heir lines. If both parents have a dominant genetic inheritable trait, the traits may become co-dominate, like in blood types."

She looked at him, her eyes narrowed and searching.

"Then you'd have inherited *both* of your parent's abilities, not just one. And your father as well?"

"Maybe," he said slowly. "Or maybe while genetically I have them both, I only have access to one, whichever is actually more dominant. My father couldn't pass on *both* of his co-dominate genes, only one. If this theory is correct, then my mother's talent is also dominate rather than recessive, and since my father could carry both, he could have passed that particular ability on to me as well."

"Where did you learn of this?"

"My mother, who has friends in Ruthenia where it's being researched. Though, they'll have to gene map for a few generations to get accurate results. The current findings are really fascinating, though."

Melody shifted her focus to the window. "There must still be something in eye color."

"I think so, too. Mine aren't mixed but split. Same with my father. You'll see others in the population with a mixture of colors. If there is blue and gold, they're all through the iris."

"Not divided as yours are," she mused, "like gold wrapped around a sapphire."

Surprised, he stared at her. "Is that what my eyes look like to you?"

She wouldn't look in his direction, instead she continued to face the window, a flush pinkening her cheeks. "How else would you describe them?"

"I don't know," he answered. "I never thought about it."

He pulled into the FIO parking lot and found a decent spot close to the side entrance. They'd still have to get visitor passes from the front, but at least if the weather became worse, the walk wouldn't be horrendous. Melody folded the blanket and laid it on her seat. After closing the door, she adjusted her jacket.

Vayden stuck his hands into his pockets and waited while she seemed to shore up her nerve. "Ready?" he asked.

"Oh!" she squeaked and then rushed to open the vehicle again. "We almost forgot the papers," her words muffled in the interior.

Vayden bit back a smile. "Can't have us looking unprofessional."

She glared and swiped curls from her eyes. "Don't mock, Dossett. We are here to ask a favor of one of the most powerful institutions in the nation. I think looking like we know what we're doing is important."

"Whatever you say, Guardian Ericksen."

His grin earned him another scowl from her. When she stomped past, her boots crushing the fragile ice settling over the brick, Vayden followed. At some point, she'd realize she had no idea where to go or what to do. Until then, he'd enjoy the amusement of a fiery Melody. She charged forward like a woman on a mission, shoulders back, chin up, the file clutched firmly against her side. The image of a Tribunii in control. Wiggling his hands in his pockets, he wondered if she'd been taught the skill by HCES or if the confidence belonged to her alone.

At the side entrance, she gave the handle a firm tug. The metal door shuddered, but remained closed. Vayden stopped behind her. "I think it's locked."

She yanked again, same result. "How do we get in?"

"The front entrance. Everyone has to sign in and be given visitors badges."

Her cheeks, already pink from the cold, flamed brighter. She released the handle and stepped back. "Oh. I should have known that. We have a similar process at division."

"You're nervous." Vayden placed a hand on her back and guided her around the imposing gray stone structure. At ten-stories, the building towered over everything else on the street. A wide row of cement stairs led to multiple glass doors. First Intelligence Office and the Sziverian national insignia were chiseled in the blocks above the entrance. "You don't need to be. Voklane is an unranked guardian. A liaison between the arch guardian and the Intel teams. A messenger, if you will."

"But Castien thinks he knows something?"

Vayden glanced at her as they walked up the steps. "A messenger would hear many things now, wouldn't they?"

She hugged the file to her chest. "I should know these things," she mumbled, so low Vayden almost didn't catch the words.

"Why? Because you've worked cases for six months?" Vayden held the door for several people exiting.

A frown bunched between her brows and bracketed her mouth. "No, because some things I should just *know*, I shouldn't have to think so hard to consider things as an enforceman. You don't."

Vayden chose his words carefully. "You didn't have to think hard at the park the other day. Give yourself more time if this is really what you want with your life. A couple of years, and you'll be seeing the bad in everyone, don't worry."

She brushed past him into the dimly lit interior. "If it's what I want? Do any Gen-Heirs have a choice?"

Yes, when they're placed on the wrong path, Vayden bit back. Instead, he focused on an open circle welcome center packed with radios, files, messengers, and receptionists. Everyone conversed in respectful, hushed tones, unlike the chaos at Enforcement Service divisions. Vayden braced a forearm on the high-polished, chestnut wood surface and smiled at an older gentleman positioning a visitor badge to write on.

"Names and guardian you will be seeing?"

"Vayden Dossett and Guardian Ericksen to see Guardian Voklane."

The man wrote in neat block letters. "Is the guardian expecting you?"

"No."

The man set a map in front of Vayden. In clear, concise directions, he showed the way to Ryan's office. "You will go directly to this location. You will not deviate from the path. If the guardian is not in his office, you will wait. If the guardian does not arrive within thirty-minutes, you will leave and make an appointment on your way out to try again another day. Understand?"

"Yes, thank you." Vayden took up both their visitor passes.

Melody clipped her badge to her jacket. "Is it always like that?"

Vayden glanced back on the way to the stairs at the now busy clerk and frowned. "No, actually. Normally, I have to wait to see if the guardian will agree to see me. Voklane must have given orders to allow anyone who needs an audience."

"Convenient."

According to the directions, Voklane's office was located on the fifth floor and down several maze-like corridors. Melody took everything in with wide-eyes and practically vibrated with uneasiness. Vayden resisted the urge to hold her hand and once again explain the people walking the halls weren't any better than her. Somehow though, he figured the rankings painted above some doors might ruin his efforts. Many turns later, Vayden finally found Guardian Ryan Voklane, Arch Guardian Synintel's liaison to deployed Intel Guardians and teams.

The door stood open, the room empty inside. Vayden motioned for Melody to choose one of the two seats in front of a well-organized desk. More seats lined the wall behind the door. A clock on a filing cabinet ticked the seconds away. Melody glanced at it, settling in the chair.

"Do you think he'll be here within the time limit?"

Vayden shrugged, leaning back and folding his hands over his stomach. "No clue."

"You aren't concerned about being kicked out?"

"We won't be kicked out. We will be asked with the utmost politeness if we will kindly exit the premises."

She cast him a suspicious glance. "You sound as if you know this process."

He smiled. Inhaling, she opened her mouth to speak when boots sounded behind them. Vayden looked over his shoulder. Tall, broad-shouldered, with close-cropped, pale blond hair and almost eerie, silvery blue eyes, Ryan Voklane arched a brow at their presence.

"Well, hello. How can I help you?" he asked, snapping a folder he carried closed.

Melody sprang from her seat, hand extended. "Tribunii Melody Ericksen, Guardian Voklane."

Vayden gave a short wave. "Vayden Dossett. Henry Castien sent me."

Ryan motioned for Melody to return to her seat, her hand ignored. "Ah. I see." He closed the door.

Melody sat slowly. "I'm sorry if we should have made an appointment first."

"Are you handling the Castien case, Tribunii?"

"Um," she glanced at Vayden, "we both are at the request of Mr. Castien."

"His daughter Lucianna was kidnapped at the scene of the crime," Vayden clarified. "And IICES lost the evidence pertaining to the case."

"And you've taken it on as a reward?" Ryan asked, perching in front of them on the edge of the desk. His slate gray slacks tightened over his thighs.

"No, Castien is a close family friend. He trained me," Vayden corrected. "He figured since you showed so much interest in the case, you must have information."

"Did he now?" Voklane asked quietly.

Ryan leaned forward. Silver tendrils sparked in his eyes. The guardian reached out and touched Vayden and Melody's hands in a flick of motion. Vayden sat back and blinked, wondering if he imagined the oddity. Ryan pulled away quickly and straightened, turning his back to them as if nothing strange had happened. "Ask your questions."

Vayden took the papers from Melody and explained to Ryan what they'd discovered, choosing to ignore the man's odd behavior. "We have the addresses here for every drop-off and were wondering if you had any information on them or if there's anything you can tell us that will help lead us to the kidnappers."

"Trust me, if I knew where to find the girl's abductors, she'd already be safe in her father's arms," Ryan said from in front of the window. Hands clasped behind his back, he seemed to look over the city as though it were his domain. "You work the streets, Dossett. Have you heard any whispers about a group calling themselves The V Alliance?"

Vayden considered the name, which wasn't familiar. "No. But I saved the Hunter women from being taken by Leone Cyrano, who admitted to Ramsey Hunter she was going to be sold. Do you think Lucianna was kidnapped to be sold? Have you heard about this?"

"Yes, I know about the trafficking. I don't believe Lucianna Castien is in danger of being shipped off. Not yet, anyway."

Vayden straightened. Adrenaline spiked through his veins. "You *do* know something."

"I know you are honest," Ryan began, turning to face them once more. "But if you repeat anything I share, I'll deny knowledge."

Melody squirmed in her seat. "Are secrets really necessary?"

Voklane's pale gaze settled on her. "You can wait in the hall if you'd prefer, guardian. Sometimes secrets are necessary for the safety of the realm, for those who risk more than you for the information to save lives. If you are uncomfortable with that, the meeting can progress without you."

She blew out a slow breath and slunk down into her chair as if hoping it'd swallow her. "I'm fine, thank you."

Ryan nodded. "Good." He propped himself on the windowsill, crossing his ankles and shoving his hands into his pants pocket. "I think a group calling themselves The V Alliance may have something to do with the Castien case. They may have everything to do with it, but I don't have enough evidence. Yet." He cast them a pointed look. "I'm hoping you both can fix that."

Vayden leaned forward, bracing his elbows on his knees. "All right. We're listening."

8

————————

Haven City dashed by in a blur of ice and muted colors. Melody tried to focus on everything she'd learned in Ryan Voklane's office. Tried to wrap her mind around a secret society, tattoos, and intrigue. But the distracting masculine scent of earthy citrus surrounded her in the Ariot. The combination of his cool authority and intelligence at the FIO left her somewhat flummoxed. Along with the genetic information he'd shared before their arrival. Her mind struggled to make sense of everything she'd been taught and everything he'd managed to contradict.

"Did you want me to wait while you're at your house?" Vayden asked.

"No, you can come in," Melody said without thought.

He slowed the vehicle to a stop. "I meant wait around or go back home, but I'd be happy to come in."

Before she could remark, he exited. The Ariot rocked at the absence of his weight. Melody took a deep breath, placing the blanket in the backseat. Cold air rushed in, ruffling her hair and sending chills along her skin. The warmth of Vayden's fingers closed around hers. For a second, she stared at their joined hands. A deep longing to know how his hands would look other places on her body tugged at her. Forcing the unwelcome visual down, she allowed him to help her exit.

Melody fidgeted with the file, which now contained the list of names and addresses Voklane had given them. She wanted to make her own copies to research but understood the need to allow Vayden to keep the originals. She didn't want the information anywhere near Enforcement. Not yet.

Silence and the chill of no one bothering to heat the house made Melody frown as they stepped inside. "I guess no one is home." She tried not to be relieved by the realization.

Vayden closed the door. The urge to fidget as he looked around had Melody heading for the stairs. She knew what he saw. A serious lack of light and color and anything remotely cheerful. Normally this time of year, most homes boasted a riot of colors and textures hanging from windows, doorways, and ceilings. Plants would sit in front of every window. Not in the Ericksen household. Decorating wasted a limited resource. Time. Something her parents refused to give up.

"I'll be back shortly," she said from the stairs.

"Do you want me to wait anywh—"

He didn't get the chance to finish as a squealing young girl launched herself at Melody, unbalancing her and sending her cascading down the stairs. Vayden rushed forward, wrapping his arms around them, taking the brunt of their fall. His hard, warm chest pressed into her back. Her butt nestled much too intimately between his thighs.

"Melody, Melody, Melody!" Lyrica squealed, oblivious to the chaos her excitement had created. She wrapped her smaller body around Melody. The file crinkled between them.

Melody tapped her sister's shoulder. Grinning, Lyrica raised her head, her leafy green eyes bright with question. "What are you doing home?" Melody asked.

"Wintervail is next week."

Melody blinked. How had she forgotten the holiday was so close? "Oh. Right. Where are Mother and Father?"

Lyrica shrugged. "I don't know. I didn't see them leave, so they must be working."

"Not to break up this sweet reunion, but do you think you could continue it while standing?" Vayden asked.

Heat suffused Melody's cheeks. "We need to get up. We knocked over my… visitor."

"Oh!" Lyrica gasped and scrambled off. Eyes wide, she looked at Vayden, then to Melody. "Who are you? Who is this?"

Melody sighed and tried to get up, but Vayden rose and wrapped her in a hug. "This is Vayden Dossett, I'm working with him."

Lyrica giggled. "He likes you."

I like him, too. Melody cleared her throat to keep the words from escaping. She elbowed Vayden in the side. He released her with an *oomph*. "Yes, well, we're solving a case together, that's all."

Lyrica stepped to the side as they stood. She held

out a small hand and twirled the long navy length of her skirt. "Hi, I'm Lyrica."

Vayden knelt down and smiled, taking her small hand between both of his. "Hi, Lyrica. How long are you home for?"

Her sister narrowed her eyes on Vayden's lips while he spoke, then she smiled and answered, "Two weeks. Melody promised to take me to the ice gardens this year!"

"You've never been?"

She shook her head, chestnut curls down past her shoulders bouncing.

"They are very pretty."

"Mother and Father say all the sculptors are Gen-Heir artists, so the gardens are always perfect."

"Ah," Vayden said slowly, and Melody's heart clenched. Then he smiled and released her hands. In elegant, unfamiliar gestures, his fingers moved in graceful motions. Lyrica gasped and then covered her mouth, giggling.

"Is that true?" she whispered and then moved her hands in a similar fashion.

"It is," he answered the same way.

Melody blinked. "Is what true? And what are you doing?"

An innocent flush pinkened Lyrica's cheeks, and she giggled again. "It is our secret, right?"

Vayden nodded. "That's right." Then he made the strange motions again.

"He said I can tell you if he can come along, but only when we get there," Lyrica seemed to translate.

"Those are words?" Melody asked in awe.

Lyrica beamed up at her. "Yes. They are my words. But no one speaks them outside of my school."

"I don't understand," Melody said, frowning.

Lyrica bit her bottom lip. "Mother doesn't allow me to use my hands to speak. She says then everyone will know… I'm not… you know."

Anger had Melody shaking and reaching for her sister. She pulled her into a tight hug and then leaned back so Lyrica could see her speak. "You are perfect, do you understand? Perfect."

Lyrica nodded, a sad smile touching her lips. "I know, sister."

Melody couldn't help but hug her again. Over the top of her sister's head, she met Vayden's troubled stare. "How did you know?" she asked.

"She watched me speak," he answered softly.

And he'd *spoken* to Lyrica, in a special way, meant only for her baby sister. To Vayden, Lyrica wasn't some genetic error. He'd been quick to go to her level and treat her with respect. Tears burned Melody's eyes, and she buried her face in Lyrica's soft hair. "And the language with your hands?"

"A family friend is deaf. He taught all of us Dossett kids a long time ago."

When Lyrica tried to pull away, Melody hugged harder. An exaggerated smothering sound muffled against Melody's chest. Her sister flailed like she was being squeezed to death. "I can't *breathe!*"

Melody laughed and released her. She bopped the file she still held on the riot of Lyrica's curls. "Can you keep Vayden company while I run upstairs for a bit?"

Lyrica looked around the sparse entryway, more of an official space than a welcoming home, and bit her lip. Melody kept a sigh internal. The rest of the house didn't offer much more. She'd given her baby sis a difficult task.

"Um," Lyrica said, "do you play chess?"

"How about we walk the greenhouse?" Vayden asked.

"We don't have one, not like that," Lyrica replied, frowning.

Vayden raised a brow and looked at Melody. "Is that right."

The words were a statement, not a question, as if they'd solved some great mystery for him. Melody lifted her chin. "Schedules run my parent's lives. If it's not part of their important daily tasks, there is no time for it."

He held his hand out and wiggled his fingers. "Chess it is then, mite. Show me the way."

Lyrica latched onto his hand with a grin. "I am the best player in my whole class."

"Uh oh," Vayden said in a dramatic fashion. "You better not leave me too long, Melody. Your sister is going to embarrass me otherwise."

Lyrica laughed and tugged him toward the front room. "Come on, wimpy-wart, I'll let you have the opening move, *and* you can play black."

Vayden clutched at his chest and waited until Lyrica looked at him. "You know how to make a man feel important."

Melody bit her tongue to keep from laughing. Her heart swelled, and she rushed up the stairs, afraid if she witnessed much more, denying the growing attraction for Vayden would become impossible. At every turn, he proved how different, how unique, how *special* he was.

Forcing herself to focus on work, an important factor in her life right now. Not some far too handsome, intelligent, sexy, probably the best kisser in all of Haven Ci—

"Stop it!" Melody chastised herself, slapping the file down on her bedroom desk. She braced her hands on the smooth surface and took several centering breaths.

An unfamiliar tension rolled through her. She needed… *something*. The desire floated like an unknown mist outside her reach. She didn't know what was pulling at her other than a deep-seated need to taste Vayden Dossett one more time. The thought of kissing him again made her stomach flutter and her cheeks flush. But the itching between her shoulder blades was something else entirely. A mystery she didn't have time to solve. Pushing the discomfort aside, she took a seat and went to work copying the information. She lost track of time, barely noticing the light fading from the room until she squinted.

"Melody Jane Ericksen!" a female screech echoed into her room, making her jump.

A flood of anxiety sent Melody's heart into her throat. Oh no. Melody shoved all the papers back into the folder and stuffed her copies deep into her bottom desk drawer. She'd hide them better later. The paranoid part of her brain insisted she take precautions due to the strangers who made appointments at and subsequently entered her parents' home.

Almost tripping over her feet in her haste, Melody ran from her room and to the stairs. Her mother tapped a satin enclosed foot, hands fisted on her narrow hips. One brown painted brow lifted in imperious anger over green eyes. Great. The queen of the house must have seen Vayden and wanted an explanation.

"Your sister informed me the gen-common in my living room is working with you?" Willow asked, her nose tilted upward in indignation.

"Yes. He has a name, mother."

"I don't care about his name," Willow snapped. She pointed at the opening for the living room. The action sent her hip-length hair swinging. The silvery threads interspersed within the deeper brown glittered in the golden light of dusk. "I care about the damage being done to your career even as we speak."

Funny how when her mother spoke the words she'd thought herself only days ago, vivid anger exploded within her. Her only excuse, things had changed. "That is ridiculous, no damage is being done. Vayden is a decorated investigator."

Her mother leaned back as if struck. "*Vayden*? On a first name basis, are we? Already he corrupts your professionalism."

Words failed to form in Melody's mind. She blinked. Rolling her eyes, she pressed past Willow. The long skirt of teal cotton from her mother's dress whispered across her pants. For the first time, Melody was thankful Lyrica couldn't hear their mother's hate-filled words.

"I am not done speaking to you, young lady," Willow said crossly. "You will explain yourself this minute. I'll not have all of Haven City talking about us and your indiscretions."

Melody stopped mid-step and swiveled on her toes. Her free hand bunched into a fist. "My *indiscretions*? It's an investigation, Mother, not a reckless liaison." Though the thought of a wild affair with Vayden had the heat of anger shifting into an altogether different form of warmth.

"Really, Melody," her mother reprimanded. "As if anyone would believe a gen-common could solve any type of crime. Assumptions will be formed."

"What kinds of things could anyone say that would hurt this house?" Melody countered.

"You have responsibilities. You have a duty to this family. If you're believed to be cavorting with some neanderthal, who will show any interest in you? Let alone what family will consider you for their son?"

"My family would," a deep masculine voice said behind Melody.

If her mother's glare could injure, Melody figured Vayden would be bleeding. "Of course, they would. Being married to a Gen-Heir, a guardian would be a step-up for your family."

Melody choked. Vayden brushed her hand in what she figured was a wish for her silence. "You are absolutely correct, Mrs. Ericksen. Having Guardianess Ericksen added to our family would improve us."

What would having a family who supported you no matter your goals or dreams or who you fell in love with be like? Melody wanted to turn and look at Vayden, knowing without a doubt, he'd meant every word. His family, a powerful shield guardian, and a successful business leader would be excited. Because Vayden would be. No other reason needed. No other explanation necessary. Envy stabbed sharply into her chest. She pressed the folder to her stomach.

Tension vibrated from Willow's slender frame. Bright red splashed across her high cheeks, too sharp from too little care for when and what she ate. "Melody would *never* lower herself to such a union, so your family can just forget their ambitions. This family is well outside your class."

Something snapped inside Melody. Like a physical string popping through her being. She spun, grabbed the front of Vayden's shirt, and pulled. Caught off guard, he fell into her, which was exactly what she wanted. Her lips pressed to his in a hard kiss. Before he could register the action, she glanced over her shoulder at her mother. Defiance stiffened her back and had her glowering.

"Too late mother, Vayden asked me to contract with him two nights ago." She smiled meanly. "And I said *yes*."

THE CRACK OF WILLOW'S PALM LANDING ON MELODY'S cheek echoed through the foyer. Pain radiated across Melody's face. She didn't even have time to gasp before Vayden growled and launched himself between her and the threat. A danger Melody never would have thought she'd encounter in her own home. She grabbed his arm to stop him.

"It's okay," Melody said.

"Like the artic it is," he rumbled out.

"She's my daughter," Willow stated with a snarl, her hand raised for another strike. "I will do with her what I please."

"And she's my *wife*," Vayden roared.

The words fragmented in the air. A validation that stole Melody's breath. Willow's hand fell to her side. Her mother's shoulders trembled. The steely edge remained in Willow's eyes as she glared at Melody.

"How long?" Willow asked.

Vayden answered before Melody could. "One year."

The hostility seemed to drain from her mother. "I see. Well then. Come with me, daughter."

Melody glanced at Vayden, who shook his head. Drawing a deep breath, Melody leaned close. "I'll be okay."

His gentle touch trailed down her still throbbing cheek. "Are you sure?"

Melody handed him the folder. "Yes. She won't get the better of me twice, I promise."

Next time, if there ever was one, her mother would wear a matching print across her face. Melody had never believed Willow capable of striking one of her children. The fall into irrational anger spoke of how dedicated her mother was to seeing the hopes and dreams she'd always placed on her daughter's shoulders realized. Shoring up her nerve and running through all the self-defense training she'd received as an enforcer, Melody followed her mother into the massive space designated as an office and research room. The musky scent of books, old paper and dust permeated the air.

Willow stood on her tiptoes shuffling, through contents on a shelf. She pulled down a box, opened it, then snapped it closed and moved on to another one. "I suppose I should have asked before losing my temper if this was a legalized affair. I apologize."

Melody blinked in disbelief. "You... *apologize*?"

"Yes, daughter. I understand the need to get the wild out before you move on to the duty. I had four lovers before I agreed to commit to your father for the required time to raise children." A noise of relief rushed from her mother. "Ah, yes, here we are."

Melody took a weary step back as Willow approached. Her mother held a small box out. "What is that?"

"A fertility bracelet. I don't see you wearing one. Hopefully, it's not too late to track your ovulation." Willow shoved the box into Melody's chest. "You need two full months to be accurate, leave a week in the middle of your cycle to be safe until you're sure the beads are properly placed."

Equal parts embarrassment and horror filled Melody. Her mother should have *no part* in her personal life. Especially where sex was concerned. Damn it, Melody wasn't even *having* sex, and she wasn't sure when she would. Sure, she'd been rash and announced a fake marriage, but she certainly didn't expect Vayden to go along with her little lie. Okay, who was she kidding? Her huge lie.

Her mother, however, couldn't know the truth, so Melody snatched the box from her hand and forced a shallow smile. "Great. Thanks."

Willow gave a curt nod. "Will you be staying here and going to his house on a schedule? My first two contracts worked that way. Very efficient."

And very cold. Melody shivered. A scheduled relationship? She wondered if her parent's marriage was so clinical. *This* was the future her mother wanted for her? Somehow, she didn't think Vayden would agree to such a ridiculous notion of a relationship. Melody looked at the box meant to protect her from an unplanned pregnancy. No, life with Vayden would be anything but boring and arranged. She figured that would include any intimacy.

"Melody?" her mother asked, exasperated.

"Yes?"

"Will you be going to his house on specific days of the week?"

"Um, no," she said, her impulsive streak running her mouth once again, "I'll be staying with him."

VAYDEN KNEW HIS JAW HUNG OPEN, AND THERE WASN'T anything he could do to change that fact. "Come again," he asked, positive this pretty, infuriating female wouldn't drop *two* life-altering decisions he had no say in on him.

"I have to pack a few of my things to bring back to your place," Melody said slowly, again because he hadn't believed her the first two times. "My mother is going to box up and courier over the rest of my clothes. She wants me to leave the rest of my things here, since we on—" Her voice failed, and she cleared her throat. "Only contracted for a year."

"Okay," he said, though he really didn't because he'd lost track of what exactly was happening when Melody's mother had struck her. The red haze that had taken over his vision still feathered in the peripheral. Lyrica had been blissfully unaware of the entire fiasco, having been resetting the chessboard. All Vayden wanted to do was grab both of them and go back to his place. One he could now at least claim to have responsibility for. The other... He glanced over his shoulder and heaved a sigh. "What about Lyrica?"

Melody licked her lips. "She goes back to school after Wintervail. I'll come see her every day."

"Your mother... treats her well?"

A flicker of something dark crossed Melody's eyes,

but she looked away before Vayden could pinpoint what. "She doesn't hurt her if that's what you're asking."

The risen red streaks on Melody's cheek made another knot of anger burn in his chest. "Just you, hmm?"

Melody fingered the damage. "She's never done that before."

"No excuse."

"I know."

"Do you?" Vayden glanced back into the living room, where Lyrica bounced a black marble knight across the board like it was a toy pony. "Harm can come in many forms, not just physical."

"I am very aware of that," Melody whispered. "And there is nothing I can do about it. She's their daughter, a minor. They don't hurt her, I swear. They don't even pay her any attention. The housekeeper mostly keeps up with her when I'm not home."

And Willow's hatred had sent Melody into such a rage she'd said something she couldn't take back. Not without losing whatever ground she may have covered with her wretched mother. Plus, Vayden didn't really see the downside to this situation for him. Yes, he'd give her an out because he didn't want a woman who didn't *really* want him. Especially a woman he wanted as much as Melody. But on the minuscule chance, she was serious, he only saw their future stretched out before him.

Lyrica flounced out as Melody ran up the stairs. "Where is Mel going?"

"To pack, she's going home with me." Vayden signed.

Lyrica frowned. "To work?"

"No, to stay. She decided to marry me." Vayden wasn't sure what emotion saying the words stirred up. Wonder perhaps. Or bewilderment. Maybe a little anticipation.

Confusion twisted on her young face. "Can you repeat?" she asked, her hands moving slowly.

"Melody decided to marry me," he signed with concise movements.

Lyrica's lashes fluttered against her cheeks as she seemed to process his answer. A slow grin spread across her face. "Really?"

"Yes."

"You're going to be my brother?" Her hands flew in a burst of excitement.

"Unless she changes her mind," Vayden amended, hoping Lyrica would keep this bit from her mother. "Which she's allowed to do."

"She'd be crazy to change her mind," Lyrica signed with an eye roll.

"You don't know anything about me, mite," Vayden felt compelled to point out.

She glanced away, her face tight. Her movements were hesitant when she replied. "I know you're good."

Vayden wanted to inquire on *how* she knew anything about him, but given her clear discomfort, and figured now wasn't the time. "And that I'm gencommon?"

Another eye roll and expression of aggravation made him laugh. "My sister sees beyond all that, even if she thinks she doesn't," Lyrica signed in short quick motions, in words more mature than her twelve years, showing how the youngest Ericksen had had to grow up far too quickly. "She loves me for me, and I am not perfect, either."

Vayden's jaw tightened. "You are exactly as you are meant to be."

"Then so are you," she quipped, her little chin lifted in defiance.

Vayden grabbed her chin and gave it a quick squeeze. "I never claimed to be anything else."

She beamed up at him. "Me either."

"You are a special girl, Lyrica." He released her chin and smiled.

Happiness shone in her eyes, and her skirts swirled around her ankles as she danced in place. "I sure am. I won both of our chess games."

Vayden laughed. "You did, but I'm determined to win back my honor." He touched a finger to his temple. "The next time we play, I'll be ready for your quick thinking."

"So you think," she said, swinging her arm as though she brandished a sword. "I told you I'm the best."

"I have been warned," Vayden agreed.

"Warned for what?" Melody asked, breathless.

Loaded down with two bursting shoulder bags, Melody navigated each step carefully. Vayden rushed forward and took a bag before she could protest.

"That your sister is the best," he answered, arranging her possessions comfortably on his person.

Melody's eyes twinkled with laughter as she stepped off the last stair. "Ah, I see my encouragement to be confident has taken."

Lyrica sighed. "At chess. He forgot to add that part."

Melody kissed her little sister's cheek and then

leaned back enough to be seen. "I don't think he forgot anything."

"Are you really going to marry him?" Lyrica asked.

Vayden tried not to hold his breath. Melody could set the record straight, or continue on with her charade. He wasn't honestly sure which one he wanted. To see if she'd go through with the declaration, or the chance to convince her.

Melody glanced in the direction her mother had disappeared to. "Yes, for one year."

Crossing her arms over her chest, Lyrica's gaze narrowed. "He thinks you might change your mind. You won't, will you?"

Ha! Called out by the twelve-year-old. Vayden cleared his throat to keep from laughing in a sort of wicked glee he didn't think Melody would appreciate. She cut her eyes in his direction and then returned her focus to Lyrica.

"Vayden and I have a lot to talk about," Melody said cryptically.

At the front door, Vayden waited while the sisters gave their goodbyes. Neither Willow nor Melody's father bothered to see her off. Lyrica stood watching in the doorway while Vayden handed Melody the file and arranged her things in the back of the Ariot. He waved to Lyrica on his way around to the driver's side. They drove off with Lyrica kissing her goodbyes.

For a long while, Melody simply looked out the window. When she finally spoke, Vayden had to lean closer to hear. "I wish I didn't have to leave her behind."

"You said she was safe, that she'd be fine." He eased

the car around a corner, breaking to a stop behind a carriage.

"She will be, I just… she's never been at home alone before."

"You're going to see her every day," he reminded her as he safely eased around a row of carriages, the horses clopping along.

"I know."

Vayden pulled into the closest parking space he could find at his building. He stared up at the five stories. Tendrils of ice spread across the brick facing and crusted the corners of the windows. Flurries of snow danced on the wind. Beside him, Melody sat unmoving, her hands clasped between her knees, knuckles white. Reaching over, he slid his hand along her forearm until he reached her hands. Startled, she gasped and glanced at him.

"We're just going up, like any other time," he said softly.

"I know."

"There's nothing to be nervous about."

An edgy chuckle left her as she looked away. "Right, only my future."

Vayden angled his body to look at her better, shifting his weight in the small space. "Nothing is decided yet. Nothing has been signed or filed. Your future is still entirely your own."

A shaky breath rushed from her mouth. Unable to stop, Vayden brushed his thumb along her full bottom lip. Her tongue darted out to wet her lips, teasing the pad. "You wouldn't hold me to my lie?"

He stared at her pout, his finger sliding along the

glossy path she'd left. "And have an unwilling wife? Hardly."

The heat of her breath flowed over his hand as she forced her head back, away from his touch. "I shouldn't have put you in this position. My mother…" She rubbed a nervous hand under her chin. "She made me so mad."

Vayden cocked his head to the side. "Was she not stating the same opinions you hold? That she raised you to feel?"

A flush spread across her cheeks, and she flexed her jaw. "She's wrong. I was wrong."

"Ah," Vayden said slowly. He leaned forward and captured her chin between his thumb and index finger, forcing her to meet his gaze. "What exactly were you wrong about?"

Fire flared in her green eyes. "*Everything.*"

Vayden grabbed the front of her shirt at the same moment she rushed at him. He caught her against his chest, ignoring the flutter and crinkle of papers around them as the file went flying. Arranging her across his lap in the cramped space, his mouth sought hers with the same reckless need she conveyed. Her arms wrapped around his neck, her fingers speared into his hair, forcing him closer. The warm, slick length of her tongue fought with his, exploring and driving him crazy in equal measures. Her knees settled beside his hips.

Unable to resist, he slid his hands over the firm curves of her butt and kneaded. A delicious whimper rewarded his action. She wiggled in a provocative manner over the proof of desire he couldn't deny. The spark of pleasure at her body moving over his hazed his thoughts. Deepening the kiss, he groaned and almost forgot they were parked in a very public location. *Almost.*

Despite every cell in his body rebelling, Vayden pulled back from the intoxicating kiss. Her ragged breath matched his as he leaned his forehead to hers. "We have to stop."

"I know," she whispered but pressed another soft, slow kiss to his mouth. "I haven't actually said yes, yet."

He laughed and gave her rear another tight squeeze. "That, and we're still in the parking lot."

Vayden kept a smile of satisfaction to himself as she leaned back and looked around as if waking from a dream.

"Oh, yeah." The alluring freckles across the bridge of her nose and cheeks stood out in stark contrast against her suddenly beet-red skin. She muttered something he couldn't catch, untangling from around him.

Vayden ignored the chill at her departure and focused on helping her gather the papers back into the file. Once she had them all, he stepped out into the frosty evening, taking a quick moment to adjust his pants and let the cold dissipate the remaining tendrils of lust burning through his system. When he was certain he could walk comfortably, he gathered all her things together and waited on her.

Loaded down with Melody's belongings, he followed behind her into the greenhouse courtyard. A couple walked arm in arm, their bodies pressed close together, their words too soft to hear. A man jogged with a medium-sized brown spotted dog on a lead. Two old ladies sat on a bench beneath a tree, brushing the top of the greenhouse with sprawling branches. They tossed bread crumbs near their feet for an eager gathering of small bouncing songbirds.

Vayden breathed in the thick, warm air and released it on a grateful exhale. Outside, the forces of winter froze the land, and anything unlucky to be caught without shelter. Safely enclosed in glass, under the tender care of humanity, life continued to thrive. Greenhouses across the nation would be the only refuge for those seeking an escape from the bleak conditions soon to stretch for months. That, along with the colorful cheer, each home uniquely created during the Wintervail season. Vayden focused on the woman walking with brisk purpose to the stairs, wondering how her family managed to ride out the winter without any of the vivid decorations meant to take the edge away.

On his floor, Vayden passed a bag to Melody and dug into his pocket for his apartment key. He held the door open for her to enter first and then closed and locked them in. Motioning at the door across from his bedroom, he led her into what would be her space for what he hoped was a short time.

He opened the door to reveal an obnoxiously pink bedroom. "In here."

She stopped at the entry to the room as if she'd walked into an invisible barrier. "Oh. My."

"My nieces decided they were better designers than me," Vayden said by way of excuse.

Melody let out a long breath. "Right. Well, it's definitely special." She looked at him. "And you expect me to sleep in here?"

He pointed to his room. "In here, or in there with me. Which is it to be?"

9

MELODY WEIGHED HER OPTIONS. THE ROOM WHERE PINK went to die, or the space where she surely would, because sleeping in Vayden's bed meant as his *wife*. And everything the single word entailed. The maddening throb between her thighs reminded her perhaps option B wasn't so bad after all... She firmly ignored her body and stalked into the explosion of ruffles and glitter.

Yards and yards of rosy tulle and silk draped over a queen canopy bed. Thick fuchsia carpet padded her steps. Silvery birds hung from the ceiling by thick pink satin strips. Even the two dressers were a shade of blush, with crystal knobs and topped with little porcelain ponies. The room was a study in indulgence. And as Melody glanced around, she couldn't help but wonder what Lyrica would have done with her space if given complete control as Vayden had allowed his clearly young nieces.

The sudden flair of light as Vayden lit a lamp brought a whole new level of brightness to the room.

Melody squinted and tried not to be overwhelmed yet again. The bed creaked with the weight of her belongings, forcing her attention to the man who could have denied every word she spoke to her mother and yet hadn't. To the man who Melody had to humbly admit might just be too good for her. A fist tightened around her heart, and she looked away, knowing the shame would show if she were to look her direction.

"We can set the record straight tomorrow if we need to," he said quietly into the silence she'd allowed to grow heavy between them.

Setting the file on the dresser next to a musical carousel, Melody sighed. "Might be too late by tomorrow. My mother is likely to set the record straight to anyone who will listen, just to be safe."

"What record?"

A wave of mortification swept through her, but he'd hear it from someone else soon, if not from her. She turned to face him, shoulders squared. "That our marriage is a legal, safe affair. Me enjoying my youth, so to speak."

Vayden shrugged. "I don't really care. I get a year to convince you to take a longer chance, that's all I care about. But I also don't care what she says to anyone else. This is *our* life, our decision, and we can tell her we changed our minds. I'm sure she won't be upset."

Melody laughed at the understatement. "No, not one bit."

He crossed the short space to her and took both her hands. "Melody, marriage is a big decision, even if it's only for a year. You know how I feel about it, but not even that matters. What you want does. There is no rush."

"If I stay here, everyone will assume our relationship is official, even though it's not," she pointed out, trying to ignore the warmth of his hands around hers and the sizzle of awareness at his touch.

Vayden released her hands and took a step back. A teasing grin played across his lips and danced in his eyes. "All my strategy to get you to say yes, eventually."

She rolled her eyes and waved at the door. "Out, let me contemplate the mess I've gotten us into on my own."

He picked up the folder and tapped it against his palm. "Aren't you even a little curious about the names Voklane gave us?"

In all the chaos of the afternoon, Melody had forgotten about their visit to the FIO guardian.

Vayden walked backward out of the room. "Because I am, and I'm planning on working some tonight, with or without you."

Melody wasn't sure if his actions were a dare or a disruption to distract her from the turmoil she'd caused in both of their lives with one rash declaration. Either way, she was grateful for the opportunity to focus on something else. Something more important than either of their issues. She took a moment to center herself. To allow the quiet and rightness of Vayden's space to settle into her. Once she was certain she could act like an adult, a professional one, Melody turned down the lamp and left the girly room.

Vayden sat at the table, papers already spread out, areas of the map peeking out through gaps in the sheets. Only light spilled from the dining area. A small glow from the woodstove cast heavy shadows in the living room. A smattering of twinkles shone beyond the wall of glass overlooking the city beyond. Ice coated the edges of windows. By morning every pane would be covered in condensation.

"Found anything?" Melody asked, peering over his shoulder as he slid papers aside and touched a finger to a street on the map.

"I don't know, maybe." A sheet of paper fluttered and appeared over his shoulder. "Check these names and addresses with your half of the list, would you?"

Melody took the paper and went to the side of the table she'd designated hers. She pulled in a chair and put the pages side by side. The two lists blurred together. She forced herself to focus but kept glancing at the doorway to the room she'd be occupying. "How often do your nieces visit?"

"Once or twice a week," he answered without looking up, paper flapping as he shifted pages in front of him.

"Really? So often?"

"Yes, Bree and her husband usually work the same hours twice a week, so I take the girls. My parents live too far to make it convenient."

No wonder he'd allowed the girls to make the room their own, they likely considered this their second home. Melody gnawed on her bottom lip and flipped a pen between her fingers. Vayden sighed and settled his forearms on the table, his gaze meeting hers.

"What is it? What's wrong?" he asked.

She shook her head and looked down at the work. "Nothing."

"Melody." His tone didn't leave room for argument.

"Do you think," she rolled the pen around, still not

meeting his gaze, "I mean, would your nieces mind if Lyrica ever used their room?"

"They will love your sister," he said gently. "She is welcome here anytime you want her to visit."

Melody took a deep breath and nodded. A rogue thought went through her mind that perhaps she wanted Lyrica to do more than visit. But since she hadn't even decided what her role would be under this ceiling, she decided to keep the idea to herself. She turned her attention back to the lists, trying once more to do something useful.

"Are you so worried about her?" he asked, arms still resting on the table, his gaze steady on her. "You said she'd be fine, that she'd be safe."

"They won't hurt her," Melody assured. "They just aren't good for her, you know?"

"Yes, you won't hear me arguing with you." His fingers drummed on the table. "But there isn't anything I can do, or even we can do, until you figure out what you want."

And wasn't she thinking the same thing seconds ago? "I know."

"But, if you do decide in my favor, and I'm not saying this to convince you one way or another, we'll talk about Lyrica's place in our home." He looked around the open space, his brows drawn in thought. "I'm sure I could figure out a way to arrange my office space in here, somewhere."

Our home. The sentiment created a warm ball in her stomach. Compiled by him already envisioning the changes he'd carry out to make room for a little girl he owed no responsibility to. Melody gripped the pen as tightly as the squeeze around her heart. "You don't even know her. Why would you do that?"

He scrubbed his hands over his face. When he looked at her again, exhaustion and frustration seemed to wear him down. "I wish you didn't even have to ask that."

Genuine confusion swirled inside Melody. "But I did, and I'm no closer to understanding. We're strangers to you, and yet, you'd offer your home to both of us? Completely upend your life? Why?"

Sighing, he shoved away from the table and went to the kitchen. "First, I *want* you in my apartment. I've somehow managed to convince myself I'll be happier." He opened a cupboard, removing cups and loose tea. He waved an empty teabag around. "I might be weaving my own illusions, who knows, but it doesn't change anything, I want you here." He placed a teakettle on the stove and opened the hatch to heat the surface. "Second, Lyrica is a great kid, she deserves to be treated like any other kid her age, which I'm assuming doesn't happen often."

When he glanced over his shoulder, a brow raising in question, Melody shook her head.

He shook out a long match. "I thought not. See, reason enough right there."

Melody found herself a breath away from saying she'd contract with him. Right now, if he had one in the apartment. First thing in the morning if not. She snapped her jaw closed and blinked away the moment of insanity. Suddenly being married to the far too sexy gen-common because of who *he* was didn't concern her anymore. No, forcing him to be part of what *she* brought to the table, the dysfunction and hatred, kept her from agreeing. The tables had been bitterly turned, and Melody wrestled with the change.

He finished toiling in the kitchen, two steaming cups of tea in his hands when he returned to the table. One cup landed in front of her, the warmth of vanilla and bite of orange wafted up, making her breathe deep.

"One of the addresses Voklane gave me matched with a drop-off from the hired carriage company."

The words were spoken so casually that Melody almost missed their significance. She choked on her tea and stared at him. "What? Are you serious? Which one? Is it in Haven City or Caris?"

"Haven City. But, the other interesting fact is according to the list, another person lives only three houses down."

"So, it could have been either location," Melody surmised, rising to join him in looking at the map.

"Yes. Both will be worth investigating first thing in the morning." He looked up at her. "When do you need to be back at South Row Division?"

She sighed and reached for her tea. "Well, technically, I'm working a case. I've let my MP know what I've been doing. But I have HRS duty in two days."

Vayden's face twisted in displeasure. "Not the safest assignment."

Melody couldn't stop a snort. "I work South Row. Crime is a sad, a daily fact of life. Our human rabies syndrome cases are actually lower than East Street or even North Bridge Divisions."

"Are you trying to convince me you won't be in danger?"

Melody patted his shoulder, ignoring the heat and

muscle beneath her fingers. "You seemed to need assurance."

"You are going to be on a team with a handful of other people, who may or not be brave enough to actually stand between an infected and its prey." He held up a finger, his expression dark. "One bite, Melody. One stray drop of blood or saliva in an open wound or splashed into your mouth, and that's it. Three weeks later, if you're lucky to be healthy that long, and you'll be a mindless zombie searching for victims to infect, too."

"I know how the virus works," she whispered, hating the shiver of dread that raced up her spine whenever she thought of encountering an infected.

To date, she'd been lucky enough to only read about the handful of cases springing up in the city, not having witnessed any personally. Her family wasn't connected enough for large parties, and she didn't do much more than go to work and return home. She'd been scheduled to work the HRS shift at Division seven times in her career, and so far, nothing had happened. Yes, they had instances of people turning while waiting to be accused or doing the accusing, or even providing witness testimony, which was why a team existed in the first place. The cramped and over-crowded halls of every Division location made an outbreak deadlier than usual. Reducing the number taken to an infection facility to safely live out the remainder of their days was the goal. The shifts were essential and part of every guardian's duty.

"I understand the need," Vayden said, shifting papers over the map as if forcing himself to think of something else. "But I don't have to like you doing the assignment."

"It's just one day. Hopefully, I won't miss anything important with our investigation while I'm sitting around reading a book in the ready room," she said with a frown.

"If something comes up, I'll have to deal with it," he replied.

She sipped her tea, relishing the sweet warmth. "I know, and I understand. Finding the girl is what matters." She looked over the visible map sections. "Will we go to the address you confirmed tomorrow after the ice thaws?"

"Yes, the moment we're able. I'll be watching the roads from up here. The Ariot should be able to move before the carriages, so we can beat some traffic, maybe."

A sense of nervous expectation trembled in her stomach. The morning would find her waking up in Vayden's home. Soon after, they would venture off in search of vital information to hopefully give them another thread to follow in finding Lucianna.

The glow of the lamps caught the rich green leaves of the little clementine. Lost in thought, Melody found herself gravitating toward the small tree. She brought the tea back to her mouth and sipped as her gaze shifted to the sparkling world beyond the glass. Her fingers brushed the leaves. A faint quiver danced under her fingertips. Soft edges curled around her hand, enrobing each finger. Melody rubbed the silky leaves, her mind wandering to the disaster of her day. The plant soothed her, seeming to absorb her cares, radiating peace and a sense of calm

The urge to sink her entire arm into the depths of the branches had Melody pulling free. At some point, she'd need to investigate further her rising obsession with the little tree. But not tonight. She had enough on her mind, enough to deal with. She didn't think she could handle another life-altering change.

MELODY BURROWED INTO THE MOUNTAIN OF BLANKETS covering her, shimming deeper into the comfort and soft warmth. Cold air permeated the room, making leaving the bed a task she found herself avoiding at all costs. That and facing Vayden. Apparently, there was a single bathroom in the entire space, and she learned last night she had to go through his room to get to it. The whisper of her door opening made her squeeze her eyes shut.

"I told you to leave the door open," Vayden said softly. The clunk of glass hitting wood sounded near her head. "Only the main room and my bedroom have wood stoves."

Since she couldn't exactly confess, leaving her door open would have been too great a temptation to wander into his bed, but she remained silent.

"I brought you coffee. I don't know how you take it."

Melody peeked out from under the blankets. Still damp from the shower, his dark hair framed his face. He wore a dark green button-up and tan pants but no shoes. She pulled the blankets down enough to sit up. "Thank you."

He shoved his fingers into his pockets. "Do you

need anything for the coffee? Milk? Sugar? I have some vanilla sugar that is great for it."

Melody brushed curls from her face. "Vanilla sugar and milk sound lovely, thank you."

He grabbed the cup and nodded, and that's when Melody realized he was nervous. She laughed and shook her head.

Vayden arched a brow. "What?"

"You. I can't believe you're nervous. Three wives, you said? Waking up with an adult female in your place isn't new. I should be the nervous one."

For several moments he was silent, staring at her with his gorgeous golden sapphire eyes. Then he shrugged. "You're different from them."

Melody tilted her head. "You hardly know me."

"You keep saying that, but I don't feel the same." With that, he turned and strode from the room.

Melody released a long breath and patted the covers to expel restless energy. "Well, okay then."

She braved the cold room, slipping from bed and padding her way on the thick carpet to her bag. A quick rifle through the contents produced a pair of dark blue pants and a cream sweater. She tiptoed with haste across the hall into Vayden's room. The scent of his soap, earthy and sharp with citrus notes, hung heavy in the air. She ignored the huge bed, covered in rich browns and reds, and kept a fast pace into the bath-room. Along with all his things, fluffy pink towels, shimmery flower-shaped soaps in a wide jar, and a white step stool painted with big pink roses revealed the bathroom was very much a shared space. Melody smiled, taking one of the pink towels. Why not? She lived among the vibrant color now, she figured it was fitting.

In the spacious white marble shower stall, the hot water took her by surprise, and she yelped, struggling to find a way to even out the stream with cold. Her parents' house didn't have a way to heat water. She was used to quick, cold showers, especially in winter, when bathing became almost unbearable. In the coldest stretch, she filled a sink and washed that way.

For a few minutes, all she could do was stand under the near scalding spray and bask in the fall of liquid heat. Tension melted from her muscles. Her brain emptied until only the pounding on her skin and along the tile under foot, surrounded her. She never imagined bathing could feel so good.

Steam rolled in the air, filling the stall and room. Melody sighed, not knowing how long she truly had and not wanting to experience the flow of familiar cold water. She quickly washed with Vayden's soap, unable to stop breathing the scent deeply. A flush that had nothing to do with the heat of the shower swept through her. Knowing not too long ago, Vayden had stood naked, soaped up, surrounded by mist as she was, and had her imagination going to forbidden places. Desire coiled tight in her belly, and Melody squeezed her eyes shut and forced her sudden rapid breathing back under control.

She shut off the water and fumbled for the towel she'd draped over the glass door. Eyes still tightly closed, she pressed her face into the softness and took slow breaths. Why did he have to be so strict in his standards? Why couldn't he just give in to the attraction weighing them both down and see how they'd be together?

Pulling the towel down, she knew the answer.

The same doubt crept into the back of her mind. Without the protection of the contract— a minimum year honored by over ninety-percent of those who entered into one— the risk of becoming infected with human rabies syndrome was a real risk. Melody's single night of hasty passion so many years ago was safe only because she knew her lover had been like her. Untouched. A contract insured they kept the promise to remain faithful for the duration of their relationship, short as they may choose it to be.

Staring at the closed door to his bedroom, Melody had a sinking suspicion a year wouldn't be long enough to learn all Vayden seemed willing to teach about the differences between a man and woman. And yet, that's all she'd be able to give, *if* she could even manage to convince herself her parents wouldn't do something rash. Like embark on an insult crusade against him that could seriously harm the professional career he'd worked so hard for.

She buried her face in the towel again, ignoring the chill in the room and the cooling water running down her skin. How in the inhabited world had she messed everything up so horribly? Hiding in the bathroom wouldn't solve a single thing. Somehow, Melody found her inner adult, squared her shoulders, and forced her mind back to the important part of the day. Finding more information about a missing teenage girl.

10

Vayden parked the Ariot two blocks from the target house, thankful to be out of the apartment, where the urge to take advantage of being very alone with Melody plagued him every second. If he'd been smarter, he'd have taken her back up to Madeleine's. But no, he'd wanted her under his ceiling, where he *might* have a better chance of convincing her to make their fake contract a reality.

Except he hadn't.

Nope, he'd kept his distance. Taken care of her. Made sure she had a good breakfast and anything else she needed before they left. Because up until yesterday, Vayden was pretty damn sure no one had ever taken care of Melody without having to be paid for their efforts. She deserved better, and he wanted to be the one to show her as much.

Melody glanced out the window. "What are we going to do? Just walk up and knock on the door?"

He glanced at her while opening the door. "If you were wearing your HCES uniform, that might have worked to our advantage. I've found most people slam the door in my face."

She blinked. "Um, okay, then what are we supposed to do?"

"Walk around the property first, see what we can determine the old-fashioned way. It's cold, still early, if anyone is up, its likely to be staff, who won't pay us much mind." He exited the vehicle and went to the sidewalk, waiting for Melody to join him. "If we're lucky, maybe there's a neighbor out, and about we can talk to."

Melody hunched deeper into the dark crimson jacket she wore over her cream knit sweater and navy slacks. While not as finely woven as what his mother, or even his sisters, wore, the clothes were nice. As with everything else about her, she took great care in her outward appearance beyond her guardian duties.

Vayden wanted to ask when whatever in the artic they were about was over if she'd still pursue finding a ranked guardian to marry. Or if she'd venture off on her own and do what *she* wanted. The thought of anyone by her side but him made him bristle, however, and he found himself picking up his pace and putting distance between them. Before he did something rash. Like demand she contract with him for a decade when she couldn't even decide if she was willing to risk a year.

The rapid fall of her boot-heels on the brick behind him mirrored his every step. "Vayden," she called out, slightly breathless.

He slowed his gait, tamping down guilt. "Sorry," he muttered.

She touched a hand to his arm. "I'm anxious to see what we can find, too. But we don't belong here, and me chasing after you will probably draw unwanted attention."

Chuckling, he shoved his hands into his jacket pockets. "No, looks like we had a lover's spat." He glanced at her and winked. "Only this time, the guy is the one storming off." He shook his head and tsked. "What did you say to make me so upset, Melody?"

She laughed, her rich mahogany curls bouncing around her face.

Sighing in mock frustration, he shook his head. "And then you go and ruin the façade by laughing."

Her smile broadened. "I guessed I laughed at you one too many times and hurt your big manly feelings."

Using his elbow, Vayden nudged her gently. "I like you this way. Relaxed. Not so serious."

Her breath puffed out in a cloud of vapor. The tip of her nose and rise of her cheeks had turned pink from the chilly air. The smattering of innocent freckles across her face practically glowed in the golden morning sun. She looked sweet and impossibly young. The coat swallowed her modest curves, detracting still more years from the very adult number he knew she claimed.

"Serious is… safe," she said softly, the wind almost carrying her words off before he heard. "When I decide to act differently, nothing seems to work out quite right."

"Maybe because the result isn't as consistent as when you do the same thing over and over again," he guessed.

She glanced at him under her long, dark lashes, her green eyes speculative. "Maybe."

Vayden slowed as a two-story tan brick house with four chimney stacks, an iron fenced in yard, and a three-story greenhouse rising from the back came into view. The white painted numbers on one of the dark wood pillars creating the front porch told him this was the house they wanted. "We're here."

Melody surveyed the house from the fence, her face scrunching. "Seems quiet."

"Like I said, early." He tested the gate. It creaked open with a subtle push. "Guess we're being welcomed in."

She followed up the narrow brick walkway behind him. "Looks like the gardener has been lax."

Vayden studied the weeds sprouting between the cracks in the path, white and glittery with frost. The struggling plants would survive much colder nights. Pots on the porch revealed brown sprigs stabbing up from barren soil. A broken chair laid overturned on the otherwise vacant wooden planks.

"I'm not sure anyone lives here anymore."

Melody walked onto the porch with him, her hand wrapping around the pillar near the steps. "How odd."

Vayden tested the door, unsurprised to find it unlocked. The door swung open. Light from the entry barely made a dent into the dark interior. Papers fluttered along the floor. "Looks like they left in a hurry."

"We can't go in, it's trespassing," Melody whispered as if anyone on the street could hear them

"Okay," Vayden said in agreement. "You stand out here."

Then he walked in on an echo of Melody's shocked gasp. A toppled side table and a half-empty box of junk sat in the middle of the foyer. Garbage littered every inch of the floor and gathered along the base boards. Vayden puffed out a breath and wondered how he was supposed to find anything of value in the mess. A faint noise had him glancing over his shoulder. Melody stood in the door, her toes flush with the threshold.

"Well?" she asked, craning her neck.

"Come in and help me look through all these papers. Maybe we'll find something useful."

She shook her head. "It's illegal."

"We're not using anything we find for evidence, guardianess. We're using it to find a missing kid."

A heavy exhale rushed from her. She looked back at the empty road. Her hands slapped her thighs. "Well… I guess I can help look, no one seems to have noticed us."

Vayden worked his jaw to keep from smiling. "I won't tell anyone."

She cast him a glare of annoyance. "Sure you won't because that would implicate you, too."

"Only if you made the decision to accuse me," he said, winking.

"You are impossible." She used her foot to close the door, removing their only source of light besides the windows.

"I prefer tenacious." Vayden fisted his hands on his hips and looked around again. "Okay, let's figure out where the office may have been, that's probably our best place to start."

After walking the bottom floor, they both agreed on a back corner room as the likely candidate for a study location. More papers littered the floor, and a broken porcelain statue that looked to once have been a decoration on the barren, and dust-covered shelves were the only things left. Vayden sank to the floor and gathered the papers nearest to him, looking each one over. Melody did the same.

They remained on the floor for who knew how long, piles of paper growing around the office as they looked carefully. Shadows lengthened across the room. Wind buffeted the windows, smacking branches against the glass. The house provided some refuge from the elements, but without fire, the cold reach of winter crept in.

Melody blew an errant curl from her face, her hands falling to her thighs, multiple papers clutched between her fingers. "I feel like everything is multiplying, and we aren't going to find a single useful thing."

Vayden shuffled through a stack he'd made, his eyes scanning each sheet and discarding it just as quickly. "Well, we're going to keep searching. Every paper scattered around this house until the moon rises if we need to." He looked around the chaotic room and the patches of now clean floor. "Something is here, I know it."

Melody went back to searching individual papers, her audible sigh of frustration filling the room. The shuffle of pages paused for a moment and he glanced up. Her brows were pinched tight, her lips set in a grim line. Vayden crawled across the distance to her.

"What have you found?" he asked, tamping down the rise of excitement over a possible discovery.

"I don't know, it doesn't make sense. I've never seen these symbols before." She held a yellow sheet out to him. "Have you?"

Vayden studied the odd ciphers. He sifted through all the unusual languages he'd seen over his many years and investigations until one clicked into place. "Markinish."

"Where is that spoken?" she asked, tilting her head to look over the words again.

"Mark Inland." Vayden handed it back to her. "Don't lose that."

"Do you understand what they've written?" she asked, turning the paper in many directions while tilting her head.

"No, I don't, but maybe Voklane can help. The FIO should have access to language experts, right?" At least, he hoped they did. If the FIO failed, he'd try Henry.

She glanced up at him, her spring green eyes wide. "You think this is it? The clue we might need?"

"I bet it's something. Whether it's what we need or not, I have no idea. Yet." He glanced around at the dying light and the endless mess. "I doubt we'll find much more."

Melody picked up a few more sheets nearby. "What about this?"

He took the paper when she held it out. Rows of neatly printed addresses with numbers written in parathesis lined the center. He glanced around where she sat. "I bet the desk was here."

She looked around again. "Then all of this may have come from it."

"Let's get them all, we'll look them over at the apartment."

RAMSEY HUNTER TUTTED AT HER NEPHEW AS HE POUNDED the dough like an enemy to be conquered. "Not so rough, Parker. We have to treat the dough nice, or we'll have mean cookies."

"Uh oh!" he proclaimed, lifting his hands away. Bits

of flour and caked-on goo dangled from his small fingers. The wooden stool he stood on wobbled slightly under his quick movement.

"Uh oh, is right. We don't want mean cookies," Ramsey said with the utmost seriousness, using her foot to steady the support.

"I spank them mean cookies!" He slapped the dough and burst into laughter.

Ramsey shook her head and chuckled. She reached for the rolling pin and patiently showed the child how to flatten the dough to prepare it for the flower and bird-shaped cutters scattered on the counter. An array of bagged frosting, special candies made just for Wintervail cookies, and colorful sugar sprinkles filled the kitchen table. All they had to do was cook the first batch. Without destroying the dough.

With her brother Jonathon in Italyssa handling a potentially disastrous situation for his wife Sylphine and her family, Ramsey found herself bringing in the holiday alone for the first time. Parker hadn't been formally adopted yet, and until his papers were legal, he couldn't leave the country to be with his new parents.

Ramsey had volunteered to care for the kidlet while they were away. Most days, life was simple enough. Others— well, she'd learned emotions weren't a solid state where Parker was concerned. They tended to be more fluid, flowing from one extreme to another with little to no warning. The trauma he'd experienced only weeks ago, being stuffed into a small attic space to be kept safe by his mother, who was then raped and murdered, had left quirks only time, support, and patience would heal.

The dough rolled out and ready, Ramsey pressed the first cutter in and waited for Parker to repeat the action. He did so perfectly, clapping in delight when Ramsey removed the shape, revealing a bird. She left him to the task while carefully using a spatula to move the ready cuts to a cookie sheet. The pan was almost full when a pounding thumped at the front door.

Ramsey sighed, setting the spatula down. "Someone must have forgotten your daddy isn't home."

"He's gone to Italweesa," Parker chirped, slamming a cutter into the dough hard enough to make a sound. He picked up the flower shape, looked at it, chortled in happiness, and repeated the action.

Ramsey brushed her hands on her apron. "Stay right here, and don't make our cookies mean."

His hand lifted from the cutter and reached for another one. "No mean cookies!"

"That's right." Knowing she had limited time before Parker's four-year-old mind became too bored to pay attention without being reminded of his task, Ramsey rushed to the door. She opened it and found herself staring at a broad chest clothed in a deep red knit sweater. Blinking, she lifted her gaze and met silvery blue eyes belonging to a handsome man. "I'm sorry, Jonathon isn't available at the moment."

The visitor smiled in amusement, the action softening the angles of his face. Not enough to make him look overly kind, but rather, less threatening. He lifted a hand and pulled off a tan ivy cap, leaving behind slightly mussed short, pale blond hair. "I'm not here for Asherwick, Miss Hunter. I'm here to speak to you. My name is Ryan Voklane, I work for the First Intelligence Office."

Ramsey frowned and tightened her hand on the doorknob. "I don't see what use the FIO would have for me."

"Oh, plenty, I assure you."

A loud *bang* sounded from the kitchen, and Ramsey's pulse spiked. "I'm sorry, now isn't a good time, I'm a little busy."

Voklane took a step forward, almost filling the entire doorway. "This won't take long." He angled his body, revealing a small figure that had been hidden behind him. "I brought someone so you'd know you're safe with me."

"Raina!" Ramsey proclaimed in surprise.

"Hello, Ramsey," Raina Merrick said, smiling. Her pale brown eyes twinkled with genuine happiness as she stepped beside Ryan. A peach skirt fluttered down to her ankles in soft waves. A peach vest over a pale blue long-sleeved silk shirt made the master guardianess look professional, as usual. Her light brown hair fell in a braid down her back, little tendrils framed her pretty face. "Guardian Voklane said the matter was urgent and asked if I'd accompany him, and I agreed. Being home alone can be stressful enough without strangers calling."

Ramsey stepped out of the way, holding the door open wider. "Please, come in. Parker and I were making cookies."

"How fun," Raina said with another smile. "Wintervail cookies are my favorite. I can't wait until Tanis is old enough for the tradition. I'll go help while you and Ryan talk. If that's okay?"

Unsure what else to do or say, Ramsey nodded in agreement. "Thank you."

Ryan glanced around the spacious foyer. "Anywhere?"

Aside from the general family areas, the downstairs belonged to Jonathon and Sylphine. Upstairs, Ramsey had transformed two of the bedrooms into her own private domain. However, this Voklane man had no need to be present in her room. Blowing out a breath, she waved toward their modest library, where Sylphine conducted her affairs when in Sziveria. "In here will work."

Ryan let Ramsey enter first. She lit several lamps on her way to the tidy desk at the back of the room. She wished, not for the first time, she weren't so awkward. Avoiding societal gatherings for most of her adult life had led to a pitiful lack of adult social skills. She put the desk between them.

"Okay, what did you need?" Ramsey asked, hating the faint tremor in her words.

Ryan reached behind his back and pulled free a folded slip of paper. "To know if you can read this."

Despite her fingers being covered in flour and crusty bits, she accepted the sheet and looked it over. Familiar characters filled the page in neat rows. Some were circled, some had been drawn through, and others had checks or stars or X's next to them. The same foreign language had been written on cargo manifests her brother had been investigating weeks ago. "Markinish."

"Yes."

Ramsey took a deep breath and sat. "There is no one at the FIO or any of the other government organizations that can read this?"

"I'm sure you know Markinish is a very unique language. There are many different dialects. And no, we have no one familiar with it in all of Sziveria." He ran his free hand through his short-cropped hair, his other fist squeezing around his hat. "Your brother told me you have a gift for languages. I was hoping you might know at least a few of the characters."

The latent talent that had seemed to surface overnight still took Ramsey by surprise. She'd found a few quirks with it, however. She looked over the sheet. "Okay, I recognize parts of this, it's very similar to what I've been helping Jonathon with. I'll see what I can manage."

Ramsey flattened the paper on the desk, her fingers pressing into the corners while she cleared her mind. Little crumbles of dried dough and gritty flour fell onto the surface. She took a slow, deep inhale and stared at the characters. The odd lines, dots, and squiggles seemed to rearrange themselves in front of her until a handful of coherent words formed. Not all. Some of the characters remained complete gibberish to her mind. She didn't question it, didn't allow herself to panic, which she'd been tempted to do the first time she'd experienced the phenomena. Most languages she understood after a few weeks. Some dialects of Markinish she had studied over a weekend, and the patterns clicked, making sense.

"It appears to be a list. Almost like a shopping list. But..." She swallowed hard, her heart jumping uncomfortably. She looked up at met Voklane's worried stare. "I think it's for people."

Ryan flew from his seat. Pressing his hands to the desk, he leaned forward. His eyes seemed to glow silver with an odd inner fire. "Show me."

Melody settled deeper into a cushioned chair, trying to focus on the words in the book lying open on her lap and not the chaos outside the door in the lobby of the South Row Division. The Boredom Room, as those assigned Human Rabies Syndrome Containment Duty, liked to call it, was a disorganized space. Two round tables sat unused in the center of the room. Empty mismatched shelves lined one wall. A random filing cabinet sat next to the door. At some point, Melody liked to think the First Prefect over the Division had grand plans to make the area fun and not so boring. But funding, and time, had waylaid the plans. The reality looked more like people threw furniture into the room when they had nowhere else to.

Since HRS incidents were low in the building, of which Melody would never complain, more often than not, the assigned guardians found themselves reading, playing cards, talking, or as one Tribunii currently decided to occupy his time, throwing a bouncing ball at the wall. The constant *thwack, smack,* made Melody twitch. Coupled with the hum of endless conversation, footfalls, and shuffling cards, her patience was on the thin side.

The radio remained silent. In another hour, someone would get up to make sure the charge was holding and crank the magnetic energy source if necessary. The small group couldn't leave, so food and drinks were delivered throughout the shift. Melody glanced at the clock and stifled a groan. They'd only been on duty for four hours; they had another eight to go.

Melody couldn't stop her mind from roaming. She wondered what Vayden was doing. Whether he'd heard back from Voklane about the evidence they'd found, and if he was chasing another thread. Without her. She scowled. Some aspects of his job were far better than hers. No zombie duty, and being able to decide what cases to take seemed pretty wonderful about now.

Once again, a weariness over her familial duties weighed her down. She plucked at the seam of the chair, frowning. Family was about more than self. All her life, her parents had drilled into her the importance of ensuring their line among Sziverla's ranked guardians.

The moment she'd been old enough to be assessed for a logical talent, they'd had her at a testing facility. Other inheritances, like sympaths, beast masters, interceptors, cryptographers, botanists, and medical talents, along with so many others, were touch-based. The Gen-Heir could handle something, and their talent would come to life. Logical talents were harder to detect and had to be placed. Like Melody, and her investigative skill. Strategy, logistics, and analytics were other logic-based inheritances the country made immense use of. She'd had her choice of places to go.

Her parents, of course, had made the decision. Enforcement Services were the easiest to be accepted into and the fastest way to earn higher positions within the Divisions, and, therefore, a chance at a ranked guardianship seat. She'd worked hard, rose in the HCES rankings, and now she sat here wondering why? For who? Because looking back at all her hard work, none of it had been for *her*. Sighing, she flipped the book closed and stared at the radio.

The door cracked opened on a burst of masculine laughter, pausing while whoever stood on the other side continued to speak and chuckle. Melody glanced at the clock again and scrunched her face. They weren't due for a refreshment delivery yet. Another shout of amusement came from whoever stood on the other side, and Melody found herself leaning forward to get a look. Everyone else had stopped what they were doing, too, waiting on their visitor to walk in.

Finally, he pushed the door the rest of the way open, and Melody almost fell out of her chair. *Vayden*. And the grin on his face made him look unbearably handsome. Judging by the vacant expressions on the faces of the other two women in the room, she wasn't alone in her thoughts. A fierce wave of jealousy made her frown. She looked back at Vayden, wondering at the sudden possessive need to yank the hair of her two fellow female Enforcers and shout in a clear, concise manner *mine!*

She blinked. Not good.

The first person to snap out of the shock was Tribunii Samuel Hadfield. He jumped up from bouncing his ball, a goofy smile on his face. He held out his hand. "Dossett! What's going on? What brings you here?"

Melody's jaw dropped. Vayden returned the man's enthusiastic welcome, taking his hand, shaking, and turning it into some weird masculine greeting ritual. The friendship between the two was obvious. Samuel clapped him on the back.

"Then it's true?" Sam glanced at Melody. "You married our Mel?"

Vayden finally looked at her and smiled. The action sparkled in his eyes, and he winked. "I brought decent food. I know what they expect you all to eat on this miserable duty assignment."

Everyone descended on him like a horde of the infected they were meant to be protecting the population from. Dropping the bag on the table, he stepped away. Melody unfolded from the chair as he crossed the distance between them. Her heart thumped a steady rhythm of anticipation. With a smile curving his lips, he leaned down and pressed a slow kiss to her mouth. Her toes curled in her boots. She had to fist her hands to keep from grasping his shirt to pull him closer and bring the kiss to depths she knew would get her in trouble.

"I missed you," he whispered against her mouth.

"You did?" She knew she stared at him like a lovesick idiot, but at the moment, she couldn't seem to help herself. Wait, lovesick? Wouldn't she need to be *in love* for that? She gasped and took a step away.

"Yes, I did. So hard to believe?"

She tucked a curl behind her ear. "I don't know, I guess." At the table, her fellow enforcemen pulled wrapped packages out of the bag, exclaiming their delight. "Did Voklane get back with you?"

"Not yet. But I'm doing some research on the properties from the list he gave us. I'm hoping something turns up."

"You mean they weren't all just homes?"

He shook his head. "No, some were holdings, others were homes, but when I started digging, they weren't all owned by the people on the list."

Melody considered his words. "How did you know to look deeper?"

He shrugged. "I'm not sure. A feeling, I guess."

An odd sense of frustration welled in her chest. She couldn't remember having a feeling about anything while she investigated. Sure, she could go to a scene and look around and spot things, but was that the same? She opened her mouth to ask when the radio blared. Frenzied screams and confused shouts sounded before the cry help. The caller failed to mention the floor and department. The enforcer closest to the door, Tribunii Ellora Cherian, ran forward and shouted at the reception desk.

Ellora returned, her face set in stern lines, her dark brown eyes filled with fear she couldn't mask. "Fourth floor, theft crimes."

Samuel ran to the cabinet behind the door. He tossed everyone a catching pole, including Vayden. Denial made her gasp in alarm.

"Tribunii Hadfield, Vayden isn't an enforcer, he can't go up there with us," Melody argued, proud of the strength in her voice. Her heart threatened to burst from her chest. She was scared. So scared.

"Do you think they're going to care who helps up

there? If any civilians are stepping in right now, no one is going to argue. You haven't faced an infected yet, have you?" Sam asked, slipping gloves onto his hands to help grip the pole better.

Melody shook her head, accepting a set of gloves from Ellora. "No."

Vayden flexed his hands around the pole. The tips of his fingers poked free from fingerless black leather gloves. "Won't be my first go-round."

Samuel sighed and tested the flex on his pole. "Mine either."

First Guardsman Terissa Pendry blinked. She hugged the wooden rod to her chest, her dark gray eyes wide. "I don't want to go up there. I can't do this."

Ellora tied her long blonde hair back and glared at the young woman. "You have to, FG Pendry. You don't have a choice. You knew when you decided to become a guardian, our lives are placed on the line to keep everyone else safe. Any Guardian of Sziveria has an obligation to ensure the safety of the population."

Terissa visibly swallowed, her already wild gaze shined in desperation. "But… it's a zombie."

"Yes," Vayden growled from the door. He grabbed a small hand radio from beside the larger one. In quick movements, he cranked the magnet inside to create a charge. He checked the unit, and seeming satisfied, slipped it into his back pocket. "An HRS victim who is currently working fast to make more victims. Get a move on, FG."

Poles in hand, the group left the room. They fought the panicked flow of traffic down the stairs on their way up to the fourth floor. Despite the situation being contained – an infected couldn't navigate stairs – the knowledge of sharing any amount of space with a deadly contagion had the occupants of South Row Division fleeing.

On the fourth floor, Ellora took the lead. Vayden fell in behind her, followed by Samuel, Melody, and a lagging Terissa. An eerie silence made tingles dance along Melody's nerves. A group of people huddled in a corner, soundless. Tears streaked down several cheeks. Ellora shooed them towards the stairs, to safety. Melody glanced back and gasped in outrage as Terissa fled with them. The little coward! She hadn't even *seen* the zombie yet and ran away.

"FG Pendry is gone," Melody told the group quietly.

"Great," Ellora muttered. "We still have four, we can do this."

Melody didn't know who Ellora was trying to convince, herself or the team. Either way, Melody took a bracing breath and followed, now as the last member, down the empty corridor. Papers, file folders, and envelopes littered the ground, along with hats, shoes, and someone's glasses, and was that— Melody tilted her head while walking. Yep, someone had lost their dentures. She tried to imagine the state of terror that would literally knock teeth from someone's mouth. The lack of noise made Melody shiver. Life usually teemed in the corridors, loud and demanding, each person challenging to be heard over another.

Doors were closed all along the hall. Likely barricaded from the inside until someone made the rounds giving the all-clear. Instead of fighting for innocence, or a conviction, anyone remaining on the floor huddled in fear, hoping to survive the event. While an infected couldn't negotiate stairs, they could still twist knobs.

An acute sense of hearing and vision, brought on by the active stage of the virus, made sensing their prey easy. Melody had heard and read of their inhuman speed to reach their victims the moment they sensed them. Moving too fast for their victims to get away unless their target happened to be an interceptor. A Gen-Heir with equal wraithlike reflexes. Melody glanced at the team in front of her. None of them carried that particular gene. Too bad.

They rounded the corner, and Ellora held her fist up. Melody almost collided with Sam, her feet slipping on loose paper. She braced herself against the wall and tried to see over the taller frames of Sam and Vayden.

"How do you want to do this?" Ellora asked so softly Melody had to strain to hear.

If the Tribunii was whispering, then the infected must be visible. Melody swallowed the nervous rise of bile in her throat and tried to calm the need to breathe much too fast. Having a complete freak out would risk not only her life but everyone else's.

"There's no easy way," Sam replied with a faint tremble in his hushed words.

"Sure there is," Vayden countered, using the cord on the end to widen the noose on the other side of his pole. "When I say *now*, don't hesitate."

Melody's world shifted to slow motion. Vayden didn't ease or even attempt to creep up on the zombie. He outright launched himself like a maniac at the monster. The infected ran faster than Melody thought possible towards the one man she realized, in the worst possible moment, she didn't want to live her life without.

• • •

SALIVA GUSHED FROM THE INFECTED MALE'S MOUTH, mixing with blood. The thing previously human had managed to get at least one victim. Since Vayden didn't see a body lying in a pool of blood, the person had escaped. Though, perhaps *escaped* was a poor choice of a word. If in two weeks they didn't check themselves into a containment facility, this would be happening somewhere else. If only one casualty came of this incident, South Row Division would be lucky. As packed as the corridors usually were, Vayden was expecting at least a dozen bodies and just as many injured.

The infected rushed at him, fingers twitching, mouth open wide. Sickness and determination rolled off the human rabies syndrome victim in waves. Vayden lifted the pole at the precise moment and sent the end into the infected's chest. The monster slammed into the wall with enough force to send plaster flying. In the split second it took for him to recover, Vayden flipped the noose around and looped it around the man's neck.

"Now!" Vayden's muscles worked hard to contain the straining infected. Gnashing teeth and curved fingers made a desperate bid to reach their target.

Melody arrived first, her attempt to loop around the zombie failing. Face pale, arms trembling, she tried again and managed, pulling the loop tight and taking some of the burden from him. Ellora and Samuel secured their poles in unison. The team separated to form an X, effectively securing the infected's movements. The zombie couldn't move even an inch without their say-so.

Bracing his pole with one arm, he reached into his back pocket to retrieve the radio he'd grabbed. "What's the front desk's channel?"

Ellora answered, and Vayden quickly adjusted the signal. He pressed the coms button and sent a message letting reception know the infected was secured and to send someone from the containment facility or health services when they'd arrived. Hopefully, somebody had remembered protocol and called in the incident. While they could technically wait it out since the active stage of the virus lasted no longer than three hours, the effort would be immense.

The group fought together to hold the much stronger male. He twisted and turned, snapping, drooling, and franticly tried to reach any of them. A gruesome ring formed around his neck from the nooses cutting into his diseased flesh. Each pole would have to be thoroughly disinfected or destroyed.

Sweat trickled down Vayden's cheeks, and he noticed he wasn't the only one laboring under the struggle of containment. The infected bucked under the restraints. Melody and Ellora stumbled into the wall but kept their holds. The echo of boots running down the hall made them all look to the left. A welcome face appeared, despite the heavy frown marring the shield guardian's features. A lab coat billowed out behind him. Black boots, slacks, and a dark green sweater made the white stand out all the more. The edges of his dark blond hair touched the collar of the coat.

"Dossett," Terran Kaine, Shield Guardian Levkaseon said with a crooked smile and head shake. Arriving to cleanly remove a viral incident was a normal occurrence for him. As a true Gen-Heir pathologist, he could detect any bacterial or viral infection by touch. Being naturally immune to everything capable of killing the rest of the human population meant whenever possible, he was responsible for getting close enough to dispatch the threat. "I thought you put infected containment behind you."

Vayden released a long-suffering sigh. The arrival of more people created movement the infected attempted hard to get nearer to. Vayden strained against the increased strength the zombie put into his efforts. "Me too, but I seem to have been here at the wrong time."

"Keep him steady," Terran instructed, motioning over his shoulder for one of his teammates. "Hollis, try to keep his attention forward."

Melody's gaze caught Vayden's. Uncertainty shone in the depths of her eyes. Tension vibrated along her entire body. Sweat dampened the hair around her face and slickened her skin. The gloves kept the pole from slipping free during the strenuous task. When Terran walked behind Ellora, Melody's attention shifted to the shield guardian.

"Should be over in a second, everyone. Just keep it up a little longer," Terran urged, slowly moving into position behind the infected.

Terran produced a heavy silver device that fit in his hand. Aligning the case in his palm, he settled his thumb over the back end. Determination hardened his features and bunched the muscles along his frame. With rapid-fire precision, he sent the metal rod into the base of the infected spine. The action broke the spinal cord, but not the skin. In the blink of an eye, the zombie folded in on himself, almost taking the unprepared holders down him. Vayden knew what was coming and kept a tight hold. The corpse's head flopped about his chest and shoulders.

"Okay, you can release now," Terran instructed,

placing the metal punch into a secure wooden container one of his teammates handed over. "We'll handle the rest." He glanced around. "Are there other bodies?"

"Not here in this hall. Maybe another. He has fresh blood on him, so he definitely managed at least one bite," Vayden said, laying his pole down. The others followed, allowing the deceased to slowly gravitate to the floor.

Terran mumbled curses, handing the box off. "I'll do a search. Hopefully, if the person survived and fled, they'll be smart enough to check in at the city containment facility."

"I had the same thought," Vayden admitted.

Terran searched over their small group. "Anyone come in contact with any fluids?"

They all answered in the negative, and Terran nodded. "Good. You're free to go, thank you."

Melody jumped when Vayden grasped her elbow. "Come on."

"Where are we going?" she asked quietly.

"Up." He glanced at Ellora and Sam, touching his back pocket. "I have the radio still if you need us again."

"Twice in one day?" Sam shook his head. "Don't speak such things over us, Dossett."

They didn't encounter a single person on their way up the stairs to the sixth floor. Vayden opened the door into a lush space. Birds trilled. Sunlight streamed through glass and dappled under trees, warming the humid space. Stone crunched beneath their boots. Vayden guided Melody to a cement bench. She sat down, heaving a long exhale, her hands bracing on her knees.

"I imagine," Vayden said, sitting beside her, "the experience was similar to your first violent crime scene."

She nodded and took another deep breath. "Yes. Only I didn't throw up over this."

Vayden couldn't help but smile. "There's still time."

Laughing, she shook her head. She straightened, pushing damp curls from her face. "You were so calm. How many times have you dealt with an infected?"

He leaned forward, resting his arms on his thighs and clasping his hands between his knees. "While I built my client list as a reward seeker, I needed a job. I'm sure you can imagine how difficult it is for a gen-common to find work in this city."

She flinched but remained silent.

"Anyway, I needed something that paid well. Risky jobs always pay the best and I found the riskiest of all."

Gasping, she turned on the bench, her eyes wide. "You did not." She punched his shoulder. "Tell me you weren't so foolish."

He chuckled. "I was nineteen. At nineteen, you think you're damn near immortal. Hunting the infected in the Old City Ruins was exciting and paid so well I had money in savings by the time I could afford to work as a reward seeker full time."

"I wish they'd send patrols to the Ruins. Maybe there'd be fewer instances if people stopped going there to use the inhabitants."

Vayden shrugged. "Maybe, maybe not. My experience has been when someone wants to do something depraved, if they think about their craving long enough to want it bad enough, they'll find a way. The Ruins just — make some things easier."

"And lead to HRS outbreaks." She shook her head. "It must have been awful."

"Well, sometimes. The area has become almost self-policing, like the Northern Boundary. If the virus becomes active, the residents flee to higher ground. Locks aren't a thing there, so anyone's space is open to others. If you've never been, it's hard to explain."

A shudder trembled her shoulders. "I've never had a reason to go. No one reports crimes there."

"No, I don't suppose they do. The only reason Health Services keeps an active containment unit there is to keep tabs on the outbreaks. If more than three happen at once, chances are one or more are going to happen in the city. They know to be prepared. Or as prepared as they can be. The residents didn't really need us except to remove the body. If no one was there, they'd wait the two or three hours for the active phase to reach its conclusion. Disposing of the contagion is their only problem. They *need* Health Services for that, and naturally, Health Services doesn't want HRS victims laying around," he said.

"That's so sad." Melody pulled her foot onto the bench and wrapped her arms around her knee. "There's so much no one talks about, isn't there? We don't read about the Old City Ruins in the paper, but we all know it exists, but we're clueless about how they live."

"Not everyone is clueless. And many of them have reached a point where they want to be left alone to live life their way. Not all of them sell themselves or other criminal services, some garden and barter their excess food, or trade skills, just like any other city. They have a small market and a little economy all their own," Vayden said.

She laid her cheek on the top of her knee, her gaze shifting over the area. "Is it safe to visit?"

He lifted his clasped hands and rubbed at the stubble covering his chin. The whiskers scratched along the leather. "I don't know about that. They have a sort of guard system in place. Containment units wear clothing clearly identifying them, so they're left alone. Everyone else has to state their purpose. If they're okay with what you're doing in their area, they let you pass."

"Wow, that's... I can't believe that's a part of our city. Sounds so..." She huffed out a breath. "Primal Years to me."

Vayden considered her comparison for a moment. "Yeah, I suppose if I had to imagine what that time in humanity was like, Old City Ruins would probably be close." He leaned close and nudged her knee. "Ready to go back down?"

"I suppose. Thank you for this." She leaned over and brushed her fingers along a thick, broad leaf. Her eyes drifted shut. The leaf's point curled around her finger.

Realization slammed into Vayden. Not a maybe. Not a suspicion. He *knew* Melody had been deceived. Whatever test she took, whatever results were handed over, whoever officiated the scores, had all been lies. She wasn't a logic-talent. Not even close. Anger over knowing she'd been denied an entire life of discovery and wonder at who she truly was had his hands fisting.

She swayed closer to the plant, which trembled and stretched. Visions of the shrub wrapping around her in an embrace she'd find as anything but loving had Vayden almost voicing his alarm. Before any noise could escape from his throat, he bit his tongue. He grasped her shoulders to keep her upright. He wanted to chastise the little philodendron, but sadly the only person who could communicate with said plant would completely freak out if she learned of the ability now.

Sighing, she lifted her hand from the leaf. "I thought we were leaving."

Vayden slowly released her. The plant seemed to tremor its displeasure. He glanced between her and the tree, looking for signs she'd noticed. As with the clementine at his house, she appeared oblivious to the subtleties. On edge, wondering to what lengths the botanical inhabitants would go to reach out to her, Vayden urged her to rise. He threaded their hands together because he wanted the contact and to keep her from touching anything else. The strand of composer he figured she clung to would likely snap if another stress factor were dropped in her lap.

"What's the hurry?" she asked, her boots kicking up pebbles as he rushed them to the exit.

"Time to get back. Don't want people talking," he said over his shoulder.

"Oh please, they think we're contracted now." Her eyes laughed at him when he glanced back. "All they'll think is you're... quick."

A ball of fire expanded in his chest. He wanted to show her just how *quick* he'd take things with her. Exploring every inch of her body until she screamed his name. But now was not the time, and this was not the place. Knowing his luck, they'd end up half buried by vines and roots near enough to the surface to reach her bare skin. He shuddered at the thought.

However, he couldn't let the comment go without a reaction. Yanking her hand, he spun and caught her against his chest. He buried his fingers into her silken curls and kissed her, hard and deep, leaving no questions about how lacking he'd be as her lover. The entire length of her body softened against him. Vayden gentled his lips over hers. His tongue caressed, exploring all the secret places of her mouth, discovering one whimper at a time what she liked. What she craved.

She rose on her tiptoes. Her hips pressed between his, nestled in all the right places to drive them both just shy of insane. Vayden's hand slipped from hers to cup her butt, holding her tighter, making him groan. Her legs parted enough for his thigh to slip in. In the rational part of his brain, he knew they should stop. Bringing her gasping on pleasure, while a definite goal, wasn't one he wanted to share with anyone else. And if they kept going, he wouldn't know *how* to stop, no matter who walked in on them.

Slowly, he untangled their bodies, then their mouths. He smiled at the dazed way she stared up at him, smoothing the hair back from her face. He touched a kiss to her nose. "At least now, when they talk, they'll be half right."

12

———————

Beyond emotional and physical exhaustion, Melody shuffled behind Vayden down the corridor to his apartment. After the greenhouse, they'd helped clean up the mess left behind once the containment unit vacated Division. The bone-melting kiss he'd given still lingered like a whisper across her lips. She couldn't stop thinking about it. Somehow, she'd managed to function during the remainder of the shift, though most of the afternoon seemed a blur.

The distraction Vayden had supplied after her sassy comment had helped keep her from dwelling on the awfulness of the HRS incident. What the event meant for a family. For the man's lover. Maybe even a spouse. Looking into the face of a human reduced to the instinct of a viral host had terrified her. All she wanted to do now was wash off in the blissful heated paradise of Vayden's shower and bury herself in the softest sheets she'd ever slept in.

At his door, his keys jingled, and he glanced over his shoulder. "Doing okay back there?"

The urge to lean into him and press her forehead into his back and rely on his strength had her swaying away from him. "I'm fine."

He quirked a brow. "Fine? I don't think so." He unlocked the door and pushed it open for her to enter first.

Melody froze before crossing the threshold. Wall lamps flickered down the entry hall and brightened the living room. In the short time she'd known Vayden, he'd never kept lights burning when they left the apartment. Warmth from a pellet stove filtered out into the much cooler corridor.

"Vayden, kiddo, are you finally home?" a lovely female voice filtered down the hall.

Kiddo? Dread had Melody's fingertips tingling. Oh no… no, no, no.

A grin spread across his face. "Ma?" he called out.

"Yes, your father and I are in the living room," she answered.

Melody whimpered and turned on her heel. She couldn't meet his parents. Especially not his mother, a shield guardian. She wasn't ready. Not right now, filthy and stressed from one of the worst afternoons of her life. Vayden's arm banded across her upper chest and forced her into the apartment backward.

"You aren't going all cowardly on me now," he whispered into her ear and then kissed her hair. The moment the door was firmly closed, he released her.

"I can't do this," she said, her chest constricting. Pinpricks began to dance across her vision. Breathing took actual effort.

Vayden changed direction, pushing her into his bedroom. "We'll be out in a minute," he called as he closed the door. Hands gripping her shoulders, he turned her to face him in the dark room. "Relax."

"I can't," she admitted, hating the tremble in her voice that revealed her weakness. "I've reached my bad day allowance. I can't handle anything else."

He rubbed her arms and sighed. "I know, but what if I promise meeting my parents won't make your day worse?"

A laugh of hysteria bubbled from her chest. She tried to turn away from him, but he wouldn't let her. "The only reason they're here is probably because of the same rumor everyone at Division believed."

"A rumor you started," he said calmly.

"I know. I know this is all my fault. That I put myself here, and I only have myself to blame. *I know,*" she snapped. Tears burned as the day, the week really, threatened to shatter the tentative hold she had on her emotions. She took a slow, deep breath. "I know I've made a mess of everything, and I need to be the one to fix it. I do. But I don't know if I can do it *right now.*"

He folded her into a hug, one she didn't realize she needed until he cradled her against his body. "No one is asking you to fix anything. I'm not. My mother is a smart woman, and so is my father. They'll figure things out for themselves pretty quick. While they might want to know what's going on, they aren't going to demand anything. You walked out of my door with me this morning and back in this afternoon. Even we can't deny *something* is going on."

Melody allowed the soft glide of his hands along her back to soothe her frayed nerves. She pressed her face into his hard chest and inhaled the dark masculine scent of him.

"Just meet them, please." He rested his cheek on top of her head, the stubble from a long day catching in her curls. "You don't even have to speak if you don't want to, I promise."

After everything he'd done for her, Melody knew she couldn't deny his request. A tremor of anxiety raced through her limbs. Vayden's arms tightened. "Okay."

"Okay to which part?"

"I don't know," she admitted, her voice fatigued. "I'll do my best, I guess."

He released his hold, and Melody wanted to protest but knew she couldn't meet his parents enclosed in a Vayden-ball, no matter how much the thought appealed. Squaring her shoulders, somehow finding the woman her mother had paid good raimarks for Melody to at least pretend to be, she forced herself to take a step back.

"Ready?" he asked, hand on the doorknob.

No. "Yes. Thank you."

He nodded, his fingers brushing under her jaw as if he knew her gratitude was for more than asking if she was ready. "It's going to be fine, you'll see."

Skepticism left Melody frowning, but she didn't argue. After being in the dark, she squinted from the burst of light as he opened the door. His hand settled at the base of her spine. Gently, he urged her into the hall and beyond, into the open space of his living area.

A stunning woman who didn't look old enough to have a son Vayden's age stood from the couch and faced them. Her hand went to her mouth, and she smiled at Melody. A real smile warmed her honey-brown eyes. Vibrant shoulder-length strands of golden hair gleamed in the lamplight. Vayden made quick work of introductions. His father, Grayson Dossett, was a prime example of how his only son would age. Strong, handsome, and stylishly mature with thick strands of silver in his dark hair, his delight at meeting her seemed as genuine as his wife, Amari's.

"We're a little drained. Melody had HRS duty at South Row Division today, and there was an incident," Vayden explained, his hand still a strong support on her back.

"Oh my," Amari exclaimed, rushing around the couch. "Come sit down, pretty girl. I know how awful that experience is." She grasped Melody's hand in hers, warm and soft. Concern pinched between Amari's brow. "Your first time?"

Melody nodded, unable to stop the shiver of horror.

Amari tutted and eased Melody onto the couch. "I'll make some tea. Grayson, my love…"

The shield guardian didn't have to finish her thought. Her husband reached for a blanket and draped it around Melody's shoulders in a fatherly gesture that brought another burn of tears. Vayden sat on the couch beside her and pulled her into the shelter of his side. Melody didn't protest. His parents fluttered and fussed around them both, taking care of Vayden's hunger and Melody's apparent need for comfort. Sweetened vanilla and lavender tea landed in her hands.

Too stunned to do much more than accept the care, Melody watched and sipped while Amari straightened what she could on the table without disturbing their investigative efforts. The surrealness of being tended to by a high-ranked guardian left Melody speechless and so humbled she found herself fighting tears for the third time since walking into Vayden's home.

"Are you helping Vayden on a case, Melody?" Amari asked, squeezing into an overstuffed chair beside her husband.

"Um, I guess you could say we're helping each other," Melody hedged.

Amari's eyebrows lifted in question.

Vayden squeezed her bicep, where his hand still wrapped around her. "As a loyal HCES Tribunii, Melody is having a hard time admitting when they've messed up. Henry's file has gone missing, he asked me to find Cia."

"What?" Grayson asked, straightening in the chair. His golden-rimmed green eyes stared at her in a way that made her forget she was an adult. "What do you mean the file is missing?"

Pulling her spine straight, she lifted her chin. The missing information wasn't her fault. She figured at this point, how and why the case had disappeared would never be discovered. "All I know is it did, and I went to Mr. Castien myself to learn what I could. I found Vayden there, and Mr. Castien said he'd only work with HCES if Vayden was included. We've been working together since."

"How does HCES feel about that if they allowed the case to fall to the wayside? Don't you have other tasks?" Amari asked.

"My MT has made it clear the case takes precedence, even if I'm working on it alone," Melody answered, hating the knot in her chest. She wished she knew why someone wanted Lucianna Castien to remain missing because that was the only logical conclusion she could come to as to why someone had removed all traces of the case from South Row Division.

"We're going to find her," Vayden said.

Pride replaced the censure in Grayson's gaze. "I know you will, kiddo."

Amari slipped her hand into her husbands. "How is Henry?"

Vayden sighed and shook his head. "Lost. You should convince him to stay at Terravine Manor, at least until after Wintervail or until we find Cia, whichever comes first."

Grayson ran a hand down his face. "I'll talk to him."

"Will we be celebrating more than Wintervail at the blooming party?" Amari inquired, glancing between them.

The dismay Melody had managed to shove down flared to life on a burst of fire in her stomach. Her mouth went dry. The depths of her tea held no answers to her situation.

"We're still... working on that," Vayden answered carefully.

Amari gasped in obvious delight and slapped Grayson's thigh. "See! I *told* you he wouldn't have contracted without telling us he'd even met someone."

"Elianna did," Grayson mumbled.

Amari waved his comment away. "Eli is more impetuous than Vayden. Even though he didn't listen when I told him the first three were mistakes, he still introduced us before they married."

Vayden groaned, his head falling back onto the couch. "Ma..."

"Don't worry, I won't say anything else." Amari stood and headed to the kitchen. She rifled around inside a large tote. When she turned back around, Melody almost leapt from the couch. Only Vayden's hold kept her pinned in place. Two thick silver bracelets gleamed in Amari's hands. "I was hoping this time, maybe you'd have a promise ceremony?"

Vayden took a deep inhale, and Amari rushed forward, the promise bands held out. His mother spoke before he could utter a word. "Please. I know it's asking a lot, but if you haven't contracted yet, or even if you have or plan to, none of my children have allowed us the pleasure of being there for their promises. All couples make them, even if just to each other, or when they sign the contract as a promise of fidelity alone. Please let us be part of yours."

The silver bracelets clanked together. Amari held them out on two open palms. "We could hold it at the Wintervail party this weekend, either with everyone in attendance or as a private affair in the library with just family."

Melody glanced at Vayden, her heart in her throat. What would he promise her? And what could she possibly promise him? A flash of whimsy had her imagining Vayden slipping the cold metal onto her wrist, holding tight and promising her more than she could hope. Before she could stop herself, Melody reached for the thicker band. Both cuffs were identical, only one heavier and broader for a more masculine wrist. Strands of silver vines wove together to form a tangled braid, a half-inch thick for the feminine version, an inch for the masculine. They were stunning and clearly represented the Terravine shield rank.

Melody noticed Amari and Grayson wore similar bands. Sliding the cool metal through her fingers, Melody met the shield guardianess's kind gaze. "Are these family heirlooms?"

A flush spread across Amari's cheeks. "Actually, and this is a little embarrassing, I had a set made for all my children. None of them have gone on to make public, or family private, promises, however. Bree wishes she had, and I keep trying to tell her just because they're contracted for another eighteen years now that she's pregnant again doesn't mean they can't make promises for their future. Anyway, I know it's presumptuous of me, but I'd love it if you at least consider having one."

Melody caressed the cuff through her fingers. "I think... I'd really like to."

MELODY'S ADMISSION MADE VAYDEN WANT TO LEAP OFF the couch and shout in victory. The slender cuff his mother had produced warmed in his hand. He wanted to slide it onto her wrist and proclaim his promises right now. However, he sensed a hesitance in her words.

"But?" he asked when she remained quiet.

"I want Lyrica there," she whispered, meeting his gaze, somehow reducing the room to only the two of them.

"Okay, we'll make that happen, then," he promised, sliding his hand along her jaw, caressing under her ear. "What about your parents?"

Her gaze darted up to his mother, who watched their exchange with a mixture of curiosity and hope. Melody licked her lips. "I'm not sure... if they'd understand."

"Your parents aren't supportive?" Grayson asked.

Vayden almost snorted. "Her parents are worse than Ma's."

Amari took a sharp breath. "Ah. Well then. We will have a beautiful evening with…." His mother's honey-colored eyes narrowed on Melody. "Your sister?"

"Yes," Melody whispered.

"How old is she?" Amari asked.

Melody held the band back out to Amari. "Twelve."

Amari took a step back, accepting Grayson's outstretched hand. "No, you hold on to that. When Grayson handed me mine and told me to think about what promises I'd make him, I did. You do the same for my son."

Grayson stood. "We'll let you two rest now."

"You aren't going back to Terravine, are you?" Vayden asked, his attention shifting to the window and the freezing landscape beyond. Only a band of brilliant orange light along the horizon remained of the daylight. Already ice crept along the edges of the windows.

"Oh no. Madeleine is expecting us," Amari answered, smiling. "I have missed her."

Vayden didn't ask why his mother assumed his nieces' room would be occupied. Then again, she was a logic-talent, and one look in the room where Melody's belongings resided, would have given even a non-logic talent a clue that he and Melody weren't sharing a room. At the moment, at least.

"Will she be at the blooming party?" Vayden asked.

"Of course. You know she and all the Ralstons are invited every year."

Amari's Wintervail irises were the talk of the city each year, and the party she threw to celebrate their height of bloom even more so. To be invited was an honor, to attend and be seen a must for anyone who considered themselves important.

Vayden grinned. "Should be fun, then."

"It's always fun," his mother said without humor. "It's *my* Wintervail party."

"Which is perfect every year," Grayson soothed, pulling his wife close.

Vayden saw his parents out and returned to the living room to find Melody enthralled with the promise band. He braced a hip against the back of the couch and flipped the cuff he'd been given for her between his fingers. "You didn't have to say you'd do the ceremony, you know."

She rose, the blanket falling from her shoulders to the couch. "I know, but the way I see it, everyone already believes we're contracted. My mother made quick work of spreading the news. And…" She passed him a fleeting glance before slowly migrating to the nearest little tree in front of the windows. "Were you serious about us contracting?"

Vayden hesitated, torn between going to her and allowing her to seek comfort in the plant, as she seemed unconsciously headed towards doing. He settled on closing half the distance between them. Close enough to reach her if she appeared ready to fall into his little tree, but far enough away to give her space. "I am very serious."

She stopped near the window, her hands sliding the cuff in a circle, studying every inch. "My mother would probably pass out if she learned of me having a promising ceremony with you."

"My mother will understand," Vayden reiterated. "I'll tell her we changed our minds."

"No," she said with a small sniff, "she was too excited." She shook her head and turned to face the window, taking a small step closer to the plant. "I don't know why, but I don't want to disappoint her by refusing. I mean, she doesn't even know me, why would she care if I made you promises?"

Vayden considered his answer. Aside from her obvious love for Lyrica, Melody had a limited concept of familial affection. He had to tamp down the tide of anger threatening to overwhelm his calm.

"Because I'm her son, and hearing the woman who has agreed to be with me for the next year make promises that remain between us and strengthen our bond, is something most mother's want to experience." Vayden grinned. "Well, that and holding a grandbaby. My mother is a serious supporter of her children procreating."

As he'd expected, a sweet flush bloomed across her cheeks. "I see."

Vayden pulled out a dining chair. He sat, reaching for her wrist. Slowly he urged her closer until she stood between his knees. She didn't protest, but she didn't meet his gaze either. He ran his hands to her biceps. The stiffer fabric of her HCES jacket crinkled under his palms. "I know it'll only be a year, but it's still a year with me. Are you sure you want to?"

"I guarantee you my mother has already begun a list with marriage matches for me for when I'm done with you," she whispered. Gradually her gaze lifted to meet his. "I don't know if I'll ever be done with you, though."

The distress and shine of tears in her eyes made him pull her into his body. He hugged her tight, his cheek resting on her shoulder. She slid forward and gave no warning when she straddled his lap, forcing him to quickly close his legs to keep her from falling. She wrapped around him, her body trembling.

"I'm scared, and I hate it," she said, her voice weak and wavering.

"I know you think we're strangers...."

She shook her head, her curls tickling his jaw. "No, I'm scared of what my mother can do. The things she'll say. You've worked so hard and—"

"Hey, no." Vayden leaned back and grasped her face in both his hands. He pressed his thumbs near her ears until she looked at him. "None of that. There is nothing she can say or do that would ruin anything for me. Your mother is... no one. Not compared to either of my parents. If she wants to take on *my* mother, she's more than welcome to try. And my father could make sure no business walks through their door again. It would not be in her best interest to sabotage anything between us."

"Somehow, I don't think she'll be thinking about that. You don't understand how obsessed they can be."

Vayden's lips quirked into a half smile. "Let them obsess. We'll be living our lives while they're panicking. Sounds good to me."

The smile she attempted was weak. She looked away from him again. Her cheeks flushed and hot beneath his fingers. "They'll never see you... fairly."

What about you? The question hovered in his mind but never left his lips. He didn't want to know if she'd forsaken her prejudice. Couldn't stand to know if she hadn't. Carefully he unwound her from his frame and helped her stand. The perception her parents had for him was nothing new, she'd made no secret of it, and neither had they. And yet, the reminder left a hollow ache in his gut. He didn't know if he'd ever be able to tolerate knowing he was less-than in Melody's eyes.

"Go get your shower," he said, urging her with a gentle nudge towards the front of the apartment. He headed to the kitchen. "I'll have another cup of tea waiting for you when you get out."

She hesitated, pulling on the bottom of her jacket and shifting her feet. "I didn't mean to upset you."

Vayden opened a cupboard and pulled out a tea tin. "I know. You didn't."

"Now who's lying?" she asked, her words laced with frustration.

He filled the kettle with water and placed it on the stove. "I'm not lying. You can't change who they are or what they think." *And I can't change you.*

"That doesn't make their views any less wrong," she said softly.

Vayden met her pure green eyes, a knot heavy in his chest. "No, I suppose not."

On a sharp inhale, her mouth opened, but no words came out. She sighed and strode from the room. The faint *click* of his bedroom door closing echoed from the hall.

Vayden pressed his hands onto the counter and let his head drop to his chest. What in arctic was he doing? Could he really contract with someone who looked down on him? Groaning, he knew the answer. Yes. If that made him pathetic, so be it. He wanted Melody. In so many ways. Yes, he desired her body and her heart, but he also longed to see her embrace her full potential. A capability she didn't even know she possessed. One her parents had gone to great lengths to bury.

The kettle let out a shrill scream, forcing Vayden's

thoughts away from darker things and onto caring for the woman who'd agreed to contract with him. Shaking his head in disbelief, he filled two porcelain cups and dropped in tea bags. The warm, spicy scent of vanilla and cinnamon drifted up on steamy swirls. Sitting at the table, Vayden set himself to the task of continuing to research the property information he'd received from Voklane. Tomorrow, when they were at the records department filing the contract, he'd also pick up what he'd requested.

Time stretched until he took a sip of cold tea. Shocked, he stared at the cup and then glanced at the still quiet hall. Where was Melody? He went to his bedroom, easing the door open. A shaft of light cut through the darkness from the bathroom, illuminating a pale swath of skin laid out on his bed. Vayden swallowed and considered backing out of the room, away from temptation. His feet had plans of their own, moving him closer to the very naked woman passed out on top of his blankets.

At some point, she'd been wrapped in a dark towel. Movement had dislodged the thick fabric from her torso. The cloth played a visual game of seduction, draped over a thigh to pool between her legs. Her arm fell across her stomach, under her pert little breasts. Wet strands of hair stuck to her shoulders and cheeks. Easy breathing swelled her chest and drew attention to all the soft female curves displayed for him to take in.

Everything male in Vayden responded. He almost sank to his knees. Knew if he didn't leave the room, he'd discover how she tasted after a shower. If her skin carried the flavor of soap and woman. How smooth and supple she'd be under his palms. How quickly he could make the curls between her legs damp for a whole other reason than a recent wash.

Jaw clenched, he yanked a blanket he kept folded at the bottom of his bed up and let it settle over her on a flutter. He made sure the pellet stove was full before dousing the lamp in the bathroom. Melody wasn't his to touch. Not until tomorrow, when they'd sign a contract the moment the records department opened. Until then, he'd wait. No matter how much doing so cost him.

13

THE HARD *THWACK* OF STAMPS HITTING PAPER AND HOLES being punched mixed with the hum of conversation and papers being shuffled in the records department. Transfixed on the clerk signing the witness line, Melody didn't notice anything beyond the narrow bubble her world had become. She and Vayden were officially contracted. No longer a rumor, but a fact. Someone touched her arm, and she jumped.

"I have the papers I need. Are you ready to go?" Vayden asked.

She nodded, looking back at the short man behind the counter. "Do we need a copy?"

"Have that, too." He held up a thick folder of papers. "That one being signed is for safe-keeping at the records department's secondary location."

Melody blinked. She'd stood like a lump through all the paper signings? "Did I sign them all?"

Vayden laughed and grasped her elbow, steering her through the lines waiting their turn up front. "Yes. Forgot already?"

"No," she denied quickly.

He chuckled. "It's okay, I know this is a lot to process."

A lot to process?

She was married.

Married.

The moment had never been one she put a lot of thought into because she'd dreaded when a man would lay claim to her. When she'd marry for position instead of love. But that wasn't her fate. Not anymore. Melody realized the significance of Vayden's contract. Freedom, if she had the courage to seize her future. While he'd insisted on a single year, there was nothing stopping them from renewing for longer when the time came. If he wanted her still. If they wanted each other. Her parents could rail and berate her as much as they pleased. She wasn't bound to them any longer.

Melody dug her heels into the tile. The soles of her boots squeaked. Vayden lurched to a stop and glanced at her in confusion. She grabbed his shirt sleeve to keep him in place and closed the distance between them. Before he could say a word, she leveraged herself on his shoulders and jumped. He accepted her weight, muttering a curse of surprise. Legs wrapped around his waist and arms around his neck, Melody closed her mouth over his. In front of every spectator present, she sealed their marriage with a kiss.

Vayden's arms closed around her, holding her closer still as her legs tightened until fabric alone separated them. He opened his lips for her questing tongue. The crowd disappeared. Only her, Vayden, and their kiss existed. Desire rolled through her belly, settling hot and deep between her thighs. In the back of her mind, she realized she should have waited to jump on him until they were alone. Very alone. And she could do something about all the layers of clothing between them.

When she'd awoken this morning, naked in his bed, she'd tried not to be embarrassed knowing he'd walked away. She hadn't meant to pass out, but the comfort of being surrounded by his scent and his sheets had been too much. Crawling onto his bed, she'd laid down and drifted into blissful sleep, only to stir at sunrise without his presence. The way he devoured her mouth now, she knew her worries were ungrounded. He wanted with the same ferocity she did, and, oh sweet summer sun, *now* nothing would stop them.

Breathless, Melody raised her head and whispered against his damp mouth, "Thank you."

"For what?" he asked, easing her down the front of his body as she unwound herself.

She forced away disappointment, knowing they'd given everyone enough of a show. "You rescued me."

He snorted and shook his head. His fingers threaded through hers. "No, I didn't."

Melody waited until they cleared the building before arguing. "Yes, you did. I married who I wanted, not who my parents expected."

"Yeah, because *you* decided, Melody. Not because of anything I did."

"You asked," she said, exasperated.

"And you answered," he replied in kind. "You could have said no, and remained exactly where you were. But you didn't." He stopped on the sidewalk and looked down at her. In the brilliant light of day, his jewel-toned eyes were devasting in their vibrance. "For the first time in your life, you've made the decision you wanted." He leaned down and brushed a fluttering kiss across her mouth. "I'm proud of you."

Joy swelled her heart. "I did, didn't I?"

He squeezed her hand and smiled. "Do you need to go into South Row today?"

"No, my MT didn't have anything new for me when I checked yesterday." Melody tried not to dwell on that too much. Her team leader, Master Tribunii Marck Rainier, wanted answers just like she did where the Castien case was concerned. Answers that wouldn't happen if she were stuck at Division. At least, that's what she kept telling herself.

"Good, you can help me sort through this mess," he said, holding up the thick folder. "I didn't think my inquiries would have such large results. We'll be cross-referencing for a couple hours, at least."

Melody could think of something she'd much rather be doing alone in his apartment. But they needed to find Lucianna and we're finally getting enough information to start actively making progress. Lust-driven ambitions would have to wait. They walked to the small parking lot a block away, filled mostly with government-issued Ariot's for the several official buildings in the area.

Inside the vehicle, Vayden handed her the folder. "Do you know the layout of the city enough to sort these by location?"

Melody blew out a breath. "I know South Row well enough."

He backed out of a parking space and shifted gears. "Okay, that's a start. See what you can find."

"While we're driving?"

"Why not? It's a thirty-minute drive when no one is on the road."

Outside the vehicle, horses, carts, bikes, and the occasional Ariot vied for positions on the road, trying to outmaneuver or otherwise go around anything slower than them, which more often than not led to no one going anywhere. People shouted. Horses neighed. Bike and Ariot horns blared.

Melody sighed. "Right."

Vayden demonstrated patience unlike any she'd ever witnessed navigating the congested city streets back to the apartment. Melody's mind kept drifting back to the comfortable morning spent eating with his parents and the moment they'd left to sign the contract. Alone. His parents had to get back to their jobs, and Vayden needed the documents and wanted to get a jump on the lines at the records department.

"Is it normal," she found herself asking while staring out the window, "to sign a marriage contract without family?"

"Yeah, it's pretty standard," he said, zipping into a left turn during a rare break in traffic. "That's what the promise ceremony is for. Family."

She brushed her fingers along the smooth top of the folder. "And you've never done one of those?"

"Nope, I have not." He glanced over at her. A small smile played on his lips. "Never met anyone I wanted to do one with."

And how exactly was she supposed to respond to that? She flushed. Pleasure and nervousness quivered in her stomach. "But you still contracted. Three times."

"Yes, true. However, you have to understand at the

time, neither of us were ready for what promises actually meant. We were being safe. Enjoying life together, for as long as that meant for our relationship," he explained.

"You never wanted more with any of them?" Melody asked.

He shrugged, turning into his building's small parking lot. "Maybe, but in the end, it didn't matter, neither of us tried hard enough to make anything go beyond the time we'd agreed to commit. When the contracts ended, so did anything we'd managed to build."

A shiver raced up her spine. "That's so… sad."

Vayden took the folder from her limp hands. "Yes, I agree. But marriage is hard, and it won't work without two people, no matter how long the agreement is for."

Warm moist air washed over as the door swung open leading into the complex. Birds trilled, and bark crunched under the tenant's shoes. A faint rustle shook the branches in the tree branches above. Melody drew comfort from the lush surroundings and resisted the ever-beckoning urge to disappear into the depths of greenery.

"You think we'll be different?" she asked.

He shrugged again. "I guess I hope we will be."

A sense of unease curled in her chest. She stopped at the door to the stairs, moving out the way when someone exited. "What if we're not? Different?"

Vayden sighed and held the door open. He motioned for her to go up first. "That's the point of taking advantage of the one-year contract, Melody. For us to decide if we're willing to put forth the effort and dedicate more. We have twelve months to learn if we can live together."

Unless she had his baby. Then Sziverian law declared them contracted for an automatic eighteen years. Each new birth renewed the family clause. Melody clenched her jaw to keep the words from spilling out. Somehow, she didn't think they'd help anything. The box her mother had given her was buried in her bag, which she'd figured she'd be unpacking soon, in the room she'd be sharing with him. Biting her bottom lip, Melody suddenly wasn't sure if she wanted to use the method of birth control. An excited rush accompanied the thought of carrying Vayden's child. Of starting a family with him. Which, she admitted, was crazy, considering up until a week ago, she'd considered him genetically unfit. Time, and knowledge, made quick work of her misconceptions.

Now the dream of a precious little girl with gold in sapphire eyes and bouncing chestnut curls had Melody's steps dragging. On his floor, she slowed until he passed. Her stomach flipped, and anticipation tingled along her nerves. His keys jingled as he slid them into the lock. Melody bounced on the pads of her feet, resisting the urge to shove him through the door to get them into privacy faster. Sending important documentation flying in her desire to have him horizontal would not endear him to her, so she waited. Patiently.

She used her foot to close the front door and followed him into his office. The second the file touched the surface of his desk, she grabbed the front of his jacket. She didn't think beyond the need to feel his mouth on hers. Beyond the taste or texture of his tongue sliding along hers as she devoured his mouth.

He groaned and grasped her hips, lifting her onto the surface of his desk. Melody didn't object. She parted her legs to make room for him, her hands desperately trying to find any expanse of his skin beneath the layers of clothing between them. Finally. *Finally.* She wanted to weep with the pleasure of knowing nothing stood between them now. They were each other's for the next year. No doubts. No fears.

His mouth slanted over hers. Devouring. Claiming. The teasing tips of his fingers slid under the edge of her shirt, brushing up her spine, leaving a trail of lightning. He hooked his hands over her shoulders and pulled her even closer. Her breasts crushed into his chest, and the hard proof of his arousal sent shock waves of pleasure through her center. Breathless and aching with need, she shifted closer. The action sent another pulsing shock straight to her toes.

"Uncle Vay-da! Uncle Vay-da! You home? Uncle Vay-da!" a sweet, young voice cried down the hall, followed by pounding little feet.

Melody gasped and tore her mouth from his. Vayden pressed his lips together, sighed through his nose, and dropped his forehead to hers. A nearly silent curse escaped from him before he straightened and made quick work of adjusting his clothes and hers.

Blinking, Melody could only stare. "How many people have a key to your apartment?"

"Our apartment now," he answered, helping her down. "And if they share my last name, they have one."

A cherub with dancing green flecked blue eyes flounced into the room. An impossibly bright pink dress swirled around her legs. Lighter pink ribbons fluttered from her shoulders to her hips. She looked like a princess. Until Melody took a closer look and noticed all the dark stains, little holes, and running threads.

Clearly, the dress was well-worn and well-loved. The little girl held her arms up, her little hands opening and closing in an obvious message between her and the big man she called Uncle.

Vayden scooped her up into his arms and tilted her upside down. She squealed, her small legs kicking at his chest. "I found you!" she squawked and giggled.

"You sure did, mite." He flipped her back around and smacked a loud kiss to her cheek. "Where's your momma and sissy?"

His niece pushed tangled blonde hair from her face. "In the living room."

Vayden situated her on his hip and turned them both to face Melody. "Amee, this is Melody."

The little girl hid her face in the crook of Vayden's neck until only one eye peeked out. Melody gave her most I'm-nice-I-promise smile. "Hi, Amee. How old are you?"

Amee flexed her fingers, touching her thumb to each one before holding her entire hand out. "I this old."

Vayden folded two fingers down. "This old."

"Twee!" Amee proclaimed. Forgetting to be shy, she straightened so fast, Vayden had to wrap his other arm around to brace her back. "But I almost four! My birf-day is almost here, isn't it Uncle Vay-da?"

"Yep, couple more weeks, and we say goodbye to three," he answered. He smooched and made silly snorting noises at her cheek. She squealed and wiggled in his arms. "Growing too fast, that's what almost here."

Melody's heart swelled at the easy exchange. Just like with Lyrica, he had no fear of children. Only adoration. With Amee still on his hip, he left the office, motioning with his head for her to follow. Melody wasn't sure if she was up to meeting more relatives. But, for the next year, maybe more, they were her family now, too.

"…not to touching anything, did I not?" a woman's frustrated voice filtered down the hall. "Krystie, these are not yours to touch. I can't believe you did this. What am I supposed to say to your uncle?"

"Look, Momma, I found Uncle Vay-da!" Amee proclaimed and shimmied to be put down.

Very pregnant, a woman turned from the table, her golden eyes wide. Short blonde hair framed her face. She touched a fluttering hand to her round stomach, smoothing down the flower print fabric. "Oh gosh, Vayden," she said in resignation, her shoulders hunched.

"What's wrong?"

The woman swept her arm backwards over the table, her hand still resting on her belly. "Krystie…"

Vayden stepped forward, frowning. Melody followed and gasped when chaotic lines of color came into view. Not a single sheet of paper, or exposed length of the map, had been spared from the artistic renderings of the child now hiding under the table.

"Krystie," the woman snapped. "Get out from under that table and apologize to your uncle. Now."

A tiny whimper and scrape of chair legs was the only reply.

"It's fine, Bree," Vayden sighed. "Melody and I will figure it out. She used highlighters; I can still see everything that's important."

"It's not fine," Bree argued. "She knew better."

"Yes, I know, but we can't undo anything, can we?"

Bree braced her weight against the table and rubbed both her hands over her stomach. "No. You sound like Daniel." A huff of annoyance puffed from her cheeks. "It's why she behaves this way, you know."

Vayden rolled his eyes and slid a chair out of the way. "She behaves this way because she's seven." His hand disappeared under the table. "Come on out, mouse."

Bree seemed to register Melody's presence. Her gaze shifted over Melody's no-nonsense work attire. Bree's cheeks flushed brightly. "Oh my goodness, I'm so sorry, I didn't realize you had work tonight."

"We're looking for Cia," Vayden said, reaching further under the table. "Melody is helping me find her. But we contracted today, so she's not going anywhere."

Bree glanced between the two of them. Melody tried not to be affected by the casual way he'd declared the status of their relationship.

"Wow, I had no idea you were even seeing someone." Bree's smile seemed more like a grimace when she faced Melody again. "I'm Bree, his sister, and these two troublemakers are mine."

"Lovely to meet you. And everything happened really suddenly," Melody said by way of excuse.

"Ah, yes, well." Bree rubbed her hands over her belly and grinned. "That does seem to happen to us. Daniel and I contracted pretty fast, too. Though not quite as fast as our sister, Eli, this last time."

Vayden snorted. "Yeah, Eli's marriage was a bit of a shocker. But they're still together."

"They are," Bree conceded. "Our family is never boring."

Melody smiled. "I can't say mine is, either."

Bree turned to Vayden, her smile fading. "I'm sorry, brother. I wish I'd have known you contracted today. I'd have tried to reschedule my shift."

Vayden waved away her apology. "You're about to have six weeks leave, I know you and Daniel are working hard to save to buy your apartment. I'll make sure they get to Terravine tomorrow for the Wintervail iris party like we'd already planned."

Bree leaned closed and pecked a kiss to his cheek. "You're the best."

"I know. You remember that when I have kids needing to be watched."

Melody couldn't stop the flush when Bree's gaze landed on her. "I will."

14

Vayden loved his nieces. He did. But, as he laid in bed next to his wife, whose body he had yet to explore, his uncle status left him with little appreciation. Last night had been a test in patience, forcing him to keep his hands entirely to himself. Amee had needed a drink no less than three times. Mr. Ice, Krystie's stuffed Icekutian horse, had disappeared, which resulted in a meltdown. Then the obligatory every-five-minute potty breaks. By the time silence had descended in the apartment, Melody was passed out, and Vayden had a headache.

Now, however... he looked her beautiful resting form over. Chestnut curls spread like a halo around Melody's head on the light gray bed sheets. The large t-shirt he'd given her to sleep in had ridden up to her ribcage, exposing the sexy curve of her stomach and hips. He'd pulled the covers down enough to get a look at her in the faint light from the woodstove.

Precious little time remained until the girls descended like a band of marauders. Despite their room not having any windows, they seemed to have an internal clock that told them the second the sun broke the horizon. Vayden eased his hand across Melody's abdomen, determined to take advantage of the quiet morning. He couldn't do much, he didn't want to have to silence her, but if he didn't taste or touch her, he'd go insane.

Easing down, he ran his tongue along the curve of her hip. She sighed, her body turning enough to make his access easier. He slid his hand up her stomach, touching over the rise of her ribcage under the shirt until the globe of her breast settled beneath his fingers. Her nipple beaded against his palm, and he ran his thumb across the sensitive tip. A soft shudder filled the air, and she squirmed. Small and firm, her entire breast filled his hand. Vayden shaped and kneaded the mound, exploring with delicate touches what made her respond.

His name left her lips on a sigh, filled with longing and, if he weren't mistaken, a touch of wonder. Vayden smiled and shifted over her thigh to settle between her legs. Sweet summer sun, he *needed* this woman. But they'd have to wait a bit longer. He didn't dare risk their first time being interrupted. Nor did he want to have to swallow the cries he intended to ensure she made. However, as he eased her panties down, sliding one leg free to expose the heart of her to him, he wasn't willing to allow her to go completely unexplored.

The delicate tremble of her limbs betrayed her nerves as he glided his hands up the length of both her silky legs, easing them open. He wished for more light than the weak glow of the pellet stove, wanting to know how she'd look, but figured the darkness eased some of her tension. If he did things right, she'd be too distracted to remember to be shy. Vayden smiled.

"Can you be quiet?" he whispered against her belly, flicking his tongue to the sensitive flesh below her belly button.

Her fingers slid into his hair, and her hips rose in an unconscious effort to get closer to him. "I don't know."

Vayden skated kisses from one smooth hip to the next. "I want you loud," he admitted. "I need you loud. However…"

The muscles of her stomach quivered. "We aren't alone in the apartment."

"Nope." He tasted the salty richness of her inner thigh. "So?"

"Maybe we should wa—"

He didn't give her the chance to finish the thought, touching his tongue to the sensitive nub between her legs. She gasped, her fingers clenching in his hair. Her response was instant. Uninhibited. She set fire to every inch of his body.

"I will," she swallowed and released an uneven breath, "try."

Vayden growled his approval. He spread her legs wider and then used his fingers to explore and tease until she squirmed and whimpered. When she was slick with need, he went in for a complete taste. With teeth and tongue, he brought her to the brink, easing her over with a well-timed stroke of his fingers deep inside her. She shattered with a muffled cry, her back arched, her heels dug into the mattress, pressing her further into his questing mouth.

The need to drive into her wet heat pulled tight on Vayden's control. He warred with himself, rationalizing at this point it wouldn't take long. He could very well be sated and content before any chance of interruption. Which perhaps wasn't the route he really wanted. He figured taking a respite and making things better for both of them when they had all the time to fully *be* had him biting her inner thigh and rising.

As he'd hoped, any lingering embarrassment over being laid out on display in front of him had melted away with her first orgasm. Vayden couldn't help but touch her again. The tips of his fingers slid over her welcoming flesh, and he was rewarded with a sweet moan. "You are so perfect," he said.

Groaning, her hands covered her face. "I can't think right now."

Pure male satisfaction swelled in his chest and made him smile. He leaned over her, pressed a kiss to her neck, and then rolled away before temptation had a chance to claim him. Searching under the sheets, he found her panties and dropped them onto her belly before pulling the blankets back up. He settled onto his side and propped his arm under his pillow.

"The girls will stay with my parents tonight. The Wintervail party lasts well into the morning, and they have a special area set up for kids," he said, brushing his fingers along the neckline of her shirt.

"How often do you watch them again?" she asked as she shimmied back into her clothing under the blankets.

"At least once a week, usually twice, though, if I can. If I can't, Madeleine or Delanee will come sit with them until I get home." He caressed up her throat to her jaw. "Bree works as a filing clerk after hours at Immigration and Import when they need the help. Her husband is a bookkeeper for a prominent lawyer's office and isn't always able to make it home in time for her to start her shift. It's easier all around for me to keep them."

"You're sure your parents won't mind Lyrica coming tonight?" Gasping, she sat up so suddenly that his hand smacked her nose. "Ow."

Vayden rose and grasped her chin. "Are you okay?"

She sniffled and wiggled her nose. "Yes… I think so. Sorry."

"What's wrong?" he asked.

"I just realized I have nothing to wear." She pressed her hands onto the bedspread. "I mean *nothing*. I've never been to a Wintervail party."

"Really? That surprises me."

"Why?"

He sat back against the headboard. "I guess I figured your parents were making efforts to get you in front of ranked guardians, therefore had you making the rounds in higher society."

Shaking her head, she plucked at the blankets pooled in her lap. "No. My parents work pretty much specifically with people like them, hoping to make an entrance and an impression on a ranked family. They have connections, but not among those they wished to persuade. It's sad, really."

Vayden took a deep breath. He'd grown up among the world she'd only ever imagined. "My mother is Shield Guardian Terravine."

"I know," she said. "I met her, remember?"

"The party is more a gathering my mother throws for all her colleagues and friends of the family," he said slowly.

"Okay," she said, puzzled. "I mean, I know I need to

look nice, that's why I'm trying not to freak out here. I have nothing. I wear a uniform to work."

Vayden waited. The real reaction he'd been waiting for moved over her like a storm rolling in on the horizon. She stiffened, then trembled. Her breathing went from slow to erratic.

"No," she whispered. "Oh no, no, no."

"My mother already said she'd handle it."

"Of course, she did," Melody breathed.

She jumped up, arms flapping, her balance wobbly on the soft mattress. She pointed at her chest. "Because what in the artic would I know about being suitable enough to be seen by an *arch guardian*? Let alone be presented in front of them all *as your wife*."

He crossed his arms over his chest.

"Vayden!" she shrieked.

"What?" he asked, looking over her bare legs and wondering if he snagged them just right if he could send her tumbling onto his lap.

"I can't go to this party. I'll do the promise ceremony like your mother asked, but that's it. I want to come home after."

"Nope. I have friends I only get the time to see at this event, and I want them to meet you."

She dropped to her knees and crawled to him. Now, wasn't *that* a pretty sight? Her riot of curls twisted and sprang in every direction around her head from sleep and their earlier passion. He figured an enticing flush pinkened her cheeks. Groaning, he dropped his head back against the headboard. At this rate, he'd never lose the erection he'd been trying to talk himself down from. Literally.

"Your mother is not responsible for me, and I don't

want to make some ridiculous social mistake because the only experience I have is in a classroom at a finishing school. Which, I'm going to assume, is wholly lacking in reality," she argued.

"Melody," he said with patience. "I don't care what anyone else thinks. They didn't marry you, I did. And while Delanee may have fun recapping the evening, which may include a line or two about you, in the end, it won't matter. I don't carry a ranking, and neither do you. The people whom I care about will love you because..."

I do.

He swallowed the words and blinked. Whoa. Okay, time to slow down. He figured dropping that truth would result in a meltdown of epic proportions. Not to mention, he needed to figure out what that meant for him, too. Love wasn't an emotion familiar to him outside of his family. Sure, he'd cared deeply for all the women in his life, but love? He took a deep breath.

"Because you're part of our family. You're already accepted by anyone who matters." He brushed a tangle of curls behind her ear. "All right? Let my mother take care of you."

"And Lyrica?"

Vayden smiled. "She's going to be so beautiful. You both are. I can't wait to see."

She grumbled and shook her head. "I don't kn—"

The bedroom door flew open, and little feet slapped against the hardwood. "Uncle Vay-da! Uncle Vay-da! The sun is up!"

"Amee!" Krystie screeched after her little sister. "I told you to knock!"

"Sowry," Amee said, her hands fisting in the blankets, pulling them down as she tried to use them as leverage to climb. "I sowry, Uncle Vay-da."

Vayden chuckled and grasped her forearms, heaving her onto the bed. "Knocking is nice, mite. I'll forgive you this morning."

She patted his arm and settled onto the mattress next to his thigh. "I'm hungry."

"Is that so?"

"Yes. For sweet toast, and eggs, and fwoot."

"You are hungry," Vayden agreed.

Amee nodded. "And juice, too."

Vayden scrunched up his face. "I don't know, that's an awful lot of sugar."

The mattress jostled as Krystie clambered up at the end and sat near Vayden's feet. The faint light filtering in from the living room windows made her nervous fidgeting visible. Melody scooted over and patted the space between them.

"You can come up here, Krystie," Melody said gently. "I don't bite, I promise."

Krystie sighed and made a slow crawl across the bed as though she contemplated fleeing instead of stay-ing. Melody smiled, and Vayden found himself echoing the reassuring gesture. They spent the next few moments negotiating breakfast. Melody suggested tomatoes and peppers in the eggs instead of a side of fruit. Krystie asked if milk would be better than juice so they could keep their sweet toast.

And as the girls left the room in a flurry of endless energy and happy sounds, Vayden's chest constricted. A man could get used to mornings like this.

•   •   •

MELODY STARED AT HER PARENT'S HOUSE AND TRIED TO tamp down the rising threat of a full-on panic attack. She barely noticed the cold, or the snowflakes drifting through the air. The horse and carriage that had brought her from the apartment clopped and rattled away. Vayden had tried to talk her into letting them all come along, arguing her parents would be less inclined to be ugly if the girls were present. Melody didn't have the heart to tell him the children would still experience her mother's contempt for gen-commons. Unlike Vayden, whose eyes, while two colors, were separate bands, Krystie and Amee's were mixed. There wasn't a doubt they were gen-common, not some possible hybrid-theory. She wouldn't allow her mother's venom to poison their minds. They were perfect as they were.

A truth Melody had accepted this morning, hoping Vayden would claim her. He'd driven her half out of her mind with pleasure, and she'd been desperate to feel his body move inside hers. To bring their marriage to full completion. If their children turned out gen-common, she'd love them with all the depths of her heart.

A sliver of anger for the prejudice her parents had heaped on both her and Lyrica consumed her anxiety. Shame followed. How could she have ever allowed them to let her feel so superior because she was a Gen-Heir? So, she had some inherited level of talent. To date, she didn't see a whole lot of evidence she was any better at anything than anyone else. Certainly not enough to consider herself above a portion of the Sziverian population.

Watching Vayden and the girls interact had been an eye-opening experience. Melody wanted the easy love for Lyrica. Her sister deserved to help make a mess in the kitchen for a meal. To feel comfortable enough to throw a fit and not wonder what the outburst would cost her. To know she was special. Unique. Cherished. All the things Vayden, by simply loving his nieces, offered. And Melody knew, without question, he'd regard her little sister the same. The problem, she had to acknowledge, came in the *how*. How in the inhabited world was she supposed to get her sister away from her parents?

Melody took a long, slow breath and shored up her nerves. The frigid wind bit at her fingertips and numbed her nose and cheeks. In a week or so, the temperatures would barely rise above freezing. A couple more weeks and travel, aside from walking and those who had the stout Icekutian horses bred for extreme low temperatures, would be near impossible. For a month or two, during the height of winter, the country practically shut down.

This year, however, the frigid season didn't have such a dim prospect. Being stuck in Vayden's warm apartment, finding pleasurable ways to pass the time, brought a curious level of excitement. The sampling of what life in his bed offered made a shiver race through her that had nothing to do with the chilly day. She knew he had more to show her and more for her to discover about him.

Forcing sensual thoughts from her mind, Melody climbed the steps to her parent's front door. Funny how only a couple days had created a separation. No longer did the home belong to her. She tested the knob and found the door unlocked. Heated air rushed out as she stepped inside. Lyrica looked up from her perch on the stairs. A bag sat near her feet on the floor. Melody closed the door, frowning.

"What's going on?" Melody asked. "Is everything okay?"

"Mother told me to pack a bag and wait for you," Lyrica said, not meeting Melody's gaze.

"Wh—"

"Ah, there you are." Willow breezed from the library into the foyer, a gray silk shawl trailing out behind her. "I received your note last night, and read about your official contract signing in *Haven City Chronicle* this morning. You should have told me of your plans, Melody."

Confused, Melody glanced between her mother and sister. "Plan? What plans?"

Willow tsked and waved a hand. "Oh, please. I raised you better than to play coy. Do you have everything you need to make a good first impression on Shield Guardian Terravine? I heard none of her children are her Gen-Heir, and so far, none of them have married qualified candidates either." Willow chuckled, the action cold and calculating coming from her. "Well, until now, that is."

Melody frowned. "Until now, what?"

"For the love of summer, Melody," her mother huffed. "You could have just told me the gen-common you contracted with was the son of Amari and Grayson Dossett. One of the most scandalous unions of that decade. I was just a teenager, but even I knew that one did not marry a gen-common when they've been approved for a ranking as high as shield guardian. And she's paid the price, too. The ranking will fall back to the Endowment and Revocation

Council to reassign when she retires. A new family would occupy her position instead of someone in her line, which wouldn't have been the case if she'd married correctly.

"And," Willow continued, "you now have the opportunity to take her rank if you make the proper impression. I'm so proud of you. I knew you had ambition, but I'd underestimated how far you'd go."

"Y-you think I contracted with Vayden because of who his mother is?" Melody asked in disbelief.

Willow's face stretched in a tight smile. She patted Melody's cheek with cold fingers. "I don't think daughter, I know. You did the right thing. I'm sorry I doubted you."

"Mother," Melody began, trying to figure out Willow's thought process. "If I had any ambition for Shield Guardian Terravine's rank, I'd have to agree to longer than a year contract. And I'd have to take the Dossett name. Vayden and I only agreed to a year, and I'm not changing anything."

Her mother's hand snapped out and snatched Melody's arm in a painful grip. "You will not get another chance like this. You *will* do what you need to do to impress the shield guardian. To prove to her you are capable, and skilled enough in your logic-based talent to take over the rank when the time comes. If that means contracting for a greater length of time or forgetting about the ovulation bracelet I gave you and allowing that man to get you pregnant, you will do so. Lyrica has been told to be on her best behavior tonight. You *will* do your duty by this family."

Melody grimaced. Willow's nails bit into the tender flesh of her underarm even through the jacket Melody wore. "I am not qualified to fill a shield guardian rank, no matter how much Amari may like me, mother."

Willow yanked on Melody's arm, drawing her to within an inch of her twisted face. "If you fail," she said, her voice pitched low, "you will find yourself homeless and without a family, do I make myself clear? Your father and I sacrificed more than you can ever understand to get you into Honor Grace Academia. If you can't convince the Dossetts to keep you around, then we have no need for you, either."

Willow released Melody so suddenly she found herself stumbling backward. Horrified, she rubbed her arm and fought the burn of tears. From a slap for marrying the man to being disowned if she didn't manage to make the relationship work, Melody's head spun from the sheer absurdity of it all. She couldn't get out of the house fast enough.

"I checked your account this morning," Willow said, adjusting the shawl over her shoulders as if she hadn't ripped her daughter's world in half. "Because we never asked for anything, you have a nice little savings. Use the money to get you and your sister a suitable Wintervail gown for the blooming party." She waved the tail end of the scarf up and down in a flutter of motion. "You can't show up looking like that."

Melody remained silent, her jaw clenched. She wiggled her fingers for Lyrica to rise.

"I want to read nothing but the best in the paper in the morning. And I expect your sister to be returned by dinner tomorrow," Willow said.

Melody managed a curt nod. Lyrica sidled up next to her but continued to remain silent as well.

"Good, I'm glad this unpleasant conversation is

over. I had hoped for more excitement, considering this entire situation is your doing. I never imagined you'd be able to marry into a shield guardian's family. Then again, I never considered offering you to a gen-common son. Brilliant Melody, simply brilliant." Willow smiled at her two daughters. "You remember this, Lyrica, when your time comes, to be open to all possibilities, not just the most obvious ones."

Melody couldn't leave the house fast enough. She ushered Lyrica out the front door and down the sidewalk. She'd anticipated the visit taking longer and hadn't thought to ask the driver to stay. She shoved her hands deep into her jacket pockets and started heading along the sidewalk toward a more populated street. Lyrica remained abnormally silent. The bag bumped against her knees, clutched in both hands.

Reaching over, Melody took the bag in one hand and her sister's hand in the other. She made sure Lyrica was looking at her. "What's wrong?"

Lyrica shook her head and looked away. The tremble of her bottom lip betrayed the distress she couldn't hide. Melody glanced behind to see how far from the house they were. Not far enough. She didn't want to see the pale blue two-story house ever again. They walked a few more blocks before Melody couldn't stand the silence any longer. She stopped at a corner, splitting her attention between her remote sister and finding a hired carriage.

She turned Lyrica to face her. "Talk to me, what's going on."

Lyrica looked away, her chin working, nostrils flaring. "I don't want to talk about it. Can we just get to wherever it is you're taking me?"

Melody grasped Lyrica's chin and turned her gaze back. "Well, I do want to talk about it. Now, come on, tell me."

"I thought…" Lyrica blew out a heavy breath and pulled her hand free with a hard yank. "I just thought you were different. From them."

"From mother and father?" Melody asked.

Lyrica nodded.

"I am," she assured. Crouching down, her heart lodged in her throat. Melody grasped her little sister's small shoulders and squeezed. "Lyrica, I am not them. You know that."

Tears glistened in Lyrica's pale green eyes. "Is Vayden's mother really a shield guardian?"

"Yes, she is."

"And you knew that about him when you said you'd marry him?"

Dread settled heavily in Melody's stomach. "I've always known."

"And she could declare you her Gen-Heir if you take their name like mother said?" Lyrica asked, her words hard with a bitterness Melody never thought to associate with her sister.

"It doesn't work like that," Melody tried to explain.

"Then she couldn't?"

Melody looked away, trying to figure out how to communicate something as complicated as rank endowment through marriage to a twelve-year-old and not clearly implicate herself as a usurper like Willow had obviously painted her to Lyrica. "She could recommend me *if* I were interested, which I'm not. I'd still have to be approved by the E&R Council, though."

"Are you going to take his name?" Lyrica

demanded, her cheeks flushing pink. "Will you do like mother said and have a baby with him so he has to stay with you? She said she has never been prouder of you, that you did exactly what they've always wanted."

Lyrica sniffled. "But you say you're not like them." She shook her head and turned her eyes away from Melody. "I don't believe you."

Melody rose and scrubbed her hands over her face. Damn Willow! How was Melody supposed to defend against such poison? Glancing down at Lyrica, Melody knew she had to find a way. She had to think of something or lose her sister's trust. Something she wasn't willing to sacrifice.

15

VAYDEN STARED AT THE PAPERS LAID OUT BEFORE HIM AND continued to ignore the banshee screaming coming from the front of the apartment. The unsuccessful attempts to quiet the girls had failed the last four times, he didn't figure try five would yield better results. So he pretended the sound didn't jar his concentration. That the lovely music of a three and seven-year-old fighting were something every sane adult wanting excitement in their life needed to experience.

An awareness niggled in his mind that had nothing to do with making sure the girls didn't murder each other before they left for Terravine Manor. Slowly, he spread the papers out that had grabbed his attention in relation to the map covering his entire dining room table. He pulled his notebook closer and checked his musings, and made new ones. Like puzzle pieces clicking into place, an image began to form. One, he didn't like the look of one bit.

"Girls!" he called. When the sound didn't lessen, he

gathered the papers together and tried again. A new urgency rode him. "Girls!"

"Yes, Uncle Vayden?" Krystie replied, appearing prim and proper in the hall. With her hand behind her back. Amee's wails of distress echoed from the bedroom.

Vayden sighed and closed the distance, holding his hand out. She bit her bottom lip and then reluctantly placed a small, wooden pony on his palm. "I need you to get your jacket on and help Amee into hers, please."

Her gaze remained locked on the polished, amber colored wood. Vayden crammed the little toy into his jacket. "Now, Krystie."

The girls emerged moments later. Amee still struggled to put her jacket on, a trail of drying tears streaking her cheeks and snot clumping under her nose. Vayden searched his pockets until he found the hanky he always kept when watching them. He wiped her little face clean and then picked her up. "Time to see Nonni."

Both the girls exclaimed their excitement. Bundled up for the cold outside, Vayden carried the documents he needed, Amee on one hip and Krystie holding his jacket tail as they left the apartment. At the Ariot, he situated Amee in the small back space, and Kyrstie held the folder for him in the passenger seat. He'd have to return his vehicle to the apartment before going back to his parents for the Wintervail party since the small ride wouldn't hold more than two and a very small person. If Lyrica returned with them for the night, they'd have to take a hired carriage. Best to plan for the eventuality.

The girls behaved on the drive, singing sweet seasonal songs about snowflakes, bright colors, and the pretty Wintervail iris. The fight over the pony in his pocket forgotten. His mother ran out of the manor when they pulled into the wide circular drive, her hands flailing with excitement in the air. The massive house loomed three stories above her in an elegant statement of red brick and carved pillars.

"Oh, my baby girls are here!" Amari exclaimed as Vayden exited the Ariot, a wide grin brightening her face.

"Nonni!" both the girls cried, jumping from the vehicle before Vayden could walk around to help. They ran to their grandmother, leaping into her waiting arms. She showered loud kisses on them, acting as if it'd been months instead of only days since she'd last seen them.

Amari rose from a crouched position and looked Vayden over. "Where are your clothes for tonight? Are they in the Ariot?"

Vayden shook his head. "No, I need to go to IIRA and see Bree really quick. I promise I'll be back in time."

"I see," Amari said, frowning. Her fingers smoothed through Krystie's dark blonde hair. "Well, in that case, will you see which gowns you think Melody would prefer before you leave? I don't want to overwhelm her with the entire rack my Stylist Elite procured for her and her little sister. Lyra, is it?"

"Lyrica," Vayden corrected, then signed, "and she'll be excited if you speak to her."

Amari's features softened, and she shook her head, chuckling. "Vayden... what were the chances of her encountering a family capable of fully embracing her?"

"I know," he agreed, running his fingers through his hair. "And I was very thankful when I realized that Henry had taught us all how to speak in signs."

A girl on each hand, Amari took the six wide steps

up to the manor. Ivy draped from massive stone urns on the covered terrace. The greenhouse branched off to the left, glittering in the noon sun, as tall as the home itself and spanning nearly an acre. Vayden couldn't wait for Melody to explore what his mother cared for. From food, medicinal, and decorative, the glass structure housed a wide variety of plant life. The girls took off running once they entered, knowing every inch of the eleven-thousand square foot structure.

The grand foyer made a sideways L shape, with the stairs sweeping in a curve to the upper floors on the left, and two entrances into a wide hall along the longest side. In the alcove of the foyer, two racks bursting with colorful fabric were positioned to make the best use of the sun streaming in through a wide set of windows. Vayden nodded to his mother's Stylist Elite, waiting patiently in the corner. She wouldn't be able to prepare her thoughts on what to do with Melody or Lyrica until she knew what gown they'd wear.

Vayden perused the selection, narrowing it down to five dresses, then two. A teal V neck with intricate beading on the bodice and hemline, and a burnt orange cold shoulder with sheer long sleeves and embroidered flowers in a rich gold. His mother approved and then showed her favorites from the girl's gowns. Vayden agreed a regal purple, long sleeved, high collar with delicate silk flowers running the length of skirt would be perfect for Lyrica. Amari handed the gowns to her Stylist and sent the woman on her way.

Once they were alone, she looked at Vayden. "How bad?"

Vayden didn't pretend not to know what she asked.

He braced a hand on the clothing rack. "Very. Neither of them knows what family love means, or I'm guessing how to accept it. Melody was genuinely confused about why you cared for her the other night."

Amari shook her head, sadness tightening her mouth. "Well, I guess it's a good thing I had your father to teach me. At least I understand what they're going through."

Vayden looked out the window, squinting in the bright light. "She's not a logic-talent like she believes."

"What?" Amari asked in shock. "What do you mean? How is that possible? She tested, right?"

"Yes, and I'm not sure. But she's definitely a botanical talent." Vayden tapped the bar. "I keep hoping she'll realize each time a leaf wraps around her finger and seeks her out, but nope. She's remaining stubborn."

"She's believed one thing for so long, how could she accept something so radically different?" his mother questioned softly. "Though, how her parents managed to keep it from her, I can't begin to understand."

"Their greenhouse is barren, and not one plant lives in their home," he said, meeting his mother's stunned stare.

Amari touched a hand to her chest, fiddling with a simple necklace around her throat. "Well, that's rather extreme. They must have known."

"Or at least suspected. I agree."

"All right," Amari began, holding her hands up, "we will worry about one thing at a time. Let's make sure she survives her first foray into ranked society. The rest, well, I'm sure you have some plans."

Vayden smiled.

• • •

Bright globes of glass glowed above, hung in uneven lengths from the vaulted ballroom ceiling. A full orchestra played to the sultry rhythm of a woman's voice projecting across the room, somehow heard even over the din of constant conversation. Couples swayed to the romantic harmony in front of a stage bursting with floral arrangements. All the doors were open, leading outside to a stone pathway to the greenhouse, where the Wintervail Iris bloomed in its full glory. Candles guided the way, twinkling like stars on the ground. An icy breeze wafted in, barely felt by the crush of warm bodies filling the room.

Melody took a healthy swallow of wine, wondering if the tall plant she stood close to was doing a sufficient job hiding her. The leaves kept tickling the back of her neck and getting caught in the intricate knot Amari's Stylist Elite had arranged on top of her head. Along with dozens of tiny sparkling crystals all throughout her hair and along the bodice of the teal gown she wore, Melody felt like a beacon. To make everything worse, she'd realized two minutes into the event the tearoom lessons she'd been given had been useless. She was fairly certain not one teacher at Honor Grace Academia had ever actually appeared at a ranked society gathering.

Every person in attendance out-ranked and out-classed her. By several ladder rungs. Melody downed the rest of her wine. She wondered if she were slightly buzzed if the night would be easier to bear. How could she ever have aspired to this? Or think she'd ever be able to belong?

Lyrica was in the playroom with all the other under-sixteen attendees. When Vayden finally arrived, and the shield guardians could excuse themselves, they'd collect the girls for the promising ceremony. Nerves jumbled in her stomach, and she pressed a hand to the stiff front of the gown. The beadwork scraped and dug into her palm. She could manage a couple hours. She wasn't a complete social pariah.

An excited flutter flowed across the crowd in a wave from the ballroom entrance. Melody leaned from around the shelter of the plant in an attempt to see what the enthusiasm was about. The guests shifted enough to catch a glimpse. She caught a flash of champagne fabric, the satin brocade pattern shifting in the light. Broad shoulders, an air of confidence, and dark hair combed back from a face she couldn't see yet, the man appeared to be an anticipated guest. Then he turned, and she swore the room tilted.

Vayden.

A high collared black shirt, open to his collarbone, displaying the thick cords of his neck, stood out in stark contrast to the pale jacket. A single button joined the two lapels over a satin vest. Her gaze wandered lower, over champagne trousers cut to fit his lower body perfectly. High-gloss black shoes completed his formal ensemble, and she realized, looking him over again, no matter what she wore, he would have looked perfect standing next to her.

He did the strange handshake, wrist bump, to forearm grasping that he'd done with Tribunii Hadfield at South Row Division with two other men who'd walked up in greeting. Melody wondered if they'd all worked together at some point on a team. The small group chatted in an easy camaraderie, joined by others until they'd had to move to keep from blocking the nearest entrance. That she stood alone, partially hidden by a potted tree, was not lost on her.

Vayden separated, shaking hands and clapping several backs before fully walking away. He headed straight for her as if he'd known where she stood the entire time without even having looked her direction. Her belly flipped and her heart skipped a nervous beat. He looked so… different. Refined. Elegant. Outrageously handsome. At complete ease with the wealth and prestige swarming around him. She had a hard time reconciling the easy-going, almost carefree man she'd contracted with to the powerful, affluent man heading in her direction.

He stopped before her, his beautiful eyes twinkling. Taking hold of her trembling fingers, he brought them to his mouth, and pressed a kiss to her palm. "You look stunning." He brought her hand to his chest and pressed it over his heart.

Melody looked him over again, having the irrational urge to mess up his styled hair. If not for his eyes and familiar smile, she didn't think she'd have recognized him. "So do you."

Tugging gently, he pulled her into his arms. "Dance with me."

The request was a statement, leaving no room for argument. With his hand resting on the small of her back, Vayden guided her through the crowd, ignoring the attempts to gain his attention. A new song began, lush notes falling over one another like a waterfall, giving life to lyrics meant to bring to the imagination cool sheets and hot lovers. Uneasy, Melody allowed herself to be swept into the slow movement of the other couples. She'd figured some form of formal dancing knowledge would be required. But as Vayden drew her into his frame until they pressed close, doing nothing more than swaying to the unhurried cadence, she realized the dancing was simple, romantic.

Before long, the other couples disappeared until only Vayden's hands resting on her hips, his thighs moving along hers in sensual slides, remained. Her arms drifted up his biceps to his shoulders. The shift of his muscles under his jacket had her fingers curling into the soft fabric. He lowered his head until his forehead rested on hers. Each slow shift of their bodies brought them closer until a curl of desire unfurled in her stomach, replacing all the anxiety of the evening. The smoky voice of the singer, weaving a suggestive fantasy of sweaty nights followed by slow mornings, made Melody envision the scenario with Vayden. She tilted her face, her mouth a breath from his.

His lips brushed hers in a teasing motion. Melody sighed, her body softening until his hold kept her from sliding into a puddle as his mouth continued a gentle assault. Unable to stop from opening for more, she almost groaned when his tongue eased inside. Their hips and feet shifted in time to the sultry beat laid by pounding drums. His mouth moved over hers in unhurried exploration. A desperate pulse throbbed at her center. She wanted more. So much more. But he refused to be rushed or do more than lightly glide his tongue along hers, keeping the kiss almost sweet. Melody didn't want sweet. She wanted the demanding, claiming, soul-scorching kisses he normally took from her.

"Ah, to be newly contracted," a man chuckled near them.

Vayden pulled his mouth free, and Melody fought to keep from glaring at the intruder.

"Enjoy such passion while you can," the man said, sending his partner in a graceful arc away from him and back into his embrace. His gaze shifted beyond them, and he smiled. "Then again, perhaps lasting desire runs in the family."

Vayden turned them until his parents came into view. Lost in each other, Grayson plucked soft kisses across his wife's lips. Amari's arms wrapped around his shoulders, her fingers playing in the hair at his collar. A smile meant only for her lover teased her lips between each kiss. Her flame red gown stood out in contrast against his black as night suit. A thin, red tie, the same fabric as her gown, was the only color on the entire outfit. They looked stunning and authoritative. In love. There was no doubt the shield guardians continued to hold a hot-blooded marriage.

Looking around the ballroom, at the stiff body language, and forced distance between other couples, she didn't see much evidence that other unions held the same attraction. "Why are your parents different from everyone else?" Melody asked before she could halt the words.

"Love," Vayden answered, leading her off the dance floor. "A rare thing in ranked society."

"You're lucky," Melody said. A sense of longing had her watching the couple. The intimacy between them felt too private to witness, even in public, and she found herself looking away. "To have them."

"I know." Vayden brought her hand to his mouth and brushed a kiss on the back. "You have them now, too."

Melody took a deep breath, the worried flutters returning to her belly. The Dossett's were a close, generous group. Melody knew nothing of those things. Kindness and familial affection were as foreign to her as the crowd she found herself swallowed by. She wasn't disillusioned. Vayden's family brought much to their relationship, and Melody had to force tears away, admitting, if only to herself, she brought nothing but animosity and grief. When they realized how undeserving she was to be included among them, would they regret Vayden's decision to contract with her?

The tone of the music shifted from adult enjoyment to one of Wintervail merriment. An excited chatter arrived at the door as dozens of children flooded into the room in search of their parents. Attendants hovered nearby, corralling the smaller ones, and helping them find their family.

Amari appeared at Melody's side, a warm smile on her face. "This will keep everyone occupied while we slip away for a bit." Her arm slid around Melody's. "Are you ready, my dear? Your sister and the girls are already waiting for us in the library."

The flutters in Melody's stomach turned into outright flips. Vayden's hand tightened on hers as they turned and headed through the crowd toward the nearest exit into the grand hallway. She'd had two days to think of what she was going to promise, had even considered writing them down. But now, her mind went blank, and she wondered if any words she said would ever be enough.

• • •

Vayden closed the door behind his father, the last to enter the family gathering in the library. He'd be lying to himself if he denied his nerves weren't as twisted as Melody's appeared to be. The faint tremor in her fingers on their way to the ceremony betrayed what she'd so bravely attempted to hide behind squared shoulders and a calm expression. Hand still on the handle, Vayden allowed his gaze to move over her again.

In the teal gown, he'd chosen, with her hair swept off her neck, tiny crystals woven between the strands to twinkle in the amber glow of candlelight, she was a vision of beauty. A dusting of freckles across her shoulders revealed what he'd been dying to know, just where the teasing flecks were located beside her nose. Smoky eyeshadow defined her green eyes, and a dusting of blush accented her rounded cheeks. He wanted to be alone with her. To peel off the heavy layers of the gown and reveal his prize. They had a bit longer before they could disappear. With a resigned sigh, he stepped away from the door.

"I hope you know I'm doing this because I love you," he growled to his mother as he walked past.

Amari patted his back. "I know, kiddo."

Grayson settled everyone down. All the family had gathered. Only Bree and her husband Joshua had kids. The girls ran in circles around the pair, Amee's hand trailing along her mother's full skirt, disrupting the layer of lace over silk. Elianna and her husband, Mitchell, held hands near the fireplace. Mitchell fixed a stray strand of Eli's short, red hair, pinning the errant lock in place, his fingers lingering on her jaw for a moment, his burnished caramel skin a contrast against her paler complexion. Luka, three years older than Melody's sister, stood near Lyrica. They chatted silently in sign. Luka noticed first when everyone quieted and told Lyrica. The preteen went to stand demurely beside Melody, but Vayden noted the younger Ericksen didn't look at her sister.

Vayden went to stand where his father motioned in front of Melody. The family closed ranks, spreading around the couple. A sense of excitement electrified the air. Amari produced the promise bands Vayden had given her earlier for safe-keeping. She handed Melody the larger one and pressed the smaller one to Vayden's palm with a kiss to his cheek.

Melody flipped the silver bracelet between her fingers, a high flush on her cheeks and chest. Vayden covered her hands, forcing her to look up at him. He smiled and stepped close, sliding his fingers to enclose her left wrist. Lyrica scuffed the toe of her beaded lavender slipper on the carpeted floor. She made no effort to move where she could see both of them speak.

Melody frowned and then glanced around at his family. "Will someone please communicate to my sister what we're saying?"

Luka went to Vayden's side. "I will."

"Thank you," Melody said softly, her gaze once again shifting away from his to the bracelet between her fingers.

Silence settled in the room. Amari chuckled and touched both their arms. "Whenever you're ready. There is no formal beginning."

Melody laughed tensely. "I've never been to one before, so I'm not sure—" She cleared her throat. "I'm not sure how to start."

"Just your full name followed by promises to Vayden," Amari instructed.

Melody nodded and blew out a long sigh. "Okay," she whispered and then raised her leafy green eyes to meet Vayden's. His heart turned in his chest. "I, Melody Jane Ericksen, make the following promises to Vayden Dossett.

"I promise to be faithful. I promise to take on your family name and, with it, honor every citizen of Sziveria with the same respect everyone should be awarded. I promise to never seek the Shield Guardian Terravine ranking. I promise to be part of this family the best way I can, to simply be Melody. Myself. I promise to never let the animosity of my parents color my world again, with your help."

Vayden glanced at Lyrica, wondering how much of that was for her benefit instead of his. A tear slipped down her cheek, and she leaned into Melody, resting her temple on her big sister's bicep. Vayden had to work hard to keep a sharp spike of anger in check. Clearly, the Ericksens had said something about Melody going after the Terravine ranking when she'd picked Lyrica up this morning. He figured they'd have learned the truth of his parentage. However, he hadn't considered their selfish hunger for prestige and what it would cost Melody. He wouldn't make the mistake again.

The heavy, cold weight of the promise band settled on his wrist. Vayden threaded their hands together and smiled. "I, Vayden Novick Dossett, promise you, Melody Jane Ericksen, to always be there for you. To help you discover new parts of yourself and let you do the same for me. I promise to never let your parents come between us."

He leaned close, pressing his forehead to hers. His heart beat so hard he thought the organ would burst through his ribs. "I promise, most of all, to love you for however long you'll let me." And then, he slipped the band onto her wrist.

16

"DID YOU MEAN WHAT YOU SAID?" MELODY ASKED THE second the bedroom door clicked shut behind Vayden.

The evening had been a blur of congratulations, meeting too many important people, and trying not to be an embarrassment to her new family. Vayden had needed to help Melody get Lyrica out of the evening gown. Never having dealt with all the tiny hooks, ties, or buttons. The gown had been put on a specific way, and when she and Lyrica tried to get her out, her little sister couldn't remember the order everything had been done in. Melody figured she was in for an equally frustrating experience.

And all through the chaos of new people, new social situations, and unfamiliar wardrobe issues, Vayden's words from their promising had left her distracted. She kept hearing them, wondering if she'd misheard in the excited aftermath of his family being far louder than she figured nine people could be.

He undid the buttons of his vest and peeled the satin off. "I meant everything I said."

Melody flicked her nails together in a nervous gesture in front of her stomach. The single lamp he'd lit near the door left his front in heavy shadows. She could barely make out his face. He tossed the vest onto the dresser and began working on his shirt.

Transfixed on the downward migration of his hand and the skin revealed with each undone button, she tried to remember what she'd been trying to get from him. "When you said you loved me?"

His hand paused near the waist of his pants. "I figured since I made the statement in front of my family, the truth of my words would be obvious."

Melody's breath grew shallow. Her heart pounded in her ears. "Tell me again," she whispered. "Say it again."

He undid the last button. The black fabric parted, framing his muscled torso. "Has anyone ever said those words to you? Your parents? Grandparents?"

Not trusting her voice to work, she shook her head.

"Come here." He held his hand out.

Melody obeyed, her fingers sliding along his palm.

He pulled her into the heat of his body. Citrus and the dark masculine scent of Vayden surrounded her. Melody breathed in deep as he buried his face in the crook of her neck.

"I love you," he murmured into her ear.

The threat of tears burned, and a sharp twist of her heart made her gasp. She sank her fingers into his hair as his lips met hers. Desperate hunger fueled her, and she took, her tongue sliding inside to claim and demand. Vayden wasted no time taking over, crushing her to his chest. Melody's hands roved everywhere. She forced the shirt off his shoulders, making him release her to untangle himself from the sleeves.

Her fingers mapped every ridge of his abdomen and then his back as he pulled her too close to allow her hands to remain between them. All the while, his mouth continued a ravaging assault, building her into a frenzy of desire. Experience may not be on her side, but Melody hadn't seduced her single lover by being timid. Her fingers sought his belt, making quick work of the buckle.

A growl of frustration was the only warning before the back of her dress was torn open. The seam ripped. Tiny beads popped and bounced all around them. Melody helped him get the sleeves from her arms and the stiff bodice down her hips. Around her legs, the heavy fabric bound her knees, and before she could catch her balance, she tilted backward. Vayden's arms wrapped around her. His feet caught in the yards of satin, and he tumbled down with her.

Somehow, he managed to catch himself on his palms, sparing her the crush of his weight. She blinked, made a quick inventory to make sure nothing hurt, and then returned to work on his pants. Once the buttons gave, she grabbed his face again and brought his mouth back to hers. Using her feet, she forced his pants from his hips. At the same time, he shoved her panties down her thighs, making her wiggle and maneuver in precarious ways under him to get them free. His fingers found her, and Melody panted. Her attempt to get out of her gown went forgotten at his touch. He groaned, and a tremor of excitement raced through her, knowing the sound came from his finding her more than ready for him.

"Melody... I can't..." he breathed in heavy puffs into her ear.

She wrapped her arms around his shoulder and drew her knees up, opening more fully for him. If she didn't feel him moving inside her soon, she'd burst. "It's okay. Just... please."

He rose enough to take himself in hand and guide his hard length into her body. Melody squeezed her eyes shut, expecting pain and discovering only a tight, pleasant sensation. In careful thrusts, he went deeper, filling her. Each flex of his hips made the movement easier. Soon, he slid in and out of her with only a growing sense of need.

Melody dug her nails into his shoulders, rising to meet him, frantic for something just out of her reach. His momentum increased until he drove into her in a hard, pounding rhythm. Melody cried out, her back arching, intense pleasure cascading in an unexpected torrent across every nerve in her body. Vayden's fingers dug into the flesh of her thigh, holding her still beneath him. He gently bit where her neck met her shoulder, sending an arc of desire straight through her torso to her center, where she screamed, shattering once again. In the midst of her personal storm, she barely registered Vayden's muffled groan and shudder. The hot rush of his seed spilling into her made her gasp and hold him tighter.

Her limbs melted like a puddle around her. Dazed, she stared at the dancing shadows on the ceiling. Vayden kissed a trail up her throat to her lips. She turned into his kiss, savoring the slow glide of his lips and tongue.

"Are you okay?" he asked, breathless, against her mouth.

She took stock of her body, a delicious shiver running up her spine at still feeling him buried deep inside her. "I might need help off the floor."

He dropped his head to her shoulder and chuckled. "That makes two of us."

Slowly, he pulled free, and Melody groaned at the loss. She sat up when he stood, kicking his pants free from his ankles. Her dress lay in a discarded mass of ruined fabric inches from them. She pushed a tangled lock of hair from her eyes and sighed.

"I hope your mother wasn't expecting that dress to be returned," she said, dropping her hands to the floor between her still spread legs.

Vayden held his hand down to her. "I doubt it."

Never having seen a man naked before, Melody couldn't stop staring at Vayden. The weak light defined all the smooth planes of his muscles and caught on the glistening sheen of sweat. Her gaze skated up from his ankles, pausing briefly at his semi-erect state lying thick and dark from their passion between his thighs. When her eyes finally met his, amusement glimmered in their depths. Flushing, she took his hand and used him for leverage to stand. A trickle raced down the inside of her thigh, and she grimaced. Vayden laughed.

"And that's why we're getting in the shower," he announced, ushering her to the bathroom. He touched her hair. "That, and without some help, I won't be able to get all this out of your hair. How much hair paste did they use on you?"

Melody touched her stiff hair. "Enough to keep the crystals from falling out, I believe."

He sighed. "All right, let's see what we can do."

MUCH LATER, WITH THE PELLET STOVE AND VAYDEN'S BODY keeping her wrapped in warmth, Melody stared at the low flickers behind the small, glass pane. She twisted the promise band on her wrist, her fingers brushing over the etched vine. Vayden's words from the ceremony kept whispering through her mind.

To help you discover new parts of yourself...

What new part did he feel she needed to find? She wanted to wake him up and ask. Wanted to know what he felt he knew about her that she hadn't figured out on her own. Restless, she slipped out from under his arm and the comfort of the blankets. Her toes touched the chilly floor. Something she hadn't noticed when she'd been lying on the hardwood hours ago. She smiled at the memory as she tiptoed across the dark room. The cotton sleep shirt she wore brushed her thighs with each step.

After checking in on Lyrica, Melody went to the windows overlooking the dark city beyond. Streetlights glittered faintly, competing with the rare cloudless night sky. The moon hung in a huge glowing orb over the rows of buildings. Ice crystals shone in the moonlight along the edges of the window frame. Melody took a slow step closer to the potted plant to her right. The avocado tree rose to just above her head, it's pretty, dark green leaves glossy in the silvery light.

She slipped her hand between the thin limbs. A compulsive need to *touch* the living branches drove her. Leaves tickled and danced along her skin. The deeper she reached, the more the urge to sink into the tree pulled at her. Subtle whispers swirled in her mind like a thousand tiny voices. Closing her eyes, she leaned closer until leaves caressed her face.

The faint murmurs coalesced into one quiet demand. Melody found herself obeying, reaching for the thin trunk in the center. The lightly textured stalk met her fingers, and she curled them around. A delicate pulse beat under her palm. She tightened her grip and squeezed her eyes closed.

Hello.

A scream lodged in Melody's throat, and she snatched her hand away and stumbled back into a solid form. Vayden's arms wrapped around her shoulders and upper chest.

"Breathe," he whispered into her ear. "It's okay."

"Th-the…" Trembling, she pointed at the avocado. Her lungs burned on a tide of anxiety. "The t-tree…"

He hugged her closer, his chin dropping to her shoulder. "I know."

Melody tried to process his blasé understanding. He *knew*? He knew a tree just *spoke* to her? Like a person? "You can hear it, too?" she asked, hopeful that perhaps she wasn't going insane. Too much happening in her life and too little time to process.

He rubbed his chin on her. "Not exactly."

She swallowed. "Then, how? How do you know what happened?"

A heavy rush of hair puffed along her jaw on his sigh. "Because I know what you are."

Melody tried to steady her breathing, unable to draw in a full lungful of air. "What do you mean? I don't understand."

"Touch the tree again," he murmured.

"I don't want to," she said, knowing she sounded like a petulant child. She couldn't help it. Fear held her rooted in place. Plants did *not* communicate with people. If she were hearing voices, Vayden would be required to take her to the nearest asylum for her own wellbeing.

Using the weight and strength of his body, he forced her forward. The foliage rustled the closer she came. Melody tried to turn and flee, but his arms remained locked in place, caging her in. Half-turned in his arms, she struggled to find a sense of calm. He waited her out, his fingers brushing softly along her upper arms in a gesture meant to comfort. She focused on the simple touch.

"You are what is known as a botanical talent," he explained calmly, his fingers still stroking under the sleeves of her shirt. "It's a touch-based talent, as I'm sure you discovered."

"No," she denied, shaking her head. "No, I'm a logic-talent. Investigation. I tested when I was fifteen. The results can't be faked."

"Up until now, I believed that, too." He pressed his cheek to her temple. "There's no denying how when you're around a plant, they seek you out. And now, well, you should have all the proof *you* need."

Air caught in her lungs and her throat constricted for an entirely new reason. "I was lied to? Why was I lied to?" she asked, more to herself than to him, knowing he couldn't possibly have an answer.

But he did. "Because a botanical talent can't become a ranked guardian."

Of course. Everything came back to what her parents wanted. The goals that meant more to them than anything else. Including integrity. Melody closed her eyes with a shuddering breath. Suddenly the lack of anything green made a sick sort of sense. At what point had her parents realized her true genetic inheritance? When in her life had they made the decision to deny who she was meant to become? Since she had no memory of having a conversation with a plant, the event must have happened early in her life.

A hot tear slid down her cheek, and Melody shook her head. A bubble of sarcastic laughter escaped from her. "Fantastic. No wonder I wasn't very good at my job."

"You rose in the Enforcement Services ranks quickly, Melody. Don't discredit yourself."

"And who do you think profited by that? We both know the easiest way to achieve a ranking is through promotions." Melody considered her career in comparison to her parents, only spending money on a chef and a bi-weekly housekeeper. Their business brought in more money than that, not to mention her own income that they'd taken to help cover *household* expenses. "They had to have paid someone to falsify my test scores. Is it such a stretch to imagine they were doing the same at South Row Division?"

"No, I suppose not," he admitted, sighing.

Melody tilted her head back onto his chest and stared at the ceiling. "Right. Everything, *everything* has been a lie."

He nuzzled her throat. "Not everything."

Heat coiled in her stomach, a welcome change to the anxiety plaguing her. She wrapped her fingers around his thick forearms and titled her head, giving him easier access. He shifted one hand to cup her breast, working the small globe in his large hand while licking a hot trail across her neck. A shiver of desire raced along her spine.

"Touch the plant again," he said against her collar.

"I don't know if I can," she admitted, hating the tremor in her voice.

His hand slid from her breast to her ribs, taking away the pleasurable distraction. "You can. I'm right here."

Melody licked her lips and reached for the avocado tree. The nearest leaf quivered. She gasped and pulled away. Vayden's fingers slid to her wrist. Gently, he guided her back to the plant, easing her hand into the foliage. Her fingertips touched the trunk. The whispering of too many words to comprehend returned a pleased, almost happy jumble of sound. Bracing for the shock of apparent consciousness in something supposedly inanimate, Melody gripped the tree.

Hello.

The surge of panic returned, but she forced her hold to remain. Licking her lips again, she whispered, "The tree spoke to me again."

"What did it say?" he asked calmly as if trees spoke to people all the time.

"Um… hello," she replied.

Hello.

"It happened again," she said, her eyes so wide she was surprised they didn't pop clear out of her head.

His chest shook against her back. "Melody. Say something to my poor tree."

"This is so stupid," she said under her breath. Then, taking a long, bracing inhale, she focused on the tree and doing the insane. "Hello, tree."

Hello.

Melody concentrated on the tiny myriad of voices seeking her out. Closing her eyes, she tightened her grasp and leaned closer. Vayden followed, but relaxed his hold enough to allow her to almost sink into the leaves. Something was definitely trying to be said to her.

"What do you want me to know?" she asked, trying not to feel completely foolish for speaking to a plant.

I bloom in five months.

"Okay," Melody acknowledged slowly. "This is important?"

Yes.

"Why?"

I do not want to bloom alone.

She tried to make sense of that. "Why not?"

I self-pollinate.

"I'm not sure I understand," she said.

The tree trembled under hand, the leaves shivering along her arm. *I do not want to self-pollinate anymore.*

Melody removed her hand and burst into laughter. "I think you have a male tree."

Vayden touched a leaf. "Why do you say that?"

"Because," she said, laughing harder, "it's tired of having sex with itself."

"My tree told you to find it a mate?" he asked in disbelief, flicking the leaf.

Melody giggled and hugged his arm to her. "Yes, that's exactly what it said."

"Huh, well, I guess I'll take you to the nursery and let you find the perfect partner for my... tree." He hugged her back to his chest. "Are you okay? Are you going to be okay with this?"

She caressed the leaves, noting how they curled and reached for her in the wake of her touch. "Do I have a choice? I mean…" She blew out a long breath. "This is pretty amazing, actually. I spoke to a tree. Actual words. I had no idea that was even possible."

"While a botanical talent isn't among the guardian ranks, it is a crucial job. Gen-Heir botanists have helped stave off diseases, malnourishment issues in food crop greenhouses across the nation, and poor husbandry situations, the list is really endless. Your gift is vital to the health of this country. I hope you will see that if you decide to explore your talent."

Melody looked over the array of plants lined up in front of the windows. Now she wanted to know what they *all* had to reveal. What secrets they'd been forced to keep because no one could ask. "How could I not?"

"I still need your help with Cia if you're willing to do that, too," he said, his hands settling on her hips.

"I don't know how much help I can be," she said, touching his face when he opened his mouth. "But, I will because I need to. I'm still a Tribunii with HCES. Her case will be the last one I work."

He gathered up the hem of her shirt. "And after?"

Melody's breath hitched as cool air touched her bare skin. "After? You keep your promises to me, Vayden Dossett."

"Gladly, wife," he growled and captured her mouth in a searing kiss that vowed her night was far from over.

17

Melody stared at the front door of her parent's house as Vayden climbed into the carriage. The file he'd left sitting on the seat opposite her fluttered. She bit at her thumbnail. A nervous habit she hadn't indulged in since her teen years. "How did it go?"

"Well enough, I suppose," he replied, closing the door against the icy wind.

"I hate leaving her here," Melody whispered against the threat of tears. "I didn't want her to leave the apartment."

Vayden's warm fingers slid along her. "I know, me either."

"How did my mother treat you this time?"

"She was much more pleasant," Vayden reported, settling in the seat across from her. "Not a gen-common insult to be heard."

"I bet. She's hoping your mother will be impressed with me enough to hand me the Shield Guardian Terravine ranking on a crystal plate," Melody said, unable to keep the bitterness from her voice.

"Well," Vayden said, drawing out the word, "she's going to be disappointed. Luka is to be tested in two months, and she's showing promise of being Ma's Gen-Heir."

Relief made Melody drop her head back on the padded seat. "That is wonderful for your family."

"Luka does have to decide that's what she wants, however. My parents won't require it of her."

Melody lifted her head and stared at him. "Why wouldn't she want it?"

Vayden shrugged. "Pressure? Finding a spouse willing to become a Dossett as my father had to do, instead of continuing their own family name."

"I'm going to be a Dossett. Your family is wonderful. The decision won't be a difficult one for whomever she chooses to contract with."

He reached across the small space between them and pulled her onto his lap. She went willingly, straddling his thighs and wrapping her arms around his neck. He splayed his hands across her back and shifted his hips under her.

"You make me feel all primal when you say things like that," he growled against her mouth. "I just want to take you back to our place and try my hardest to contribute to the population of the inhabited world."

The sudden, drenching need his words called forth would have been embarrassing if not for the very clear evidence of his own arousal between her spread legs. She groaned and shifted over him. "We have somewhere we have to be, don't we?"

He gave her a hard, carnal kiss and then set her off him. "Yes, damn it, we do."

Melody settled on the plush seat next to him. The

hired carriage was considerably nicer than anything she'd ever called from off the street. Clearly a private company Vayden relied on to get him places when his Ariot wouldn't, or in their case, couldn't due to space constraints.

"Where are we going?" she asked, trying to keep her hands, and legs, to herself. The urge to climb back onto his lap had her returning to her seat across from him.

"Do you remember about a month ago I'd been hired to seek a reward on Sylphine Seartavos?" he asked, settling back in the seat and folding his hands over his stomach. His jacket fell open to pool on the seat at his hips.

"Key Guardian Asherwick's wife?" How could Melody forget? She'd almost made a complete fool of herself flirting with a man she hadn't known was already taken by the stunning Italyssian shipping heiress.

"Yes. After they contracted, the reward became void. I ran into her and Asherwick's sister outside Mr. Harold's Book Emporium. Mr. Cyrano, the man who'd offered the reward, was attempting to kidnap Guardianess Asherwick. He, and his men, also revealed their plans to do the same with Ramsey Hunter for trafficking purposes," he explained.

Melody gasped. "They were going to sell her? To who?"

"That I don't know. But, it had me thinking about the properties Voklane gave us information about. I did a little digging and found three of them are owned by Cyrano Shipping and Trade, in the care of one of the men on Voklane's list. I sent him a message yesterday afternoon. He directed me to a man who may have more information about additional properties. That's where we're going."

Melody's heart tripped. "Cia might be at one."

Vayden nodded. "That's what I'm hoping for, yes."

"Well, let's go then!" she said, nearly bouncing in the seat.

He leaned to the side and slid the window open to speak to the driver. After he muttered directions she couldn't make out, the carriage lurched into a gentle roll. Almost an hour later, they pulled into a parking loop in front of the records department. Vayden told her to wait inside and jumped out, file in hand. Aggravated, Melody settled back in her seat. She knew they both didn't need to go inside, but being left behind, to sit in boredom inside the carriage, irritated her. Too bad she didn't have a little plant to talk to and begin learning the aspects of her talent.

Melody must have dozed, for she was forced awake by a draft of cold air and the jarring crash of the carriage door slamming shut. She sat up, expecting to see Vayden, but only the empty seat greeted her. Confused, she pushed aside the curtain over the door window. Pedestrians strolled by, huddled in their jackets against the chill. Who had opened the door? She leaned across the space and reached for the window to speak to the driver. Her foot caught and slid on something along the carpeted floor.

Confused, Melody lifted her foot and glanced down. A small, white envelope stood in stark contrast to the dark maroon flooring. A tight fist knotted in her chest. She didn't want to pick up the note. Didn't want to know why someone would have thrown it at her and run off. She might not be a true investigative talent, but she didn't need to be to know nothing good was inside.

Shoring up her courage, something she seemed to be doing a lot lately, she picked up the letter. A thick seal on the back kept the envelope shut. Nasturtiums inside wings forming a V shape was pressed into gold wax. Careful not to ruin any part of the seal, remembering what Voklane had described the afternoon they'd met him, Melody used her finger under the end to pop the signet free. A small folded piece of linen paper waited inside.

Everything in her rebelled at pulling the note free. She laid the envelope on her lap and stared straight ahead. Maybe she should wait for Vayden. Whatever was inside would likely involve him, too. Last night he'd made his stance on their relationship clear. They were a team. They handled life together, no matter the obstacles. With a sinking sensation in her stomach, Melody knew what she held would indeed be such an obstacle.

The time dragged until Melody bounced her knees in nervous energy. The sun moved in a slow arc across the sky. She switched sides to keep from being blinded. Lazy snowflakes sparkled in the clear air, floating in the faint breeze. She followed the delicate swirl of the larger clusters of diamond dust, a common occurrence as ice crystals formed near the ground, being picked up by the arctic winds blowing in from the north.

The deep rumble of a familiar voice outside the carriage had Melody straightening. Frigid air swept in as Vayden opened the door. He met her gaze and leapt in. "What's wrong?"

Melody swallowed and handed him the note.

Frowning, he sat beside her and set the file he'd been holding to the side. "Where did this come from?"

"I don't know, someone just threw it in the carriage. I didn't see them."

He inspected the seal. "It's that symbol Voklane was telling us about."

"I know." Melody rubbed her damp palms on her pants. "Do you think it's about Cia?"

"Unless they have a defector, if it is, it's nothing good," he said, slipping the note free.

The frown on his face darkened. Cursing under his breath, he handed it to her as he twisted in the seat and reached for the window. Melody accepted the paper and read the hastily scrawled letters.

Stop looking for the girl, or the next one we take won't hear us coming.

– The V Alliance

The carriage ambled into traffic. Melody stared at the note, her brows drawn tight. *...won't hear us coming.* Did they mean... She gasped and grabbed Vayden's jacket sleeve. "Lyrica!"

"I know," he said, his face pinched. "I wish we would have gone back for my Ariot, but I didn't anticipate taking hours here."

Melody stared out the window, the note grasped so firmly in her hands the paper crinkled. "My parents won't let us take her. You know that, right?"

"Let me deal with your parents."

Breath refused to enter her lungs. "They won't keep her safe. They won't even notice she's missing until it's too late, and then they may not even say anything."

"Melody," he said softly, and she looked at him. Tears clouded her vision. He caressed her jaw, swiping a spilled tear away. "We're going to get her right now, okay? They just made the threat. They won't do anything else until they see if it worked."

"But it won't work, we're still going to look for Cia," she argued.

"We'll make it in time."

She clung to his words like the lifeline they were. "I knew we should have kept her," she whispered.

Vayden took hold of her hand and laced their fingers, but remained silent. What else was there to say? The sun had almost completely set by the time they pulled up to the Ericksen residence. Melody tried to jump out before the driver had a chance to fully bring the horse to a stop. Muscular arms wrapped around her waist and halted her mid-leap. Squirming, she tried to pull free. Only once the vehicle came to a full stop did Vayden release her. Melody flew from the carriage and to the front door. She didn't bother to knock. The door bounced back, and she slammed her palm on the wooden surface to keep it from closing in her face.

"Lyrica!" she called out in instinct, heading for the stairs.

"What in the inhabited world!" her mother barked from the library door. "I am here with a client, Melody."

"Where is Lyrica?" she asked, her breathing ragged.

Willow crossed her arms over her chest and straightened her back. "I don't see how that's any concern of yours." She turned and flicked her nails over her bony shoulder. "Now go."

A red haze crossed over Melody's vision. She screeched and slammed into her mother's back, sending the slender woman crashing into the nearest wall. In a move learned during her training with HCES, Melody held her mother pinned and helpless, an elbow to the neck and her hip pressed into the small of Willow's back. *"Where is she?"* Melody screamed.

"At school!" Willow wailed. "We sent her back to school. She needs all the instruction she can get. I will not have two failures!"

Melody was out the door before Vayden made it to the top step. "She's at the school, let's go."

THE DRIVER PULLED INTO LYRICA'S SCHOOL NEAR midnight. Melody suspected after spending the day with them, Vayden had agreed to pay the man a week's salary to chauffeur them all day and well into the next. The man hadn't complained, saying it was a good thing he'd slept the afternoon away and was well rested. Melody agreed, a good thing indeed.

Vayden helped her down from the carriage and kept her arm as they walked up the long path to the entrance. She figured her uncharacteristic outburst at her parent's house may have something to do with his behavior. He didn't want her making a scene at the school. Or maybe he needed the contact, because she certainly didn't complain having him so close.

The locked front door surprised neither of them. Vayden pounded loudly, not letting up until noise sounded on the other side. Melody squared her shoulders and put on her best, *I mean business* expression. She wouldn't allow her thoughts to venture into darker territory, where Lyrica was already missing from the school.

A harried older woman answered the door. Her silver-streaked brown hair fell in a messy braid over her shoulder. She held a thick, sage green robe closed at her chest. Untied boots covered her feet. Something between a squint and a glare twisted her aging face. "Why are you knocking on this establishment's door at midnight?"

"I'm Tribunii Ericksen," Melody stated, thankful the only coat she'd managed to pack had been her official HCES jacket. "I'm here to collect Lyrica Ericksen."

The woman looked Melody up and down. Her gaze flickered to Vayden. "I haven't heard a word from her parents about an enforceman being on the way."

"There wasn't time," Melody said. "Please go and collect Miss Ericksen."

An icy breeze swept by, billowing loose snow around. The woman shifted out of the doorway, holding her robe tighter. She motioned to a corner in the foyer. "Wait right here."

Vayden entered first, then pulled Melody in behind. Melody took in the darkened interior, barely warmer than outside. The woman disappeared up shadowy stairs to the right. Glancing around the sparse entry, Melody noted the lack of color and life. No paintings graced the walls. No plants filled the corners. No drapes covered the windows. Solid, dark carpet runners covered well-traveled paths. The building felt more like a tomb than a school for children. At least at Honor Grace Academia, the proprietors had kept their girls in a sense of lavishness to help prepare them for the world they were supposed to enter into someday. This institution seemed something else entirely.

Melody frowned. "This isn't a school."

"No," Vayden agreed, looking around. "This feels like something else."

Annoyed, muffled voices and banging sounded up the stairs. Melody moved closer to the steps and craned her neck to see up the inky depths. A blur of pale fabric swept around the banister and down the stairs. Melody barely had a chance to brace before Lyrica launched herself, her thin arms wrapping tight around Melody's neck.

Lyrica trembled. "Are you really here for me?"

Melody hugged her close, relief flooding her so strongly she almost collapsed to the floor with her baby sister. She brushed Lyrica's soft curls. "Yes, we are taking you from here." She leaned back, cupped Lyrica's face, and tried to search her eyes in the darkness. "What is this place?"

Lyrica looked away. "Can we just go?"

Vayden's hand touched Melody's shoulder. He made a motion, and Lyrica looked up at him. "Yes, we can go. But you'll tell us in the carriage. Deal?"

Lyrica gave a short nod.

"Do you have anything you need to pack?" Melody asked.

"No."

Choosing to focus on the positive, they had Lyrica safely with them, and not the negative, where in the inhabited world had her parents sent her little sister, Melody held Lyrica's hand on the way to the carriage. Her sister huddled close, still only wearing her nightgown. A plain, gauzy garment that did little to keep out the blistering cold. Vayden helped them into the vehicle. Once inside, he lifted the seat he'd occupied and pulled out two thick, woven blankets. He wrapped one around Lyrica's shoulders and draped the other over her shivering legs.

Keeping a hand on her knee, Vayden crouched in front of Lyrica. When she looked at him, he used his hands in the beautiful gestures. Melody wanted to demand they speak so she could understand. But Lyrica trembled and wouldn't meet Vayden's gaze as she replied using motions, and Melody realized whatever her sister had to say wasn't good. She waited patiently while they conducted an entire conversation without her. When Vayden finally settled back in the seat and told the driver where to go, dread settled in the pit of Melody's stomach.

Lyrica wrapped her arms around Melody and laid her cheek on her shoulder. Melody held her sister close and met Vayden's stark gaze across the distance, lit only by the silvery moonlight streaming in through the windows. He held his hand up and shook his head slowly, and the alarm turned to outright fear. What had he learned that he couldn't even put a voice to?

18

HOW DID ONE REVEAL INFORMATION SO AWFUL, EVEN IF HE didn't want to speak it out loud? Vayden scrubbed his hands down his face, knowing what he was about to tell Melody would rip her up inside. He wanted to hold her, hold them both, actually. But Lyrica had buried deep in Melody's side, seeking comfort only her big sister could provide. Later, he'd have his turn with his wife, he had no doubt. If there was one thing he knew about Melody, she would remain strong for Lyrica. Part of him wanted to wait for the privacy of their bedroom, where she could have any reaction she needed, and he could be there for her. Melody, however, wasn't patient enough.

She nudged his booted foot. "Out with it," she said softly.

There was no easy way to deliver the news. He took a deep breath. "It was a mental institution."

"What?" she asked in confusion. "A what?"

Vayden glanced out the window at the white landscape glowing in the moonlight. Anger punched his

263

gut. "Your parents placed her in a mental facility, not a school."

Melody took a shuddering breath and looked away. A tear sliding down her cheek tracked silver. "Why would they do that? There is *nothing* wrong with her."

"I don't know," Vayden confessed. "She was well cared for, and they did educate her daily and taught her how to communicate with her hands. I think they were as confused about her placement there as we are, but as a private establishment, the release is determined by the admitting family."

"Well, I'm part of the admitting family," Melody said, her voice shaky. "And she *won't* be returning."

"I want her at Terravine Manor," Vayden said quietly, meeting Melody's gaze in the shadows. "She'll be safe there until this is over, which hopefully will be soon. We're going to check those addresses I received at records yesterday afternoon."

"You think we're going to find something," she stated.

"Yep." He rubbed the back of his index finger under his chin, catching the stubble along his jaw. "I have no doubt we will."

Melody nodded. "Okay, we can take her there. But..." She blew out a heavy breath. "I want her, Vayden. She can't go back to Gregory and Willow."

They'd been married three days, and already they had to handle a crisis together. One that would change everything, make them both responsible for the life of a child, which also altered things legally in their relation-ship. "I don't know if we'll be bound to the eighteen years or just until her eighteenth birthday."

She chewed her bottom lip. "Does that bother you?"

"No. I love you. I'm not going to stop loving you in a year." He rubbed the inside of her calf, aware that while his words seemed to have brought her a sense of security, she hadn't returned the sentiment. "What about you?"

"I wish I could kiss you right now," she revealed, a smile toying at her lips in spite of the tears still streaking her cheeks. "Is that a yes, then?"

He knocked his boot between hers. "You have to ask?"

"Confirmation is nice."

"Yes, of course. I don't want her returning to the Ericksen house, either."

They pulled into the curving wide drive of Terravine Manor. Vayden leapt out, asked the driver to wait one more time, and motioned for the sisters to exit. Melody kept the blanket securely around Lyrica's shoulders. At the front door, Vayden used his house key to let them inside. He placed the girls in the formal sitting room and then went upstairs to wake his parents. Amari met him in the hall. A dark silk robe billowed out behind her as she rushed to them.

"What is it, what's wrong?" she asked, reaching for him. Vayden took a deep breath and informed his mother of the situation. She squeezed his hand. "She will stay here, where else would she go? Henry is here, too. Perhaps interacting with the girl will help pull him from his sadness."

Vayden pulled his mother into a tight hug. "Thank you. I think finding Cia will be the only thing that can help Henry right now."

Amari shrugged. "I am willing to try anything at

this point. He sits in the greenhouse. Just sits there, Vayden. It's hard to see him this way."

"I know," he said. "I need you to research how Melody and I can gain custody of Lyrica, too."

"I know her parents will have to agree."

"I'm hoping you can do that, too. The Ericksens have an unnatural obsession with ranked guardians."

Amari frowned and crossed her arms. "And you think I should pull rank and get them to agree?"

"Yep."

Amari rolled her eyes and dropped her hands at her sides. "You are impossible."

"I'm taking care of my family," Vayden said softly.

Grayson came up behind his wife and wrapped his arms around her. "Sounds like a reasonable request to me, my love."

Amari grasped Grayson's forearms and leaned back into him. "I know. You know how much I hate having to act all superior."

Grayson chuckled and rocked with Amari. "Never mind that you are."

She slapped at his arms. "I am not. Not really."

Grayson smacked a loud kiss on her temple. "Right." He looked at Vayden. "Take us to our newest family members, son."

VAYDEN CIRCLED ANOTHER ADDRESS ON THE MAP AND consulted his list to make sure he'd identified the correct location. Melody wrote the information down on a separate piece of paper that they'd take with them when they left. An arc of sizzling sensation seemed to zip from one cell of his body to the next, alerting him that he was close. So close. He couldn't give up now, couldn't allow anything to distract or delay in finding Cia.

Neither of them had slept since leaving Lyrica at his parents. Melody didn't complain. She drank the stout coffee he'd set before her and ate a sweet roll and a tangerine. A paper fluttered as she pulled one free from one of the many files on the table.

"What's this?" she asked, snapping the bright green sheet.

Vayden gave the page a cursory glance. "I asked Bree to get me a copy of all the ships arriving in all the nations ports."

"This late in the season?"

"Yeah, it's why there's only one sheet," he said, marking another address.

Melody frowned and leaned closer. "Wasn't the name of that shipping company you were worried about Cyrano?"

He braced his hands on the table. "Yes, why?"

She angled the paper so he could see, pointing to one line. "Look."

Vayden read and then cursed. He gathered up all the papers, including what Melody had been working on. "Come on, we don't have time to strategize anymore, we have to check out these locations. That ship is scheduled to make port in a matter of hours. They may have already moved them. We'll start with the closest one to the MagnaRail station and work our way out."

"You think they load them on the rails to bring them to Port Tabria?"

"Yes, they'd have to load too many carriages. They

can just charter a railcar and load them all into one. Faster, too."

Melody shook her head and clenched her jaw. "People are not cargo."

Vayden crossed the room to his jacket. "Not to us. But to them…"

"What about the roads?" she asked, hastily donning her jacket while simultaneously shoving her foot into a boot.

He grabbed them both thick, knit scarves, throwing one to her. "I've driven on worse. Luckily the ice will mean less travelers."

She wrapped the scarf around her neck twice and then accepted the papers he held out to her. Shuffling through them, she moved them around in a new order. "Okay, the first one is about six blocks from the station."

Outside, the sun kissed the horizon, blending dark blue twilight into shades of gray and pink. Wispy orange clouds glowed in contrast to a brightening sky. Snow crunched under their boots and swirled around their legs. At the Ariot, Vayden scraped off the buildup of ice on the windows while Melody worked inside, arranging the papers further so they could move directly on to the next location if necessary. While Vayden wanted to be optimistic, he knew better than to believe their first stop would be the only one they needed to make. He wouldn't even consider all of them would prove useless. Cia *had* to be at one of the addresses he'd narrowed down.

Melody huddled under the blanket, the pages on her lap when he finally climbed inside. She told him the address, and he pulled out, taking the icy roads slowly on the way toward the MagnaRail station. The pastel shades in the sky morphed into vivid hues of orange, pink and yellow, casting the city in warm tones. Vayden located the address, an apparently abandoned building. Broken windows yawned in the three-story brick structure. He parked in the alley opening and then stared at a padlocked side door.

"Why lock the building when the windows are busted out?"

"Make it harder for someone to squat?"

"Or harder for someone to discover something they shouldn't," he said quietly.

"Or escape," Melody surmised, frowning. "Though, I can't imagine much of value is in there if they didn't even bother to cover the windows and attempt to secure the building."

"All true, unless they're so sure of their ability to keep whatever is inside locked up and hidden."

Melody let out a dramatic breath. "Only one way to find out."

Vayden found a half-busted crate near an open window and helped Melody inside first. He followed her in, cautious of any stray broken glass fragments. Carefully, they searched every corner of the decrepit building. Only a few broken wooden crates with shards of picked over pottery pieces were found. Vayden kicked at the splintered wood.

"Hey, we still have six other addresses to check," Melody said, touching a hand to his upper arm. "We're going to find her."

Vayden threaded their fingers together and brought her hand to his mouth. He kissed the back of her hand. "I know."

The next location took them further from the station

but closer to the warehouse district of the city, where rail lines ran to load or offload cargo. They parked near the site, a sprawling single-story cinderblock structure with high windows and thick wooden doors. Chains and padlocks were wrapped around every handle. A flash, not unlike lightning, surged through Vayden.

"This is it," he stated, closing the Ariot door.

Melody scrambled out. "How do you know?"

"I just do." He studied the building. "Let's go around back, see if there's an easier way in."

They squeezed between buildings in the confined walkway. Another narrow door was near the end of the long wall. Vayden examined the lock and found it without rust, the keyhole worn from frequent use. Whatever was inside, someone checked on it often.

"How do we get in?" Melody asked, hunching against a sudden burst of wind down the narrow alley.

"I have cutters in the Ariot."

She arched a brow at his revelation. "Cut open locks often, Dossett?"

He shrugged and headed back for the vehicle. "You never know. I once had a piece of wire wrap around one of my tires outside the city. If I hadn't had cutters, I wouldn't have been able to get free. There are many things I store in the back of this thing that always seem to come in handy."

"Like the blanket," Melody commented, stopping behind him as he crawled in enough to search the back.

"Yep." He moved things around to reach his toolbox. Anything he may need for roadside repairs were neatly arranged in the box to maximize how much he could squeeze into the small space. He found the cutters and backed out of the cab. "All right, come on. If anyone is being held here, someone will be along shortly if they plan to prepare them for transport to Port Tabria."

Melody fell in step behind him, having to almost jog to keep up with his longer, hurried strides. Air left them both in thick puffs of vapor. At the door, Vayden looked around again before bringing the cutters to the lock. A quick snap of metal and the lock broke free. Melody caught the heavy latch before it could fall to the ground. The chain rattled and clanked as he slid it free. They lay both on the ground near the door, the snow swallowing the steel. Vayden slid the door open and waited a second, listening, before venturing inside.

Cold darkness filled the open space. Melody closed the door silently behind them. In the quiet, they stood and listened for any hint of where to search. Any noise out of place. Vayden wished he had some glow vials used by First Intelligence when on critical missions. The two serums, when mixed, produced a volatile chemical reaction that glowed in a glass tube. Pining for what he couldn't have wouldn't do any good, so Vayden pushed ahead, his vision adjusting as pale light filtered in from the high windows.

He moved slowly, scanning the floor, noting a path in the heavy dust on the floor. Remaining silent, he pointed the trail out to Melody. She nodded that she understood. Vayden wished he had a gun or that Melody had thought to bring hers. In hindsight, they should have grabbed one, but they'd been in such a hurry, neither had. He positioned his fingers along the handles of the cutter to use it as a weapon if he became desperate enough.

They followed the footprints until they seemed to

disappear into a wall. Vayden looked along the wall, noting in the growing light, only one wall of the entire building was improved. The rest were cinderblock. He handed Melody the cutters and then pressed his fingertips to the wall and closed his eyes. Slowly, he moved over the wall, paying close attention to the awareness in his body. Like the vibrations of a tuning fork, he always felt the closer he was to a substantial clue, the more *something* vibrated inside him. The crackle along his nerves danced the further to the left he touched. On a hunch, he applied pressure. A faint hiss sounded as the door slid open, and warm, mildewy air escaped from a staircase leading down.

Vayden stared into the inky depths. No light glowed from below. Whatever, or whoever, was down there was in complete darkness. Sighing, he flexed his jaw. "Do you think they have a lamp on the stairs?"

Melody stepped beside him. "Unless they always bring one, they must. How far down do you think it goes?"

"A story? Maybe more, I have no idea." He glanced back the way they'd walked. "We better find out, though, I don't think we have long."

Vayden eased down the steps, his hands skimming the rough, block walls, seeking a lamp. About ten steps down, he touched cold metal and glass. Melody bumped into his back. He steadied himself on the wall while she used his hips to keep from stumbling further.

"Found the lamp," he muttered. He fumbled around until he found the small box of matches on a shelf for them below the lantern. A quick shake revealed the contents. Using the cinderblock wall, the match tip flashed to life. Vayden lifted the glass and lit the burnt tip of the wick. The bottom of the stairs came into view, along with another mounted lamp.

Soft whimpers drifted up to them, stressed and scared. Melody's grip tightened on his waist. She pushed, but Vayden didn't need any further encouragement. He took the remaining stairs two at a time, landing on a dirt-packed floor. Melody lit the second lamp and gasped at what the fall of light revealed.

Lining the entire wide corridor were cages with three to four children or young adults per unit. Melody ran along them, checking each lock as tiny hands poked out in desperation. Calmly, she spoke to each group, telling them she'd get them out, they had nothing else to fear, they were safe now. Vayden went the other direction, not wanting to dwell on the truth, or the lie, of her words. He had no idea how they were going to get them all to safety.

"Cia!" he called, searching each cell. She *had* to be here. "Lucianna Castien!"

Bars rattled at the end of the long row, and Vayden sprinted. He reached the final cage and knelt down, his hand reaching inside. "Cia?"

"Uncle Vayden?" a weak voice asked.

His hand brushed cool skin, and he wrapped his fingers around her wrist. Dropping his forehead to the bars, he closed his eyes against a rush of emotions. "Yes, baby girl, it's me."

"What are you doing here?" she asked, and Vayden had to repeat the question in his mind to make sure he'd heard correctly.

"To get you," he said as if she should have known the answer already.

Her wrist tugged free. "I need to stay here."

Vayden sat in the dirt and tried to peer into the dark shadows. The lamp light didn't reach this far down. Only the vague shift of shadows met his efforts. "Cia, come on, that's ridiculous. You can't stay here, and you can't mean that."

"I can, and I do," she said, stronger, more defiant. "They are going to help me find Mom and Joshua's killers, as long as I do what they say. They're going to train me."

Vayden touched the icy bars. "They've kept you caged. *They* are the ones who took Fiona and Joshie from you, Cia. They are lying to you. Your father needs you. I'm taking you home."

"They did not, they are helping me!" she screamed. "They told me they saw everything, and if I shoot like Daddy, I will be able to avenge our family."

A sliver of pain pierced his heart. He reached for her again. "Cia, baby girl, they kidnapped you after killing your mother and brother. We don't know why, but they need you for something. All these kids you're here with? They plan on selling them. Do you really want to be part of that?"

The echo of chains clicking through steel traveled through the gloom. Vayden glanced down the length and noted Melody cutting locks free. She went on to the next and let the young occupants finish freeing themselves. They didn't leave the area, just the cages, grouping together near the light. Vayden wanted to leave Cia to get the cutters, but he feared if he did, she'd either panic or continue to convince herself she needed to stay. If he had to carry her screaming and fighting from the building, he would. Her father could sort her out if she wouldn't see reason. The young woman had gone through a deeply traumatic event and had obviously been fed lies. She was clearly coping the best she could, by latching on to the false promises she'd been given.

Melody reached them and handed him the tool before rushing to the group of distressed children. Vayden stood and snipped the lock, not bothering to keep it or the length of chain from crashing to the ground. Dust plumed as the heavy metal landed. He yanked the door open and reached for Cia. She hesitated for a fraction of a second before launching at him, sobbing. Vayden caught her against his chest and lifted her into his arms. He buried his face in her tangled hair, not caring about the thick scent of dirt, sweat, and the sharpness of fear left behind. He knew she was a mess. Her thin body shook. Hot tears splashed onto his neck, where she buried her face.

Melody appeared at his side. "The kids say there's an exit down here that the men use when they bring more kidnap victims and when they leave. They use the stairs rarely, it seems."

Vayden considered that and the worn trail. "They use the stairs more than the kids realize. We'll take the exit down here, though. Maybe it'll let out near an enforcement radio box."

THE BOX HADN'T BEEN RIGHT OUTSIDE THE DOOR BUT rather two blocks down. Melody had run the short distance, leaving Vayden behind to care for the large group of scared children. Since he had more experience with kids, they'd decided she'd call for help while he kept her. A tall, wire-thin young woman hadn't stopped clinging to Vayden's side after they left the tunnel behind. Most of the kids weren't dressed for the blistering cold day. The sun, a white ball in the brilliant blue sky, provided no warmth. Melody conveyed the concern when she placed a call to HCES to ensure they brought coats, shoes, and blankets.

Workers in the area had taken note of the disturbance and were lending a hand by the time Melody returned. Vayden spoke with two men and a woman, while making sure a young three-old-girl didn't fall while attempting to climb his leg. The filthy teen stood in the shadow of his back; her hands fisted in his coat. Melody's heart went out to her, and she wished they could take her home right away. Too much still needed to be done, however, before they were able to walk away from the crime scene. And a crime scene the area was, indeed.

Melody glanced around, tucking a curl behind her ear as a brisk wind rushed by. Bitter-sweet emotion squeezed in her chest. This case would be her final as an enforceman. After the last paper was filed, she'd hand in her gear and start a new chapter with her husband and sister and a new, unexplored talent. She didn't quite know how to feel if she should even be feeling anything other than a faint nervousness and a lot of excitement.

A long line of black carriages ambled down the road, the vivid yellow of HCES and the crest painted on each door and across the back identifying their official status. The first to jump down was a familiar face. Master Tribunii Marck Rainier, her team leader. He stalked up, his expression a mixture of grim acceptance and respect.

"Tribunii Ericksen, I knew you'd be the one to figure this mess out," Marck said, shaking his head.

Melody motioned to Vayden. "I didn't MT, Mr. Dossett did."

Rainier quirked a brow. "Is that so?"

"Yes, MT."

Her leader's lips twitched in a smile. "I'd heard about him. The infamous gen-common son of a shield guardian that can solve cases fast enough to keep him comfortable in reward fees."

"Yes, MT," Melody confirmed.

Rainier's eyes slid back to her. "And you married him?"

"That's correct, MT."

Melody stayed back as Marck made his way to Vayden, issuing orders on his way. Several young guardsmen leapt into action, taking care of scared children, getting them into warmer clothing and into the shelter of carriages. From there, they'd be identified and returned to their families, or taken to orphanages if they had no family. One particular child would remain with them.

Two Ariots drove up the long line of carriages, moving slowly through the packed crowd. The pale blond head that emerged didn't surprise Melody. Ryan Voklane took in the scene, spoke to a few people, and then walked away, disappearing into the chaos of people. Melody blinked and looked around. She should have been able to find the large, pale guardian with ease, and yet, somehow, he'd blended in. The second man to emerge wore a jacket and badge that revealed him to be with the Sziverian National Investigative Division. Vayden waved to the handsome stranger, a look of almost relief on her husband's face.

Melody moved closer, trying to catch a glimpse of the SBID investigator's name. The harsh morning sun caught on the silver threads. Darius Ralston. Melody's attention flew to his face, to the strong masculine features, dark hair, and ocean green eyes, a colorful contrast to his deep bronze skin. One of Madeleine Fenwick's many grandchildren. The men spoke in low tones. MT Rainier nodded occasionally, adding to the conversation now and then. Vayden pointed at the exit, and both the men headed for the underground tunnel.

Fatigue etched hard lines in Vayden's face. He pulled Cia around under the shelter of his arm and beckoned Melody. "We're done here if you're ready to go. MT Rainier said to come to South Row tomorrow to make your statement. I asked him to give you the day since we haven't slept in over twenty-four hours."

"Thank you," she said, avoiding being run over by many of the rushing enforcemen covering the area.

"Are you okay to drive the Ariot?" he asked. "I'm going to ride in a carriage with Cia. If you aren't, we can come back for it."

Melody took stock of her own level of exhaustion. "I should be all right. But, if we're going to your parents, we may want to leave the Ariot there."

Vayden nodded. "Agreed."

THE MOMENT LUCIANNA SAW HER FATHER, SHE CRUMBLED into his arms, taking him to the ground with her. Sobs wracked her too-thin frame. Vayden held back, though he wanted to comfort them both. Amari had no such qualms. Wrapping the remaining members of a grieving family in her arms, stroking both their heads as she made soothing sounds, tears flowing freely down her cheeks. Melody wasn't immune to the emotional reunion either, turning from the sight, her chin quivering. Vayden wrapped his arm around her chest and pulled her into his side, allowing her to keep her back to the heartbreaking scene.

"Thank you for helping me," he whispered into her hair.

She sighed and leaned into him. "I don't know how much help I really was. You did all the work."

Vayden kissed the top of her head. "You did more than you realized."

She leaned back enough to meet his gaze. "You should go test, Vayden, for a logic-talent. Prove them all wrong. There is nothing *common* about you."

He cupped her jaw and touched a gentle kiss to her lips. "I don't need a test to reveal who I am. I never have."

"But—"

He kissed her harder. "No," he whispered against her mouth.

"I love you, Vayden Dossett," she breathed across his lips.

Vayden pressed his forehead to hers. Inside he rejoiced. "Took you long enough."

She laughed tearfully, her fingers gripping his forearm tightly to her chest. "Will you take us home?"

Vayden's heart clenched. Home. With the woman who loved him. With his family. "Let's go home."

EPILOGUE

Two weeks later
  Wintervail

Melody blew on the steaming cup of tea in her hands, holding back laughter. Lyrica danced and clapped around Vayden as he pulled his beautiful Wintervail Chest to the center of the living room. The lid wouldn't close fully, revealing glimpses of colorfully wrapped packages. The sun had fully set, signaling the start of a world-wide celebration of life continuing for nations that had survived the Primal Years and had managed to build sustainable civilizations. They'd endured another year.

The months of Arctic wind, ice, and snow, would test them all. But as Melody looked around the cozy apartment, filled with healthy plants, colorful paper birds, and sparkling glass flowers, she knew *this* family would be just fine. All the paperwork had been filed for custody of Lyrica. Gregory and Willow hadn't given much of a fight when Shield Guardianess Terravine had shown up at their door requesting their signatures. Melody smiled into her tea, sipping the spicy warmth.

Vayden motioned her into the living room. He signed to Lyrica, and she clapped in delight and traded places with him in front of the chest. Melody was slowly learning her sister's language, but the two of them still spoke too fast for her to catch much. Lyrica had become so comfortable speaking with Vayden using her hands that she often forgot to speak out loud, too. Such as now, her small fingers shaping into words of obvious excitement.

"Yes," Vayden nodded, laughing. "All you, so come on, mite. Start passing them out."

Lyrica clapped again and then opened the lid to the chest. Vayden settled on the couch, and Melody curled into his side. Lyrica exclaimed in joy at each brightly wrapped gift she pulled free, read, and then set in front of whoever's name was written on the present. Her pile quickly outgrew the two adults. Melody's heart swelled so much she feared it might burst in her chest.

She leaned her head on Vayden's shoulder. "Thank you."

He rubbed her upper arm. "Everyone should experience Wintervail. I'm choosing not to think too hard about this being the first time for both of you. It'll ruin my day."

"Yes, and I know you usually share this day with your entire family, weather permitting. Thank you for allowing her first Wintervail to be a bit more private."

"My family understands you both are adjusting and accepting. Next year, we'll do the big, loud gathering.

This year," he shrugged, "we will enjoy as our small, new family."

Anticipation fluttered in her stomach. She glanced at him and smiled when he turned to meet her gaze. "I have an unwrapped gift for you."

He raised a dark brow. "You do?"

"Yes." She kissed him, staying close as she whispered, "But it won't arrive for eight more months."

Confusion slid into disbelief. His gaze flickered downward and then back to her in question. She nodded, tears gathering in her eyes.

"Really?" he asked, breathless, his eyes wide in surprise.

"I think so. I don't want to say anything for another month, just in case," she cautioned. "But yes. I'm a week late."

He crushed her to his chest in a tight hug. "I love you so much."

Melody laughed, returning his hug. "I hope so, you're going to be stuck with me for eighteen more years."

He pulled back, his beautiful eyes bright. "I plan for much more than that, my guardianess."

SURVIVE PREVIEW

Releasing April 27, 2023

Haven City, Sziveria
  June 3rd, 830 P.C.E (Post-cataclysmic Event)

The woman huddled on the wrong side of the bridge guardrail almost went unseen. Little more than a black shadow against an even darker river flowing below, Caidon wouldn't have noticed her if she hadn't moved. But she did. A small shift closer to the edge she barely fit on. And he stopped.

She hadn't realized she was no longer alone, giving him a chance to strategize. If a river fifty feet beneath seemed a better option than life, things weren't looking too great for her. He approached slowly, not wanting to spook her, an action that may send her plummeting before he had a chance to diffuse whatever situation she seemed to have found herself. Providing he could say anything useful. He didn't understand people, didn't have much in common with most.

A gentle mist fell, floating in a haze through the meager street lamps. The night was thankfully warmer for the season and his hands didn't stick from ice build up to the rail when he leaned on his forearms and looked over. She hadn't moved anymore, just seemed to watch the flow of inky darkness rolling past. Closer, and with enough light reaching them, he could make out the smooth angles of her face and dark curls tamed by water. She was young, and pale, and too curled up for him to know much else.

"How old are you?" he asked, leaning casually onto the rail, watching the water disappear into the foggy void beyond.

Her gasp made him tense. "Who are you?"

Still gazing at the rippling water, he clasped his hands together. "Caidon Survaine."

When she remained silent, he glanced down at her. "This is where you answer my question because I answered yours. How old are you?"

If possible, she shrank more into herself. "Nineteen. Why are you asking me that?"

Caidon considered her reply. "Nineteen. Young. Lots of possibility still. Are you all by yourself? No family?"

"I have family. I have… my brother."

"Is your brother a good man?"

She glanced at him, a quick cut of her eyes and fidget of her shoulders. "My brother is an enforceman for Haven City Enforcement Services. A prefect."

Caidon opened his hands in supplication. "Okay, he protects people." He looked at her, waited until she met his gaze. "Does he protect those at home?"

She blinked and quickly looked away. "Yes, my brother is a good man."

"What is your name?"

A breeze blew up from the river. The chilled edge carried the scent of stale water and algae growing under the bridge. She pressed closer to the rail, her fingers wrapping around a bar at her shoulders. "How old are you?"

"Twenty-five."

Her fingers flexed on the rail. "Ramsey."

"Is that a first or last name?"

"First."

"How intriguing."

"Many people seem to think so."

Caidon lowered himself onto the wet cement bridge, his shoulder near hers. "So, Ramsey with the good brother, who is nineteen, why are you on the wrong side of the bridge?"

When she went to pull her hand free, he covered her cold fingers with his. She trembled under his touch. "I'm... scared."

The tremor in her voice made his grip tighten. He considered their conversation until this point, limited as it'd been. Since she'd climbed over the rail and settled herself on the other side, he didn't think she was scared of her current position. No, something else had her running. "Why? Will your brother not help you?"

"My brother can't help me," she said, her voice cracking. Against his shoulder, he felt more than heard her deep inhale. "He is more likely to do something stupid."

He shifted closer, until his head was near hers. "Like you're about to?"

"At least I'll only hurt myself."

"Is that what you think?" he asked quietly. She

loved her brother. He could work with that. "There is no hurt for you here, either. Only an end. They might find your body before you reach the Black Ocean. Give your brother something to bury, at least."

The gentle burble of water sweeping between pilons filled the quiet night. The distant, unhurried clop of hooves and clatter of wheels told him they wouldn't be alone on the bridge for much longer.

"Perhaps," he said, "you'd consider giving me your brother's name. I can at least do him the courtesy of letting him know what happened to his sister. As an enforceman, he'll search the city for you, I'm sure."

"You aren't going to try to talk me out of this?" she asked sharply.

"Were you hoping some stranger would walk by and stop you?"

"I don't know," she said in a mixture of wonder and hint of anger. "I didn't *want* to be here at all."

"Then don't be." His words held a biting edge. A challenge.

Tense seconds passed and then she shifted and Caidon moved with her, ensuring she didn't fall when she stood. "Help me over?" she asked, completely calm, as if she sat on the wrong side of safety every day. Maybe she did for all he knew.

Caidon grasped her elbow and held out his other hand to steady her if she couldn't make it over on her own. One leg swung over the rail, she balanced using her palm and teetered precariously. She pivoted, reaching out blindly, her tongue stuck out the corner of her mouth. While a figure of grace she was not, there was no mistaking her stunning beauty.

Somehow, he managed to grasp her hand while staring. She lifted her face to him and the glow of the nearest street lamp caught in her violet eyes. The familiar sensation of time slowing, coalescing around him, the very droplets in the air hanging mid-fall, he looked over her round face. Regal, exotic, unique… they all applied. He wanted to memorize the smooth angles of her cheeks and jaw. Trace the delicate slope of her nose. Lick the water from her full lips. Caidon blinked at the foreign burst of desire. Lust and romance had no place in his life, and he took great care to keep both tightly reigned.

The harsh clatter of the approaching carriage pulled him back to reality. Caidon inhaled and rushed to help her down before they had unwanted attention. She squeaked and gripped his shoulders. Her feet tangled in the wet folds of her skirt. Fabric ripped and she tumbled against his chest.

"Shoot," she muttered, lifting the heavy black length. "I liked this skirt."

"I'd hope so," Caidon said, "since you'd planned on it being the last thing you wore."

"Ha, ha," she said in sarcasm. "I wasn't going to jump. I just needed…." She shrugged and straightened. He swallowed the disappointment of losing her soft curves. "Some time to think. This bridge is pretty far from everything, but not too far from my house."

"Pretty risky."

She shrugged. "Maybe." When he lifted a brow, she rolled her eyes and tsked. "Okay fine, so I didn't make the smartest choice to wallow in self-pity. I'm okay now."

"Yeah?"

"Yes."

The carriage ambled by, the heavy wooden cab rocking gently behind the slow walking horse. The driver lifted a hand in greeting, but didn't stop. Either off duty or he already had a fare. Caidon watched the coach fade into the mist and redirected his attention to the barely visible three-story building on the corner across from the bridge.

"I'm staying there, in that hotel. The owner keeps her kitchen open all night and a fire burning in the lobby. Do you want to go warm up or do you want me to walk you home?" he asked, pointing at the corner.

She looked at the building, then over her shoulder in the opposite direction, then back. Pressing her lips together she met his gaze. "Just the lobby?"

"Yes."

Crossing her arms over her small chest, she nodded. "Okay, that sounds nice. Thank you."

The urge to slide his arm around her waist had him shoving his hands into his pockets and falling in step beside her. He wasn't tall, or overly built, but beside her, he very much felt like a man. While she had full hips, her waist was narrow and her breasts small. He figured he outweighed her by fifty pounds, maybe more. Black curls fell in clumps around her shoulders and down her back, heavy with water. Dry, he imagined they were chaos. What had he been thinking to spend more time with her? Nothing good would come of learning more about this enigma of a woman.

And yet, he held the door open for her when they arrived. He settled her on the couch with a blanket, and then went to get her something warm to drink. When he returned, two steaming cups in hand, he found her curled up and staring into the massive fire. Angling himself on the couch so he could still see the doors and stairs, he relaxed and allowed himself to look once again.

She turned and met his gaze, a small smile curving her tempting mouth. "You're staring."

He shrugged and kept looking. "Not often I find something worth staring at."

A subtle flush blossomed across her cheeks. "Well, aren't you a charmer."

"Not usually."

A delicate black brow lifted. "No?"

"Nope."

She returned to watching the dancing flames. Silence descended around them, only disrupted by the pop and hiss of burning logs. The moving shadows caught on her drying curls, and as he'd suspected, they were wild. Her chin rested on her drawn knees, the blanket acting like a cloak.

"Why did you stop on the bridge?" she whispered. "Why did you help me?"

"Would you have preferred I left you there?" he asked, genuinely curious.

"No." She scrunched her nose. "At least, I don't think so."

"Things are so bad?"

Her chin dropped further between her knees. "Yes."

Caidon waited. He was a patient hunter, an ingrained ability of his inherited talent.

"My name is Ramsey Hunter." When he didn't respond how she seemed to expect he would, she turned her head, laying her cheek on her knees. Her hair fell in a cascade of across her back and he tightened his grip on the back of the couch. "Don't you read the papers?"

"Not unless I have to. Have you been in the papers?"

She nodded. "I helped send a very bad man to prison."

"That's a good thing."

"Most people didn't seem to think so," she said softly. "I've lost all my friends." Her left hand slipped free from the blanket. In the amber light he could see the pale band around her wrist where a thick bracelet had once been. A promise band. "And *he* left. Decided I wasn't worth the trouble."

Caidon leaned forward and slid his fingers between hers. A sizzle of awareness raced up his arm. Like a magnet, he shifted closer, until his hip pressed to hers. His arm stretched out behind her, cocooning her into his side. "I guess he did you a favor then. Marriage contracts aren't for the weak."

"You've been married?" she asked, her eyes bright.

"No, not me." He pulled her hand into his chest. "Not yet."

"I wasn't sure if I was ready." Her fingers tightened around his. "Now I guess it doesn't matter."

"He wasn't the reason you were contemplating the river to sweep away your worries."

Her gaze fell to their clasped hands. "He was part of it, yes. My parents were in Monaco Sands when the hurricane hit. You know the one? From a two months ago?"

"I heard about it."

She nodded. Tears shimmered in her eyes. "I wanted

my mom, and she wasn't here. Won't ever be here again. My brother can't help. He's so… proud of me. For standing up against Joel Blackbain and fighting for all the girls he assaulted. I didn't know Blackbain was keeping half of Haven City wealthy. With him in prison, he won't be able to do business."

"I should hope not. And if money was more important to everyone than a rapist receiving justice, then why would you want to be around those people?"

"I don't, I just…" She took a shaky breath. "I didn't expect to be shunned you know? And…" She sighed and looked away, a flush darkening her face. "Ditched. He made so many promises. You aren't supposed to break those." Her face dropped onto her knees. "I can't believe I'm telling you all this."

Caidon gave in to the urge and swept her hair from her face, his fingers lingering in the silken length. "I'm glad you told me."

She settled her cheek onto her knees again, her hand flexing in his. "So, tell me something about you."

"I received a ranked guardian position today."

Shock widened her eyes. "Really? Wow… congratulations." Then her gaze shuttered. "Be careful who you make friends with."

"I won't be staying in Sziveria. I sail out tomorrow."

"Where are you going?"

He shrugged. "Don't know yet."

Understanding dawned in her gaze. "Oh, you signed on with the FIO then, didn't you?"

"Yes."

She pressed her lips together. "I guess we won't have much to talk about."

He caressed another curl behind her ear. "You can keep telling me about you."

"I'm boring."

"You're pretty interesting from where I'm sitting."

She laughed, a sweet musical sound. "Not a charmer? What a liar you're turning out to be."

Caidon leaned in until his nose nearly touched hers, knowing he was getting too close, knowing better than to learn anything more about the vulnerable beauty. The compulsion outweighed his common sense. A first, and he couldn't seem to care. Not tonight. "I leave tomorrow. I don't know when I'll be home. Give me something good to remember. Talk to me, Ramsey Hunter."

"Okay," she said quietly and relaxed back, closer to him.

As she spoke, random bits of information about herself, getting lost in memories with her parents because it was all she had anymore, Caidon shifted until he held her fully in his arms. He couldn't make himself stop touching her. Small caresses where she'd let him. He knew he was a poor substitute for the man she needed, the one who should have been strong enough to hold her in the midst of sorrow. Gladly, he took the man's place, soaking in a moment he knew he'd never share with a woman again. Just existing. Learning. An indulgence he didn't deserve with a woman he could never hope to have.

"What rank were you endowed with?" she asked, her fingers sliding through his in a back and forth that caress that left desire knotting in his gut.

"Master guardian," he answered.

"Whose seat were you assigned?"

He twisted a curl around one of his fingers. "No ones. It's in-name only. I'm not filling a seat in the House of Laws, nor will I have one once I'm done working for the FIO."

She shifted until she faced him, but didn't move away. One of her knees rested on his thigh, the blanket pooling on both their laps. "I didn't know they could do that. I mean, I knew they could create new seats, but not temporary, and without an option for how you serve, in the house or in-service to the country."

Caidon wondered if she'd let him slip his hand under her rain-dampened skirt. Touch her bare calf. Continue up to her thigh. If she'd be warm to his touch, or cool from the wet fabric against her skin. "I'm a unique situation."

"A unique *Sziverian government* situation," she clarified.

Then she looked around, as if assuring herself they were truly alone. The night had given way to early morning. Perhaps some stragglers would venture in, but Caidon figured not.

Ramsey leaned closer, and beyond the scent of rain still lingering on her skin he caught a faint hint of lavender and vanilla. Warm, calm and inviting. He wanted to press his face into the curve of her neck. How in the inhabited world was this woman, whom he'd only known for hours now, able to make him forget every carefully laid barricade he'd erected to keep from wanting anyone? She'd been nothing more than a shadow on a bridge, and yet here he sat, having a conversation he should not be having, distracted into needing things he should not be needing.

"Can you tell me? Why they made such an exception for you? Why you can't do something as easy as sit in a chair and help pass or amend laws, but are required to serve your nation to have a ranking?" she asked, her gaze searching.

A suspicion took root in Caidon and he narrowed his eyes. "You are inquisitive by nature, aren't you? That's the reason you're in the papers. You learned, or saw, something and couldn't help but look deeper."

Her cheeks flushed as she blew air into them and glanced at the weakening fire. "So my brother tells me. Though he said he blamed our very strong justice gene."

He smiled and brushed hair over her shoulder so he could see her face fully. "Ah, but I have a suspicious feeling it goes well beyond righting wrongs."

Red suffused her entire face and she audibly swallowed, remaining silent, her attention forward. How intriguing.

Caidon brushed his fingers along the softness of her neck. "What have you done, Ramsey Hunter?"

She squared her shoulders and faced him once again. "An answer for an answer."

"Sounds fair," he agreed, then guessed, "and you want to know what I do for the FIO."

"Yes."

Curiosity and amusement shone from her eyes. Whatever work she believed he did, had zero effect on her. Caidon frowned, realizing he didn't want to change her perception. He didn't want her to look at him in fear, or horror. And if she knew his genetically inherited ability to connect on a cellular level with a gun, therefore making *him* the perfect weapon, she might. For some reason, he wanted her to be different, like his mother, who could accept a monster for a mate. Since Caidon only had tonight, he wouldn't take his chances.

Smiling with the sadness he couldn't bury, he put some distance between them. "Perhaps another night."

"Ah," she said, pulling the blanket tighter around herself. "Not a good job, then."

"No," he said softly.

She glanced past him and scooted to the edge of the couch. "I should probably be getting back home. My brother keeps odd hours, and if he realizes I'm gone…"

"He'll have his entire division out looking for you," Caidon finished for her.

"Yes," she said, chuckling. "Probably. And since you outrank my brother, who is a key guardian, I don't want to cause any trouble."

"Your brother is an enforceman. Key guardian or not, everyone has to obey his order if he opts to give one, me included."

She slipped the blanket off and folded it carefully. "Not many guardians feel that way."

Rising on a frown, he held his hand out. "Only nineteen and already jaded."

"I suppose helping convict a guardian of multiple counts of rape, when he's apparently managed to be ignored for years, will do that to a girl," she said dryly, accepting his help.

And what would she say if she knew she held the hand of a man who killed in service to their country? Would he be placed in the same category? A guardian who didn't truly guard much of anything… Caidon kept the struggles internal, making sure his expression revealed nothing as he helped her stand. His father had warned him of the lonely path to becoming an assassin, and the decision hadn't been an easy one for Caidon. He alone would have to live with the consequences.

Cold air swirled past when he opened the door. Ramsey shivered, causing Caidon to hesitate.

"What's wrong?" Ramsey asked.

"If you wait here for a minute I'll run up and get you a jacket. You can't walk home in a damp clothes without anything else to keep you warm."

She shrugged. "I'll be okay."

"I'll be right back."

Not allowing her a chance to argue, Caidon ran up the stairs to his room. He grabbed the jacket he'd worn yesterday, locked back up, and returned to her side. Laughter danced in her eyes and she shook her head on a smile, accepting the jacket.

"I was about to jump off a bridge when you found me. I wasn't concerned about the cold then, I'm not now," she said, slipping into the too-large covering.

Caidon waited for her to walk past him into the now icy night. "You wouldn't have jumped."

"You don't think so?"

He matched her shorter stride on the glistening sidewalk, shoving his hands deep into his pockets. "No. You would have thought of your brother and changed your mind on your own."

"I hadn't," she said so quietly the soft burble of water under the bridge almost took the words away. "Thought about him. I don't know if I would have. I was too lost in my own self-misery to consider beyond everything I lost so quickly."

An unwarranted, and unexpected sliver of jealousy made Caidon frown. "You loved him?"

"I'm not sure." She wrapped the coat around her

and crossed her arms. "I think I liked the idea of him. Of the security. All my frien—" She sighed and shook her head. "All the girls I know are married and seem to be happy."

"So young?" he asked in shock.

"Well, sure. I mean they're only yearlong contracts, or maybe up to three years, but why wait? It's the safest way to have a relationship."

The words hung in the air between them. A reminder, he supposed for them both that having a sexual liaison outside the safety of a marriage contract could prove deadly. Human rabies syndrome was passed on through sex in its dormant stage. Within two weeks, the virus would go active and turn its victim into the equivalent of a zombie for a couple hours, forcing the infected to seek out other hosts by biting. A monogamous relationship ensured the safety of both parties, and could be committed to for minimum year and up to a lifetime, depending on the couple.

"Plus," she said, "depending on the marriage, it can elevate one's social standing. The next contract could be to someone with more wealth, more power, or whatever."

"Is that what you were doing?"

"No, but I think maybe he was," she said, her focus somewhere off in the distance. "When he told me he wouldn't be honoring his promises to me, he also let me know he was marrying a primary guardianess. When my father died, my brother inherited his seat as Key Guardian Asherwick. Unless something awful happens to Jonathon, Tobyn had no hope of having access to my family ranking."

"He couldn't have found another woman to marry so soon."

"No, likely not. I'm sure he'd been wooing her for some time. My… scandal was the excuse he needed to end things."

Shops gave way to neat rows of two-story brick houses on either side of the wide road. No lights burned in the windows. A few houses had greenhouses built higher in the back than the houses roofline. Caidon took in the tranquil, safe atmosphere. "It wasn't your scandal."

"To some, daring to go against a ranked guardian, a figure in society, was a disgrace. I betrayed one of our own."

Caidon rolled his shoulders in discomfort. *This* was the world he'd just signed into? Thank goodness he was leaving in a couple hours. "Good thing he saved you from learning his true nature until after you were stuck in a contract with him, hmm?"

Laughing, she tugged on his forearm and pulled his hand free. She laced their fingers together and slipped their joined hands into the oversized coat pocket at her hip. The action created an intimacy and a sense of comfort he wanted to fall into. How could anyone have let this woman go?

"I hadn't looked at it like that," she said, her fingers tightening around his. "But I think you're right. I bet he would have been looking to trade up even if he'd married me."

"He would have been a fool," Caidon said before he could stop.

She laughed again and bumped her shoulder to his.

"You don't know me well enough to know. He could have made a very wise decision."

Regret filled Caidon. He'd never have the opportunity to know. Never get the chance to learn what kind of match she'd be for him. If a year would be too long, or not long enough. He kept silent, not wanting to give voice to the disappointment unfurling inside. Thankfully, Ramsey didn't push for further conversation. He didn't know whether his silence at her response upset her or not. Decided not knowing was for the best.

They turned a corner and she squeezed his hand again. "That's my house, the third one here on the right."

Caidon noted all the dark windows. "Your brother still appears to be oblivious to your disappearance."

"Small favors," she said on a chuckle. "I have to go in through the greenhouse. I have a key hidden under a small rock at the back door."

"Sneak out often, do you?" he asked, casting her a sideways glance, hating the curl of jealousy that once again snuck up on him. There were limited reasons she'd have ventured off in the middle of the night, and her former promised was one.

"A few times. Jonathon would have a fit if he knew I kept a key hidden. He takes our security very seriously."

Caidon breathed cold air in deep. "Understandable when you see the worst of your society."

"I know, and I probably will take the key in with me tonight." She stopped at the small alley that ran between houses and gazed up at the dark, cloudy sky. "I don't really have a need for it anymore."

The murmured words confirmed his suspicions.

She'd taken off in the night to see her lover. Past lover. He pushed away the urge to learn where the man lived. When he'd decided to followed in his fathers' path, he'd made a vow to only take those deserving a fatal sentence. A broken heart, while a travesty, didn't usually warrant death. Nor did jealousy.

"I'll walk you to the door," he said, stepping into the alley.

She led him to a gate in a tall wooden fence, which left just enough room to open the greenhouse door. Darkness loomed inside, the house cutting off any residual light from the street and the clouds too thick for much moonlight to filter through. Caidon paused, listening, a habit he couldn't afford to break. The musky scent of earth and sharp tang of fertilizer filled the moist air. Something small scuttled in the brush next to the door. Ramsey yelped and grabbed his arm, pressing into his back.

"Oh, summer sun, what is that?" she squeaked, ruffling the hair at the back of his neck.

Caidon pulled her the rest of the way into the glass structure, trying to ignore how good his arm around her waist and her body fitting to his felt. "Probably a mouse, or small bird, wanting to get out and explore for the night, or back to its family."

She tensed further. "A mouse?"

Caidon laughed. "It won't hurt you."

"Killer mice, they could exist," she said, easing around to the other side of him. "We do live in a strange world."

Ramsey guided the way, her hand wrapped around his. Even in the dark, she seemed to know where to step to keep from tripping or walking on precious plants.

Another testament to her *few* nights of sneaking out. Three narrow stone stairs led to the back door, and beside them she released his hand to tilt up a small stone.

"Ah ha!" she declared, raising with her hand fisted. "He hasn't discovered it. I always worry Jonathon will figure out my little secret and leave me locked out in the greenhouse all night."

"He'd do that to you?"

"Sure. Well maybe." She laughed on a huff. "Okay, probably not. But he'd make me think he would." She turned to face him. "If you had a sister, would you torture her in such a way?"

"I have four," he said. "And I don't know. I'd like to think they'd be more careful with their safety."

She groaned. "Not you, too. If they are adults, they are capable of making adult decisions, I promise."

"None of them are adults yet, of which my father is thankful."

"Really? I wish we had more time. I bet there's a story there, why you're very grown and yet your sisters are not."

Caidon couldn't help but reach out and brush a knuckle across her jaw. "Not really. When my parents met, my father still had an obligation to his ruler. My mother wouldn't allow him to her bed if there was a chance of conceiving another child. She told him when he was home to raise them, they could make more babies."

"Well," she said, "he took her seriously, didn't he? Four daughters."

"I think it was a matter of him being thankful she'd waited."

"She loved him."

"Very much."

"I wonder what such love feels like," she said quietly.

His chest constricted and he dropped his hand. "You'll learn some day."

"I wouldn't think less of you." She stepped into his space, her hands pressing to his chest. "If I knew whatever it is you do for the nation."

Caidon fisted his hands to keep from wrapping her in his arms. "You say that…"

"No, it's true. You're a good man, Caidon Survaine. Whatever choice you made to become a master guardian, an important rank, is one we must have great need for."

"A good man?" he asked with a head shake. "To repeat your earlier statement, you don't know me."

She moved in closer, and despite knowing he should, he didn't move away. "A bad man wouldn't have helped a woman unable to see beyond her own misery. A bad man wouldn't have sat on a couch and listened to silly memories, doing nothing more than sitting. A bad man wouldn't have walked me home without expectation."

"Why would I expect something?" he asked and then snapped his head back, staring down her shadowed face. "You… you have been pressured into doing more than you wished by someone?"

"I was curious," she said carefully, "and he was convincing in his reasons."

"You mean convincing in his *expectations*," Caidon said, anger tinging his voice.

Her cool fingers traced his jaw, catching on the stubble. "See? A good man. You care about the past, now gone, never to occur again. I learned. I won't be so naïve next time."

Next time. He didn't want her to have a next time, unless it involved him. And how ridiculous was *that* thought?

"I should warn you," she said, breaking into his wayward reflections, "I am curious now."

Caidon barely had time to blink before her lips, soft and yielding, pressed to his. Teasing, her mouth sought more and Caidon stood frozen, his heart pounding in an uncomfortable mixture of anticipation and remorse. He wanted more than he could ever hope to give. He could give this girl nothing of himself, had no future to offer. Grabbing her shoulders, he took a bracing step away, breaking the courage of her kiss.

"No," he whispered.

"Why?"

A dozen reasons swam through his mind. All of them valid. None of them worth losing the kiss he knew he'd carry with him for months, if not years. Taking a deep breath, he leaned in close, sinking his fingers into the thick curls at the base of her neck. He crowded her, forcing her to step back into the brick wall.

"You want me to kiss you, *zlanishka*?" he asked on a growl, his nose touching hers, his body pressing her to the wall. "I don't think anyone has kissed you the way I will."

Her swallow was audible in the quiet greenhouse. "You expect me to say no to that?"

No hesitation went through Caidon as he took her mouth. To his shock, and the delight of the Ruthenian beast inside that ruled him, she offered no resistance, opening to his onslaught with a murmur of welcome. Of desire. Caidon's tongue swept inside on a claim of possession, hunting every secret of passion she'd reveal in the moment he stole. Sweetness exploded across his senses, from her scent, her taste, to the feminine curves crushed against his body. All of them competed with the whisper of *more* in his blood. A demand he found he had no control to ignore.

His mouth slanted over hers, as he kissed her, and kissed her, and *kissed her*. He broke the embrace only long enough to alter their position, to lift her higher, to be able to feel the *more* his body required. She made no argument, her legs wrapping tight around his hips, her hands seeking with the same urgency riding him. The tangled fabric of her skirt did little to hinder his questing touch. Only when her firm thighs were under his palms did he reign in some semblance of control, knowing to go any further would risk too much.

Ramsey squirmed, a hard shift of her hips into his arousal, an answering shudder racing through her body. Caidon knew by instinct the faint motions felt good, to them both, and he was undecided about making her stop. By her quickening movements, the shift in their breathing, and the building inside him, he was seconds from coming, and she'd likely take the journey with him. She knew more about intimacy than he did, a self-imposed decision he'd made when he choose his career. If he allowed himself to give into the temptation, she'd show him what he had to lose. The cost of his future.

He pressed harder and tightened the grip on her thighs, forcing her to stop. No. This was not the time, and he would rather this not be the place. She cried a denial and he deepened the kiss, then pulled back. He wanted her. And he'd have her. But only when he could have all of her, and she could have all of him.

"Wait for me," he rasped. "Will you? I don't know how long I'll be gone. Could be a year, could be ten. Wait for me, Ramsey. Promise me."

She pressed her forehead to his, her body trembling, her gasps mingling with his. "Yes."

ABOUT THE AUTHOR

SARAH WESTILL lives in Alabama with her US Army-retired husband. They have two sons – one they've successfully raised to adulthood – the other is still a work-in-progress, navigating middle school. As a full-on creative, Sarah lives to write, paint, teach, and meet amazing people while doing portrait photography. A veteran in the publishing industry working as a cover artist under the name Elaina Lee, she has been blessed to help hundreds of authors to achieve their own publishing goals for over a decade. To learn more about Sarah as she blogs her adventures, and about her Guardians, please visit her at sarahwestill.com or follow her on Instagram @authorsarahwestill

www.ingramcontent.com/pod-product-compliance
Lightning Source LLC
Chambersburg PA
CBHW010841190726
48286CB00012BA/2936